The Vatican Cameos

A Sherlock Holmes

Adventure

By Richard T. Ryan

For True Sherlockeans,

The game is always afoot!

Best,

Rick

Paperback ISBN 978-1-78092-989-7
ePub ISBN 978-1-78092-990-3
PDF ISBN 978-1-78092-991-0

Published in the UK by MX Publishing
335 Princess Park Manor, Royal Drive, London, N11 3GX
www.mxpublishing.co.uk

Cover design by Brian Belanger.

Grateful acknowledgment to Conan Doyle Estate Ltd. for the use
of the Sherlock Holmes characters created by Sir Arthur Conan
Doyle.

This book is dedicated with love my wife, Grace, who has been an unwavering source of support in all my literary efforts, and to my children, Katlin and Michael and my sonin-law, Daniel.

Introduction

Playing the Old Course at St. Andrew's probably ranks pretty high on every golfer's bucket list. Having recently retired after nearly 30 years as a newspaper editor, I decided to visit the birthplace of the game and fulfill a dream I had harbored for many years.

Making things considerably easier was the fact that my older brother, Ed, had purchased a small cottage in St. Andrew's, not too far from the course, some 20 years ago.

I planned carefully because getting to play the Old Course is no easy task. I decided to shoot for a round in the late fall, after the local tournaments had been concluded. My brother was all in because while he had played St. Andrew's many times, we had never done it together.

I arrived in Scotland on Monday and Ed picked me up at Edinburgh Airport. I prevailed upon my brother, so that even before we drove to his cottage, we stopped by the course and entered the lottery for Wednesday. I checked online that night and learned to my dismay that we had not been selected for a tee time.

On Tuesday, we played the Castle Course, and I had one of the best rounds of my life. Feeling psyched, we entered the lottery for Thursday.

Tuesday night, I saw that once again we had not been selected. So, on Wednesday, we played the new course, and although it is a great layout and quite challenging, it's not St. Andrew's.

After finishing, we swung by the Old Course and I entered the lottery for Friday. And so it was that that on Wednesday night, I checked online and learned that we had been chosen to play on Friday.

We had been assigned a 10:10 a.m. tee-off time, and my excitement was nearly palpable. All day Thursday, I busied myself with helping my brother in his garden, reading and watching the sky.

Even though the forecast called for showers, my enthusiasm remained unshaken. That night, I felt like a youngster waiting for Christmas morning. As you might expect, I slept very little.

On Friday, we rose at 8, enjoyed a hearty breakfast of pancakes and coffee and then drove to the course where we were joined by Mike and Daniel, two Americans, who like myself were living the dream.

After arranging for caddies, we headed for the first tee. The first hole at St. Andrew's is a fairly short par 4. The tee shot is one of the easiest in golf. Feeling loose and relaxed, I placed my drive right in the center of the wide fairway. Although the clouds looked ominous, I stubbornly ignored their threatening presence.

As I walked to my ball, I recalled a college philosophy course from my youth. Channeling either Hume or Kant, I couldn't remember which, I reasoned that if I denied the existence of the clouds, they would cease to be. However, as I stood over my ball preparing for my second shot, there was no way to ignore the clap of thunder and the jagged lightning bolt that ripped across the sky. As the rail began to fall in buckets, I stood there adamantly refusing to admit defeat.

After an agonizing five minutes, during which I saw other foursomes fleeing for the shelter of the clubhouse, I gave in to the urging of my brother and our caddies. I finally decided there was no logical way that I could continue to deny the existence of the storm. After all, I was standing there soaking wet.

After trudging back to the clubhouse, we sat around waiting patiently for the storm to pass, but it never did. Eventually, we drove home where I enjoyed a hot shower and a change of clothes. Then I asked my brother for suggestions on how to kill a rainy day in a small town.

He told me there was an estate sale that afternoon. The contents of a large Victorian home on nearby Bogward Road, were being auctioned off. With nothing else to do but read and wallow in self-pity, I said, "Let's go."

Thirty minutes later, we were standing inside the auction room at MacGregor's on Largo Road. There were only a few other people at the sale.

Most of the people there seemed to know exactly what they wanted because the bidding on some of the various pieces of furniture and artwork was spirited while other items attracted few, if any, bids at all. Eventually, my brother got involved in trying to obtain a Tiffany lamp, which he eventually lost when the price reached 25 pounds.

As the sale wound down, the auctioneer produced a small trunk.

"We are taking a chance with this piece," he intoned. "It is locked, and the contents are unknown. Let's start the bidding at 5 pounds, shall we?"

After no one matched his opening bid, he dropped it to 4 pounds. I nodded, and he said, "I have 4 pounds. Will anyone bid 5?" Looking across the room, I saw a man on the other side of the room gesture discreetly, and suddenly I realized that I had competition.

Despite my brother's protests, I won the bidding war and paid 22 pounds for the trunk.

As we drove home, I offered to split the contents with him – for 11 pounds.

"It's all yours," he replied.

The rain had slowed to a steady drizzle as we made our way into his garage. The locks on the trunk couldn't hold up under the pry bar I employed on them.

Lifting the top, I saw a tin dispatch box inside. Odd, I thought – a box within a box. After wiping away layers of caked on dirt and grime, I saw the name "John H. Watson" painted on the lid. Although faded, it was clearly discernable. This can't be *that* box, I thought.

Opening the latch, I saw that the inside was crammed with papers and folders. I picked up one of the folders and upon opening it, I was greeted by a title page that read:

The Vatican Cameos: A
Sherlock Holmes Adventure by
Dr. John H. Watson.

Having been a devotee of Conan Doyle's great creation my entire life, I knew that this tin box must be the same one that Dr. Watson had kept locked securely away in the vaults at Cox and Company.

The deep disappointment I felt earlier about St. Andrew's had been eclipsed by unbounded joy as I realized that I was holding one of the untold tales of Sherlock Holmes.

From my reading, I knew that the great detective had handled several cases for the Vatican, and later, I checked and verified that the case of "The Vatican Cameos" is referenced by Watson at the beginning of "The Hound of the Baskervilles."

After another sleepless night – this one spent reading – I was determined to share this untold Holmes' exploit with others. I can only hope that you derive as much joy from this story as I did.

Richard T. Ryan

Chapter One – London, 1901

"Two weeks, Watson! We have been two full weeks without a case!" exclaimed Sherlock Holmes. "Is the entire criminal underworld so in awe of my abilities that its members have given up their nefarious enterprises? Does the world no longer need Sherlock Holmes?"

He cast a surreptitious glance at the mantel where he had once kept his syringe and a vial of cocaine.

"Well here's one criminal who appears to be going about his business as usual," I remarked.

"What on earth are you talking about?"

"Police discovered the body of a teenage Asian boy floating in the Thames yesterday," I said, referring to an article in the Guardian. "His hands were tied and his face had been disfigured with some sort of sharp instrument."

"Let me see," Holmes exclaimed, snatching the paper from my grasp. Throwing himself into his chair, he began perusing the report. As the minutes passed, I could only assume that he was reading the article several times over.

Finally throwing the paper aside, he remarked, "This is not a case for us, Watson."

"What do you mean? A young boy murdered and mutilated and you have no interest? I must say, I am rather surprised – and disappointed – at you Holmes."

"Lestrade stopped by earlier while you were out. In addition to his face, the young man's stomach had been cut open, a fact either ignored or omitted by the Guardian's reporter. Obviously, the boy had smuggled something into this country, concealing it by swallowing it. Whoever he was working for wanted the goods immediately, and the young man paid dearly for his criminal tendencies. The good inspector informed me that the Yard has a pretty fair idea of who is running the smuggling operation, and they are merely crossing their I's and dotting their T's before making an arrest. So I say again, this is not a case for us, Watson."

As Holmes resumed his pacing and I retrieved the paper and returned to my reading, there was a knock on our door. Mrs. Hudson, our landlady, poked her head in. "Mr. Holmes, you have a caller. Shall I show him up?"

"By all means, Mrs. Hudson," said Holmes, "and please be quick about it. We don't want to keep our visitor waiting."

I could hear our caller long before I saw him. Heavy footfalls on the stairs indicated a large man had come to see us, and the fact that he took several minutes to ascend the single flight indicated to me, at least, that our visitor was not in the best of physical health.

I felt vindicated when I answered the knock on our door and was greeted by a small mountain of a man. He stood around five-foot-seven and was quite corpulent. He wore a black morning coat, a beaver hat and was clean-shaven with a rather dark complexion.

Having been proven right about his physical condition, I thought to myself, after taking in his well-tailored clothes and glistening boots, this must be a banker or some captain of industry come to call on Holmes for assistance.

He looked at me with clear blue eyes and then fixed his gaze on Holmes, who had risen from his chair as the man entered.

"Good morning, Your Eminence. How may I be of assistance?" asked Holmes.

"Have we met?" asked the man incredulously. He spoke nearly perfect English, but I could discern a slight Mediterranean accent.

"Not that I can recall," smiled Holmes amiably, delighted by the effect he had achieved.

"Then how on earth could you know that I am a prince of the church?"

Holmes smiled. "If you are going to dress like a layman, in an effort to travel incognito, may I suggest that in the future you wear something slightly heavier than those linen gloves. I am sure even Watson can see the rather distinctive outline of your ring through the material. Barring that, you might consider removing it altogether."

Looking over, I could discern quite clearly the oblate shape of a cross on the man's ring finger of his left hand.

"Also, your shirt appears tighter than it should which tells me you are not used to wearing garments of that ilk. Exacerbating the condition is the fact that beneath the shirt, you are no doubt wearing your pectoral cross, which renders the garment even more constricting.

Finally, your skin while generally tan is quite a bit lighter for about an inch above the collar. I can only assume that your usual attire has a much higher neck – perhaps a Roman collar?"

"Well, Mr. Holmes, I must say that if first impressions are any indication, I think I have come to the right man for assistance."

"Would you like some tea, Cardinal …," Holmes left the sentence unfinished.

"It's Cardinal Oreglia, Gaetano Oreglia. Tea would be fine. Although I must admit that I would much prefer coffee."

Holmes went to the door and yelled down, "Mrs. Hudson, please put the kettle on, and if you would, try your hand at a pot of coffee as well."

"Won't you be seated, Your Eminence?" said Holmes gesturing to a chair.

As Cardinal Oreglia sat, I started to follow suit, only to receive a reproving glance from Holmes. "I can vouch for the tea," Holmes said pleasantly, "but as for the coffee, well that's anyone's guess. We are in England, after all."

The cardinal smiled and, noticing my indecision, he laughed – a deep, rich laugh. "Mr. Holmes, please, let's not stand on formality. After all, I am here as a supplicant to seek your assistance. Please be seated, gentlemen. I think you'll want to be sitting when you hear what I have to say anyway."

"I am the camerlengo to His Holiness, Pope Leo. In that position, my primary responsibility is to look after the finances of the Vatican. I was here in London to discuss some rather delicate fiscal affairs with several of your bankers."

"This morning I received a rather cryptic telegram from His Holiness. It said simply, '*Egeo auxiliante amico platea pistorum.*'."

Holmes smiled, "I must confess that Mr. Samuel Johnson's description of the Bard as a man of 'small Latin and less Greek' might be applied to me as well. Although I have been working on my Virgil as of late."

"Watson, care to venture a guess?" asked Holmes.

"I believe I see the word 'plate' there in *platea*," I ventured.

Holmes smiled again, "Watson, not quite. *Platea* is not a cognate for our word plate. I think in this case, we must translate *platea* as 'street' rather than 'plate.' So, unless I am badly mistaken, the telegram reads, 'I need the help of our friend in Baker Street."

"You have it exactly," Mister Holmes said Cardinal Oreglia.

"Did His Holiness say anything else?" asked Holmes

"Just one other word – *prudentes.*"

"Be discreet," said Holmes aloud. "Well, that would explain the layman's garb employed by Your Eminence."

"As you might expect, given my position, the pope and I are old friends," said Cardinal Oreglia. "He has dispatched me here to request your assistance in a matter of what I can only assume must be extreme delicacy, Mr. Holmes."

Holmes said, "I am flattered. Still, surely, there are others far closer to home who might have rendered a service similar to mine."

"Mr. Holmes, you have been of enormous service to our Holy Father in the past. He still marvels at the ease with which you discovered the causes behind the death of Cardinal

Tosca. I believe that he is hopeful that you can bring this assignment to a swift and discrete resolution as well."

Looking at Holmes, I thought my friend was as close to blushing as I had ever seen him. Nothing could get to the man so thoroughly as an earnest compliment from someone he respected.

"I shall do my very best," Holmes promised.

"Before we continue, I have a small admission to make," the cardinal said. "Shortly after the first telegram arrived. I received a second."

"And what did that one say?" asked Holmes.

"Just two words – *cameos furatus*."

"Stolen cameos?" asked Holmes.

The cardinal gazed at me, and before I could speak, Holmes said, "Your Eminence, you may rest assured that anything you say to me, you may share with Dr. Watson."

Cardinal Oreglia nodded. "May I ask you a question Mr. Holmes?

Holmes nodded.

"Have you ever heard of the Vatican cameos?"

"I must confess that I have not. May I ask about them?"

"There is not much that I can tell you except that legend has it that these cameos were handcrafted by the artist Michelangelo and that they have the potential to do enormous harm to the Church."

"Are they the cameos to which the pope alludes so cryptically?"

"I cannot say for certain, but I believe they are. I am aware of no others, and although I myself know very little about them, I can tell you one other thing Mr. Holmes.

Through the years, the cameos have become associated with Pope Alexander VI. Are you familiar with him?"

Holmes nodded, "Alexander VI, better known as Rodrigo Borgia, was the second and last of the Borgias to be elected pope. He served at the end of the 15th and the beginning of the 16th centuries, did he not?"

I was astounded at Holmes' knowledge of the papacy. After all, the man was neither religious nor intrigued by history – except as it served his needs.

The cardinal nodded. "Those years are some of the darkest in the history of the Church. Ruling from 1492 to 1503, Rodrigo is said to have reveled in every vice imaginable. If you believe the worst about him, his sins ranged from avarice and simony to incest and murder. Although centuries have passed, he remains a blot on the papacy."

He continued, "As for the cameos, the only person ever permitted to look upon them is the pope."

"I also know that His Holiness has weighed destroying them, but the fact that they were created by the same man who painted the ceiling of the Sistine Chapel and sculpted the Pieta has prompted him to exercise due caution, and thus far given him pause. Now, I am afraid that ambivalence appears to have manifested itself in a very real threat to the papacy and the church as a whole."

Holmes exhaled, and I could see the light in his eyes as he anticipated a contest of wits with an as-yet-unknown adversary.

"As you know, you will be well compensated for your labors," said Cardinal Oreglia, "but I also must insist that if you do accept this commission, you bear in mind the need for absolute secrecy. Even the hint of a scandal could cause irreparable damage to everything His Holiness is trying to accomplish."

"I understand your concerns, Your Eminence, and you may place your trust in both Watson and me," Holmes replied.

The cardinal heaved a sigh of relief and said, "I hope you do not mind, but I have taken the liberty of arranging passage for you and Dr. Watson to Rome. I shall be returning with you."

"As it happens, I am quite free at the moment, Your Eminence. Watson, can you clear your calendar?"

Before I could answer, Mrs. Hudson knocked and then entered with a tray containing two cups of tea and assorted biscuits. "Your coffee will be along presently, sir," she said to the cardinal, and then she was gone as suddenly as she had appeared.

"Let us savor the fruits of Mrs. Hudson's labors," Holmes said to me. Smiling at the cardinal and then at me, he added, "It may be quite some time before we are able to relax with a proper cup of English tea."

Mrs. Hudson reappeared a few moments later, carrying a steaming cup of coffee on a small tray with lemon twists, cream and a bowl of lump sugar.

The cardinal looked at the tray, appreciating the aroma of the coffee and then smiled at Mrs. Hudson gratefully.

"I hope you approve of the coffee," she said, curtseying and then she was gone again.

"Gentlemen," the cardinal said, "we just have time to enjoy this and then we must be on our way. I am sure you will want to get to the Vatican as quickly as possible, Mr. Holmes. I have a first-class compartment booked on a train leaving Victoria for Dover in," he pulled out a heavy gold timepiece from his vest and glanced at the face, "just 90 minutes."

"Well then let us be quick about it. Watson, pack a bag, and we shall procure anything else we may need along the way."

As I headed to my room, Holmes looked at me, and without the cardinal seeing, mouthed the words, "Bring your pistol."

I nodded and then proceeded to pack, putting my sidearm in the bottom of a carpet bag, and covering it with shirts and various other garments.

As I readied for our journey, I could hear Holmes and the cardinal speaking. A few minutes later, I returned to the sitting room, and Holmes left to pack his bag.

Within 10 minutes, we were standing in Baker Street and Holmes was hailing a hansom cab.

"Victoria Station, and there's an extra pound in it for you if you get us there quickly," Holmes said.

"Righto, guv'nor" replied the driver and we were off.

Chapter Two – Rome, 1501

Standing in the light that streamed through the skylight, Michelangelo tilted his head to the side and studied the face of the Madonna staring back at him from his easel.

After several moments of intense scrutiny, he decided that she did indeed look a bit too joyous. Picking up his palette, he prepared to rectify the error when he heard a loud knock at the door below.

"Are you home Michelangelo?" asked his apprentice, Paolo.

The artist thought about remaining silent, but decided the place needed cleaning. "Uno momento, Paolo," he yelled back.

"Hurry, master. I have big news," the boy exclaimed.

Descending to the first floor, Michelangelo strode to the door and yanked it open.

"Master," Paolo said, "Everyone in the plaza is talking. They say the Borgias are looking for you."

"What?" exclaimed the artist. "I have no dealings with them. I think you must be mistaken my young friend."

"No, master, I am not mistaken. You are the greatest living sculptor, and no one can deny the beauty of the Pieta."

"Yes, but the Borgias have their court artists. Unless, of course, Cardinal Riario has hired me out to the Holy Father. But then, why should he? If I am doing work for the pope then

I cannot be doing work for Riario, and that man wants to keep me all to himself for as long as he can."

Michelangelo continued, "I think if he had his way, I would be a servant in his palace, painting and sculpting night and day *ad maiorem Riaario gloriam*."

Looking out the window, Paolo turned and said, "Master, soldiers and a great carriage are coming up the street slowly. I think they are looking for this house."

"Well, if they are, you tell them I am very busy." With that, Michelangelo bounded up the stairs and resumed his consideration of the half-completed Madonna.

"The Borgias looking for me," he mused. "I wonder what the Holy Father could possibly desire from me."

For the second time in minutes, a knock on the door interrupted his reverie.

"Can I help you, sir?" he heard Paolo ask.

"Is this the home of the artist, Michelangelo Buonarotti?" he heard a gruff voice ask.

"It is sir, but I'm afraid that he is far too busy at the moment to talk with you."

"Is he far too busy to refuse a request from Pope Alexander? Get him now before I box your ears, you impudent scamp."

"There will be no need for threats captain," Michelangelo said descending the stairs again.

"How may I be of service to His Holiness?"

"Pope Alexander requests the pleasure of your company in the papal apartments. That is all I can tell you. He has sent a carriage for you and asked us to escort you there." Grabbing his cloak, the artist said, "I am at your service."

Turning to the boy, he said, "Paolo, after you are done cleaning, you must fend for yourself tonight I am afraid. It is nearly three, and I have no idea when I shall return. Captain, I am at your disposal."

Climbing into the carriage, Michelangelo thought of all the stories he had heard of Pope Alexander. How he had bribed his way to the papacy then secured his position by packing the Curia with newly minted cardinals, including his own son, Cesare, there only to do his bidding.

His mind racing, he thought about the other stories, the mistresses, the bastard children, and he shuddered. How such a man could rule Holy Mother Church baffled him, but what that man wanted with him went beyond that – it terrified him.

After some 20 minutes, the carriage stopped in front of the papal palace. As Michelangelo stepped down, a young priest, no more than 30 years of age hurried forward to meet him.

"Signor Buonarotti, I am Father Ferrante. I will escort you to His Holiness."

Entering the palace, Michelangelo and the young priest exchanged pleasantries. "I have been so looking forward to meeting you," said the priest. "I must confess that every time I gaze upon your Pieta I am moved to tears. That is surely your greatest work."

"You may be right," the artist said, "but I truly hope that you are mistaken. After all, I am only 26. I would like to think that my best works are yet to come."

At a pair of large wooden doors, the priest knocked, and a rich baritone voice from within bade them, "Enter."

As they did, Pope Alexander VI turned to face them.

The first thing that struck Michelangelo was the intelligence of the pope's eyes. Dark and brooding, they saw everything – and quite possibly behind everything.

Tall and strikingly handsome, it was easy to credit talk of the pontiff's many dalliances despite his priestly vow of celibacy.

Michelangelo approached, knelt and when the pontiff offered his hand, he kissed the Ring of the Fisherman.

"Now rise, young Buonarotti. Leave us, Ferrante; Michelangelo and I have much to discuss." Ringing a bell, the pope ordered the servant who appeared, "Bring us some wine. Signor Buonarotti, is there anything special that you would like?"

"No, Your Holiness. The wine is more than enough."

When they were alone once again, the pope turned to him and said, "Michelangelo, I have great plans, and I want you to be a part of them. I know your work, and I am inspired by it."

After a pause, he continued, "I believe that just as I am God's representative on Earth, placed here to do his bidding, so too are you a representative of Our Lord and Savior." The pope blessed himself. "In a very real sense, Michelangelo, you are an agent of the Lord, and I believe that your destiny – at least in part – is to serve Holy Mother Church with your gifts."

"You leave me speechless, Your Holiness," said the artist.

"You have talent and I believe that you are a good son of the Church. Loyal, faithful, devout and modest. May I ask you a personal question?"

"Of course, Your Holiness."

"I am given to understand that you never sign your work. Is that true?"

"Generally speaking, it is, your Holiness."

"Yet you did sign the Pieta, did you not?" he asked laughing.

"Indeed, Holy Father. That is the only piece to which I have ever affixed my name. Shortly after the statue was installed in the Chapel of Santa Petronilla, I went back to see how it looked in the late afternoon light. I heard a group of people talking. They were admiring my work. When one asked who the sculptor was, another answered Solari. I consider myself a modest man, your Holiness, but to hear *il Gobbo* given credit for my work infuriated me."

"So what did you do, signore?"

"I returned that night with my tools and broke into the chapel. Visitors the next day were soon made aware that I had sculpted the Pieta – and not that hunchbacked fool."

The pope applauded as he laughed. "Bravo, Singor Buonaratti. I may disagree with many others here, but I believe

22

that it is possible for a man to be too self-effacing. I am glad that you are not of that ilk."

"Now to the reason that I asked you here. I am planning to redesign St. Peter's, and I need your assistance. I want to continue the work begun by Pope Nicholas. To bring my plans to fruition, I need a visionary. I need someone who is not afraid to break with tradition – even as I have done. I need a man who shares my dream of creating a church that will serve as a fitting resting place for the bones of St. Peter – the rock upon which our church is built. Are you such a man, Michelangelo?"

Before the artist could answer, the pope continued, "I think you are, and I am seldom wrong in my assessments of men."

At that moment, there was a knock on the door.

"Enter," intoned the pope, and a servant carried an ornate tray into the room with two bottles of wine and a pair of silver goblets. He was followed by a second servant bearing a salver laden with fresh fruit and several types of cured meats.

"We will enjoy our wine on the balcony," the pope said. The servants nodded and headed for the balcony. After a minute, the pope followed them and the artist fell in line behind him.

They sat at a table overlooking the gardens, and the pope said, "I love this view. It's so serene. I often come here to escape the politicking that divides the Curia and to reflect upon how best to do God's work here on Earth."

"It is a lovely spot," Michelangelo said, taking in the view and wondering what lay ahead.

"Red or white?" asked the pope, and again, before Michelangelo could respond, the pope answered for him. "Red, I think!"

"You are a man who strives mightily. You spare neither yourself nor your workers when you are creating. Such a man would drink deeply of life, and life is best captured in the richness of a robust Chianti! Am I right signore? Am I right?"

Although he would much have preferred the lighter white on such a warm afternoon, Michelangelo could only nod and say, "We have just met and yet you know me so well, Your Holiness."

"Now, before I assign you a major commission, I am going to start with something smaller. Something a bit more personal. I hope you understand, signore."

"Of course," said Michelangelo although he found the notion of having to prove himself – even to the pope – repugnant

"Ah, wonderful," exclaimed the pontiff. "Here is what I was thinking." And Pope Alexander then began to explain exactly what he wanted Michelangelo to do.

When the pope had finished outlining his plans in broad terms, Michelangelo was simultaneously excited and repulsed.

"So, are you up to the task?" asked the pontiff.

Knowing that his future might well be determined by the next words he uttered, Michelangelo paused.

Gathering his thoughts while trying to marshal his emotions, the artist looked into the pontiff's eyes, and said simply, "I am yours to command, Your Holiness."

Chapter Three – Rome, 1901

The journey to Rome took us approximately three days. We boarded the train at Victoria and made our way to Dover. We then crossed the Channel to Calais, and headed south via rail to Lyon and then to Turin.

We might have gone through the Alps using the Frejus Rail Tunnel, but I suspect that after his near-fatal encounter with Professor Moriarty at the Reichenbach Falls a decade earlier, Holmes was inclined to give the Alps a wide berth whenever possible.

During our journey, Cardinal Oreglia proved an excellent traveling companion.

He told us that after becoming a priest, he had studied the classics and theology at Oxford. He was, I thought, extremely well-read and quite cultured.

We discussed Renaissance art and architecture, the museums of Rome, and the culinary differences between Italian and English kitchens. I knew that most of these subjects were of little or no concern to Holmes – but he feigned interest and, skilled actor that he is, managed to deceive the cardinal, although I could see quite clearly his mind was elsewhere.

While only minimally intrigued by the bulk of what we discussed, Holmes did become quite animated when we touched on the subject of music, and he and the cardinal engaged in a spirited debate about the virtues of a Stradivarius as opposed to a Gunari.

That discussion segued to a consideration of various composers and operas. I must admit at this point, I was having difficulty staying awake, and I am not nearly so deft a dissembler as Holmes. In truth, I missed a portion of the conversation as fatigue overtook me.

I was jerked awake when the car came to a sudden stop, as we pulled into Marseilles.

"Ah, Watson, I see that Morpheus has finally relinquished his hold over you," Holmes said, smiling.

I looked at Holmes and the cardinal rather sheepishly.

"No need to apologize, Dr. Watson. I, too, have been a sojourner in the land of dreams," said Cardinal Oreglia. "Apparently, only Mr. Holmes here is immune to the blandishments of sleep."

Holmes smiled again, and I thought of the many times that I had seen my friend go two and three days without rest.

After lunch in the dining car, we returned to our compartment, and Holmes began to smoke while the cardinal and I continued to discuss the art of the Eternal City.

It was only when the cardinal began to discourse about the current political situation in Italy and the threat posed to the Catholic Church that Holmes fully involved himself in the conversation once again.

"As you know, gentlemen, Pope Leo and his predecessor Pius IX have been virtual prisoners inside the Vatican for the past three decades. In Italy, the situation is often referred to as the *questione romana* or the 'Roman Question'."

The cardinal began to elaborate: "When the process of Italian unification began, Rome was declared the capital of Italy. However, the temporal ruler at the time, King Victor

Emmanuel II, did not immediately take up residence in Rome; in fact, it would be some time before he moved into the Quirinal Palace. The building, which had served as home to 30 popes, and its importance as a symbol of the power and independence of the papacy cannot be underestimated. Given the delicate situation, you can understand the reluctance of the king."

"Eventually, however, King Victor did take up residence in the palace. Legend has it that after the city was occupied but before he moved in, the king sent an emissary to Pope Pius to request the keys."

The cardinal continued, "A man with a temper, Pius is rumored to have replied, 'Whom do these thieves think they are kidding, asking for the keys to open the door? Let them knock it down if they like. Bonaparte's soldiers, when they wanted to seize Pius VII, came through the window, but even they did not have the effrontery to ask for the keys'."

"Prior to the arrival of King Victor, the pope had been under the protection of the French, and a garrison provided by Napoleon III. Considering himself the sovereign of a Catholic country, Napoleon had regarded it as his duty to support the pontiff. In fact, it was only after the outbreak of the Franco-Prussian War that Napoleon recalled the garrison."

"Once Rome was vulnerable, it was attacked. Pius IX had his forces put up a show of resistance so that the world could see that he was in no way allowing himself to become little more than a chaplain to the newly crowned King of Italy."

"As you might expect, there were negotiations in an effort to reconcile the sudden takeover of the city by a temporal ruler and how best to accommodate the pope as the spiritual ruler of the Church and the ruler of what had been the Papal States with the sudden arrival of the King of Italy. To this date, the papacy has refused to recognize the legitimacy of the Italian government."

"In fact, in 1871, Italy passed what it called a Law of Guarantees. Under the law, the pope would have had honors and privileges akin to those enjoyed by the king. He would have been allowed to dispatch and receive ambassadors; he would have enjoyed diplomatic immunity; and he would have had all the appearances of temporal power that his predecessors enjoyed as rulers of the Papal States."

"Although it was generally viewed as an attempt to avoid further antagonizing the pope in the aftermath of unification, the law was roundly criticized, both by those who supported the king as well as those backing the pope. As you might expect, the Vatican looked upon it as an encroachment upon the power of the papacy. In the opinion of many canonical and legal scholars, such a measure would have subjected the pope to a law that could be modified or abrogated at any time by the Italian parliament. As I am sure you know, it was rejected by the Vatican."

"Since that time, the tension between the papacy and the Italian government has ebbed and flowed. In fact, on more than one occasion, Pius IX had considered leaving Italy altogether and seeking asylum in a foreign land. Truth be told, gentlemen, yours was the first country he contacted with regard to that matter. He also spoke with German officials, but in the end, he remained in the papal palace, as has Pope Leo, with neither setting foot outside the walls of Vatican, fearing that leaving in any manner might be misinterpreted by those who would like to see the pope stripped of his power."

"I am well aware of the pope's quandary," said Holmes, "and I wonder if the past might not have found its way to the pontiff's doorstep."

"That is my fear as well, Mr. Holmes. Although His Holiness has provided us with precious few details, the terseness of his communication would seem to indicate that whatever has happened is weighing heavily on him."

"Well then, let us hope that we are not too late," said Holmes.

When our train finally pulled into Turin, the cardinal said, "I am going to see if there are any telegrams. The Holy Father knows our itinerary. If he should need to contact us, this would have been the place to leave instructions."

As the cardinal wandered off in search of the telegraph office, Holmes turned to me and said, "I fear this is going to be a very dangerous affair, Watson. We are fighting an enemy who has no regard for the pope, so obviously we are dealing with fanatics of some sort – whether political or religious or both remains to be seen."

"I quite agree."

"Keep your wits about you then, and trust no one," he added.

At that moment the cardinal returned. I could see he was grasping a telegram.

"Mr. Holmes," he began, and my friend promptly cut him off.

"Unless it is urgent, wait until we are on the train to discuss it. We do not know our enemy, and we can only hope that they do not know us – yet. Still, their ears and eyes may be everywhere."

We returned to our compartment, and it was only after the train had pulled out of the station and Holmes had checked the compartments on either side of ours and the corridor one last time that he returned and said, "Now, Your Eminence. What says the Holy Father?"

"The telegram reads *properamus placer*."

"Please hurry," said Holmes and the cardinal in unison.

"We shall be in Rome by early afternoon," said Holmes.

"When we get there, Your Eminence, you go directly to Pope Leo. Watson and I will find a small out-of-the-way *pensione* near the Vatican. I will telegraph you our location."

"May I suggest that you stay at the *Suore Francescane dell'Addolorataon*? It is located on the left side of the Colonnades of St. Peter's Square. You will be very close to the papal apartments, and I somehow doubt that our enemies would think to look for you in a convent run by the Franciscan Sisters of the Sorrowful Mother."

"I like the idea of being close at hand, but you must not make the mistake of underestimating an enemy that we do not know, Your Eminence."

"Of course, you are quite correct, Mr. Holmes. But you may enter the convent through the rear. That way you can avoid being seen in the square if you wish. When you arrive at the kitchen door, ask for Sister Angelica and tell her that you are friends of Gaetano."

We spent the next few hours trying to familiarize ourselves with the layout of the Vatican.

Holmes, I knew, possessed an uncanny sense of direction, so I was not terribly worried.

As we pulled into the Rome Termini, Holmes said to the cardinal, "You leave the train first, Your Eminence, and go to the left. After you have collected all of our bags, get a porter to help you carry them to the curb and then take a carriage to the Vatican. Watson, you will follow five minutes later and go directly into the Piazza del Cinquecento. Take a carriage to the convent. I shall be along presently. If either of you should see me, though I doubt that you will, pray take no notice."

Looking at Holmes, I saw that he had thrown off his indifferent demeanor much as a snake sheds its skin, and I thought I detected the glint of anticipation in his eyes.

Cardinal Oreglia departed first, as we had planned, and his final words to us were, "I will be in touch shortly."

I looked at my watch and after five minutes departed, saying to Holmes, "I am quite hungry, old fellow. Please don't be late for dinner."

He laughed, and said, "Good old Watson. How glad I am that you are here. Just to be on the safe side, why don't you first pay a visit to the Spanish Steps? Play the tourist for a bit at the Trevi Fountain and then make your way to the convent."

"Whatever you say, Holmes."

As I left him sitting in the compartment alone, I saw him light a cigarette. I could only wonder what thoughts were running through his mind.

Making my way through the station, I looked for anyone who might be following me. Seeing no one, I hailed a hansom cabriolet and followed Holmes' instructions.

"Spanish Steps," I instructed the driver, all the while looking for suspicious faces and quickly averted gazes.

Chapter Four – Rome, 1501

"Father, are you absolutely certain?"

"Yes, Lucrezia," answered the pope.

"But what will you do with them all? And do you really need 50?"

"I have told you what I desire. Now, my dear, can you handle the business or must I ask someone else?"

"I will take care of everything," she said, "And cost is no object?"

"The coffers are yours, Lucrezia. Take what you need. But you have just a month to secure their services."

"And do you think Cesare will enjoy it?"

The pope smiled lovingly at her. "I think if all goes according to plan, it will be a night that your brother never forgets."

"Who else will be there?" she asked.

"I am inviting all of our closest friends – Cardinal Sforza, Cardinal de Medici and of course, Cardinal della Rovere."

"You say our 'friends' and yet you include both della Rovere and de Medici. You know that both would like nothing more than to see you dead and to assume your place as pope."

"How can you speak ill of such devout clergymen? You are a wicked girl, indeed," laughed the pope.

"I speak the truth, and you know it," she replied.

"Indeed, you do. I doubt either will attend, but I rather hope they do. Perhaps we can discuss our philosophical differences as we plan each other's demise," he said.

"At any rate, I like to know the whereabouts of my enemies, and if they are under my roof and in my sight, they cannot be plotting against me, can they?"

She laughed, "Father, you are insufferable. Whom else will you invite?"

"All of our true allies," he laughed.

"Can you be specific?" she persisted.

"Are you hoping for a name in particular? Or is this just general interest on your part?" asked the pope.

"Oh father," she said blushing.

"I think a certain artist or two may be invited. Are you looking to have your portrait painted again, my dear?"

"No, father,"

"I think I may also include young Machiavelli. I find the man possesses certain insights into the machinations of rulers and the workings of government."

Lucrezia made a face.

"You do not like Nicolo, or has he proven immune to your charms?"

"I do not trust him," she replied. "Besides, he is married. And if I were you, father, I would watch him very carefully."

"Well, I find his cunning admirable. But I must admit that I do not trust him totally either. Still, up until now, he has shown himself a faithful adviser and given me no reason to doubt his loyalty. But he is a Florentine and the influences of the Medici and the late, unlamented Savonarola may run deep. We will keep him close – but not too close. Will that make you happy?" he asked with true fatherly concern.

"Yes, father. You know there are conspirators all around us."

"I am all too aware of that fact," said Pope Alexander. "My hope is that this upcoming banquet may provide us with some small degree of leverage against our enemies and an increased hold over our allies."

"Just once, father," sighed Lucrezia, "I would like for a ball to be nothing more than a ball."

Looking at his daughter, the pope said wistfully, "I, too, often yearn for simpler times, but such occasions are becoming more and more infrequent."

He looked at her and said, "And on that note my daughter, I must go. I think I have kept the ambassador from Narvarre waiting long enough."

"Oh, papa," she laughed.

As he reached the door, the pope turned and said, "And you haven't forgotten the other thing I asked about. The decorated bags?"

"No father. They will be taken care of as well. Though why you need those is a mystery to me. Just to be sure, we have a month before this ball is to take place?"

"Yes," replied the pope, "and I am counting on you to keep this a secret."

"I understand completely, Your Holiness," she said, curtseying and laughing.

Smiling, the pope looked at her and whispered conspiratorially, "Here's a hint: All shall be revealed in due time."

Before she could protest, he was gone.

* * *

Michelangelo awoke with a headache of epic proportions.

As he lay in bed, he thought back on the day before.

He had indeed received a papal commission. In fact, he had actually received seven commissions if one wanted to be technical. Following wine with Pope Alexander, he had headed to a tavern to celebrate his fortune.

As he rose and busied himself, his head slowly began to clear, and he reflected on everything that Pope Alexander had said to him.

Before the pope had gone into the specifics of his plan, he had asked, "Do you carry prayer beads, Michelangelo?"

"Yes, your holiness," the artist answered.

"Why?" asked the Pope.

"They remind me of the sufferings that Jesus Christ endured for us," said the artist, crossing himself.

"Yes, exactly," said the pope. "Like you, like all men, I too need to be reminded of the agony Our Lord had to undergo.

"Are you tempted, Michelangelo?"

"Every day, Your Holiness. But I do my best to resist."

"Like you, Michelangelo, I too am surrounded by temptation. And like you, I do my best not to succumb. That is why I should like you to create something akin to the rosary – but just for me and those who come after me in this

office." "I am not certain I follow you, your Holiness."

"I want you to create a collection of visual reminders so that when I look upon them, I can see the temptations of the flesh. And I hope that by gazing upon them – and praying – I shall be given the strength to resist such snares. Do you understand, my boy?"

"I think so," said Michelangelo.

"Does Your Holiness know exactly what he wants, or would you like me to develop some rough sketches for you?"

"It's certainly open for discussion," the pope said.

He continued, "I must admit, in some respects, I have planned these to the last detail, but I am aware that if I impose too many limitations on you, I run the risk of strangling your genius in its infancy. So, I think it best that what we do here is collaborate – in the truest sense of the word."

"I understand, Your Holiness."

"Well then, Michelangelo, here is what I have in mind."

The pope then began to outline his ideas in such detail that the artist could see immediately that the pontiff had been planning this for quite some time

Listening intently, Michelangelo was shocked as the pope moved from generalities to specifics and then, in a few cases, to extremely detailed instructions.

After the pontiff had finished, he asked, "Do you think you are up to the task?"

Michelangelo could only nod – he was so stunned by what he had just heard.

"One more thing, Michelangelo. This must be done in absolute secrecy. No one must know – or ever learn – of our endeavor. I understand that you usually work in secret. Keep that in mind, as we go forward, and I have no doubt that more papal commissions will find their way to your door."

Thinking about what he had been asked to do, Michelangelo decided that it was sheer madness. However, he was just as certain that to refuse would have meant the end of his career as an artist – and perhaps his life as well.

With his mind racing, Michelangelo dressed, ate and decided to visit his old friend Stefano. Without telling the miniaturist what he had in mind, he needed to see what hints or suggestions he might pry from the man.

Although he thought he had the tools necessary to carry out the task at hand, he wanted to check with the craftsman to see if there were something special he might require, and if so, the best place to procure it.

Although he had no doubt of his skills, he was venturing into new territory here, and while he preferred working alone, he was fairly certain that he was going to need, if not the help and skill of his erstwhile assistant, at least his advice.

Recalling Stefano's fondness for Chianti, Michelangelo decided that another visit to the tavern might be in order as well. After all, he reasoned, this vintage was being purchased by the pope. How many other artists could make that claim?

Chapter Five – Rome, 1901

After disembarking from the train and making my way through the station – occasionally looking back – I hailed a cabriolet. Fortunately, the driver was fluent in English.

"I should like to go to the Spanish Steps," I told him.

"Is this your first visit to our city, signore?" he asked.

"It is," I replied.

"Then you have chosen a wonderful place to begin your stay. Where will you go after that?" he asked.

"I thought I might walk to the Trevi Fountain and take in the sights along the way."

"An excellent plan, signore. Would you like directions?"

I nodded and as we drove, he explained how to get from the steps to the fountain. "And remember, this is Rome – not London – so take your time, and savor the journey," he laughed.

Twenty minutes later, we arrived at the top of the steps. After departing the cab, I checked to see if other carriages were depositing passengers – none was. I also scoured my surrounding, looking for Holmes, to no avail.

After descending the 135 steps in a leisurely manner, I glanced over to see the house where the poet John Keats had once lived.

The notion that Rome is the Eternal City washed over me, and I was suddenly struck by the lines from his "Ode to a

Nightingale," a poem that had made quite an impression on me as a youth:

"Thou was not born for death, immortal Bird!

No hungry generations tread thee down;

The voice I heard this passing night was heard

In ancient days by emperor and clown."

I had heard there was a movement afoot in England to turn the building into a museum for Keats and Shelley. Although my taste in poetry ran more to contemporary works such as the efforts of Tennyson and Kipling, I could still admire the Romantics, and I must confess, their passion had always stirred something within me.

Turning left, I immediately came to the Plaza Mignanelli, over which towered a statue of the Virgin, which my driver had told me the locals called the Immaculate. I stopped to admire the four statues at the base – Moses, Isiah, King David and Ezekiel – before proceeding up the Via Propaganda toward the Trevi Fountain.

Despite my driver's admonition to go slowly and bask in the warmth that is Rome, I found myself walking at a rather brisk pace, so I forced myself to stop along the way to admire the various buildings and landmarks – and to check periodically to make certain that no one was following me.

Long before I arrived at the Piazza di Trevi, I could hear the rumble of the water. The sound increased in volume as I approached until it had reached a deafening roar. When I finally set eyes upon it, I was stunned at its magnificence.

As I stood there in rapt admiration, I heard a voice at my elbow exclaim, "It really is worth a trip to Rome, is it not, Watson?"

I turned to find Holmes standing next to me, a big smile on his face.

"We are going to have to work on your skills of observation, my friend," he said.

"Have you been following me since we left the station?" I asked.

Holmes nodded. "Almost. I left the station by a different door and watched the cardinal ride by in his carriage. After I was able to make certain that he was not being followed, I took a cab to the base of the Spanish Steps and watched as you descended. Again, I made certain that no one was tailing you, and then I took up the pursuit myself.

"Incidentally, Watson, what aspect of your military career were you reflecting upon a while back?"

I must admit that Homes never ceases to amaze me. "How on earth could you possibly know what I was thinking?" I asked.

"Simple, old fellow. As you walked down the steps and across the square, your pace was that of a tourist taking in the sights. Suddenly, your posture changed, your back straightened and your walk became that of a soldier. I can only deduce that something spurred memories of your days in the military."

"Holmes, you are truly incredible." I then outlined my reflections upon Keats and in turn Tennyson. "I guess the thoughts of Tennyson's 'Charge' and Kipling's 'Gunga Din' found their way into my walk. I suppose that I am an open book," I said.

"Not always, thank goodness," said Holmes. "Now, let us admire this incredible work of art before we make our way to the convent."

"It's all about the water, isn't it?" I asked Holmes after a moment or two.

"Indeed. We have Oceanus in the center being drawn by two seahorses – one calm and obedient, the other restive. I believe the artist has captured perfectly the duality of water. I must admit that I am rather fearful that we shall find ourselves tempest-tossed long before we are able to enjoy tranquil seas again."

As we walked down the cobblestones of the Via Delle Murratte, I took one final glimpse over my shoulder at the majestic creation, and though I hoped Holmes was wrong, even I could not anticipate the perils that lay before us.

We hailed a carriage and Holmes told the driver to take us to St. Peter's Square. We crossed the Tiber and a few minutes later arrived at the edge of the square.

I must say Cardinal Oreglia's description had not come close to doing it justice. I marveled at the enormouds size of the square and estimated that it had to be close to a thousand feet long. I knew that it was capable of holding thousands upon thousands of people. As I gazed at the rows of columns that seemed to reach out and embrace us as we made our way toward the obelisk that stood in the center, I realized that it wasn't so much a square as a long elliptical.

As I was taking in the sights, I heard someone ask

Holmes, "Excuse me, sir. Do you speak English?"

"I do," replied Holmes to a young couple.

"Can you tell me what time it is? I seem to have forgotten my pocket watch."

Casting a sideways glance, Holmes told the couple, "It is just a few minutes before four. As for your watch, I hope it wasn't expensive, because unless you have left it in your hotel room, I'm sure your pocket has been picked."

As we walked across the square, I said to Holmes, "That was rude."

"What was?"

"Pretending to know the time when you didn't even check your watch. You could have asked me. I have my pocket watch right here."

"Then if you will check your watch, you'll find that my estimate was fairly accurate."

Opening my own timepiece, I saw that it was two minutes before four. "How on earth?" I asked.

"The section of St. Peter's Square in which we were standing, the *piazza obliqua*, is actually a giant sundial and the obelisk, which gives the section its name, does double duty as a giant gnomon. I merely checked the shadow against the meridian line and told our acquaintances the time with relative accuracy. Now, had we been deeper in the square, in the *piazza retti*, which is actually more of a trapezoid than straight, I would have been forced to consult my timepiece." "Holmes, is there anything that you do not know?" I exclaimed.

He smiled and said simply, "A great many things, my friend."

Having crossed the square, we arrived at the door of the Suore Francescane dell'Addolorata. As I was about to knock, Holmes reminded me that Cardinal Oreglia had instructed us to use the rear entrance.

We walked around to the back of the building, to what I can only guess is the tradesmen's entrance. There Holmes used a much smaller, less ornate knocker to announce our arrival and almost immediately we were greeted by a nun.

Before I could say anything, she said, "You are welcome, gentlemen. We have been expecting you."

"You have?" I blurted out.

"Indeed. Cardinal Oreglia stopped by a short while ago. After delivering your bags, he told us that you would be along presently. I am Sister Angelica. Did you have a pleasant journey?"

"Indeed, we did," I replied. "And may I say that your English is impeccable."

"It should be," she said, "I was raised in Bath before I became a nun and was assigned to this convent."

Holmes could barely contain his laughter, as Sister Angelica smiled sweetly at my embarrassment.

"Let me show you to your rooms," she said.

We followed her along a long hallway and up a flight of stairs.

"Mr. Holmes," she indicated a door on the left, "This is your room."

Going to the next door. She said, "And Dr. Watson, this is your room. And may I say what an honor it is to meet you both."

"You will find dining hours and a small information booklet on the nightstand," she added.

"We normally close the doors at 8 p.m., but in your case I was told that exceptions would be made. So, I've also left a key to the door by which you entered the convent in each of your nightstands.

"If you care to join us for dinner, we will be eating around six," and then she curtseyed and was gone.

"Let's freshen up and see if the cardinal doesn't send for us," said Holmes. "If we fail to hear from him, we can dine with the sisters."

As I expected, my room was rather spartan, but it was immaculate. The white plaster walls looked as though they had just been scrubbed and freshly painted that day. Aside from a crucifix hanging over the bed, there were no decorations of any sort.

On a small night table next to the bed, I saw the list that Sister Angelica had mentioned. On the dresser were a basin and a pitcher. Outside of a single chair, the only other piece of furniture in the room was a *prei-dieu* made entirely of wood – and without a pad on the kneeler.

Walking to the window, I pulled back one of the heavy linen curtains and saw with a little disappointment that our rooms overlooked a small courtyard. I had rather hoped for a view of the square. Studying the scene below in more detail, I noticed a small fountain in the middle and a few benches on the paths. "What an excellent place for a cigar," I thought, before I remembered where I was.

After washing up, I looked at the list on the night table and saw that breakfast was at 8, lunch at noon and dinner at 6, as sister had said.

"At least I won't go hungry," I thought.

I sat on the bed. The mattress was somewhat thinner than I would have preferred. Still, it would have to do. I was thinking that I might remove my shoes and take a short nap when suddenly, the trip caught up to me. I was overcome by fatigue and no sooner had my head touched the pillow than I was fast asleep.

I have no idea how long I slept, but I woke to a hand shaking my shoulder and Holmes' voice saying, "Come Watson. We have a very important meeting." I saw too that Holmes had placed a plate of sliced fruit on my night table.

"That should tide you over," he said, "and then we will enjoy a fine dinner."

"What time is it? How long have I been sleeping."

"It's just eight o'clock. Now, eat the fruit and let us be on our way. I don't want to keep Pope Leo waiting.

Chapter Six – Rome, 1501

Michelangelo knocked on the door of his erstwhile assistant and waited. He knew Stefano was a heavy sleeper, but it was now after noon. A second knock brought no response. Finally, Michelangelo began to pound on the door. "Wake up, you lazy bastard! I need your help."

Stefano stuck his head out the second floor window. "Is that you, Buonarotti?"

"Yes. What the hell are you doing that you make me wait in the street?"

"I am busy," smirked Stefano.

"You old lecher. Have you got a woman in there with you?"

Stefano simply smiled.

"You do, don't you, and no doubt, she's married, and you thought I was her husband come a calling. Oh Stefano, will you never change?"

"No, my friend, I am afraid not."

With that, the front door opened and a beautiful young woman with a torrent of red hair – easily 20 years younger than Stefano – strode out.

"Thank you very much, signore artist," she hissed. "You have ruined what had the makings of a wonderful afternoon."

"My deepest apologies, signora," he said to her back as she stormed off down the street.

Entering the house, Michelangelo laughed and said, "And my apologies to you Stefano. Had I known…"

"She's right you know," Stefano mused. "It could have been an afternoon for the ages." And then he laughed, "But there is always tomorrow, no?"

"I did bring you a present," Michelangelo said, holding up the wineskin.

"You are a good friend. I forgive you – almost," laughed Stefano as he fetched two cups.

"And how may I be of service to the great Michelangelo?" he asked as he set the cups on the table.

"I have a commission. I have been asked to carve a number of miniatures. As you know, I prefer working on a slightly larger scale, but if I can manage these, it may lead to even bigger assignments."

"And who is your new *patrono*?"

"Leave that for now," said Michelangelo. "When the time is right – if it ever is – you shall know all."

"Sounds rather serious. In that case, how may I help?

Michelangelo decided to play to Stefano's ego, "You are the greatest miniaturist I know – perhaps the greatest in all Italy."

"I should think not," said Stefano, feigning modesty, "but continue."

"I must confess, Stefano, I am worried. This may be the most difficult undertaking of my life. Will I need any special tools for such miniatures."

Stefano thought a moment and then said, "No. I shouldn't think so. The gravers that you use for detail work on your larger pieces should suffice. Just make certain that you keep the cutting edges as sharp as possible at all times."

"I will do that," Michelangelo promised.

Steafano asked, "Exactly, what kind of miniatures are you talking about? I've seen your intricate work. It is magnificent."

"I have been asked to create a series of cameos. Anything you can tell me would be of enormous help."

Stefano smiled. "Now, that changes things somewhat. Do you have any idea what medium will you be working in?"

"What are my options?" asked the artist.

"Well, cameos are generally made from either stones or shells. If you have a choice, use stone. It's more plentiful for one; it's obviously more durable; and it is certainly more forgiving."

"Forgiving?"

"Yes. Consider the thickness of stone as opposed to that of a shell. You want to carve to the point where the stone or the shell changes color. That way your image sits on an intaglio. And you get the positive-negative effect. To that end, I suggest you use either onyx or agate. Of those two, I would always opt for agate. Of course, any stone where two contrasting colors meet will do, but there really aren't all that many from which to choose."

"What are the subjects?" asked Stefano.

"I'd rather not discuss that now."

"You're making it awfully difficult to help you, my friend."

"I know, but I am hoping that my discretion will insure your safety. I pray you will understand."

"I understand your *patrono* values his or privacy and has plenty of money to spare. By the way, this is excellent Chianti. The best I've had in quite some time, and since I know you wouldn't ply me with something this good under ordinary circumstances, I can only assume your sponsor is paying for it. Please extend to him – or to her – my deepest gratitude."

Stefano continued, "Speaking of patrons, you are still friendly with the Medici, are you not?"

"Of course. Why do you ask?"

"Because Lorenzo had one of the most beautiful cameos ever created in his private collection."

"The *scutella di calcedonio!*" exclaimed Michelangelo. "How could I have forgotten!"

"Yes. That cup is perhaps my favorite piece. As soon as I saw it, I knew that it was the work of a genius," Stefano added.

"I never did get to see it," Michelangelo explained.

"How is that possible? You lived in the Medici palace."

"Yes. However, art was Lorenzo's passion. He loved the great pieces almost as much as he loved his children –

perhaps more," laughed Michelangelo. "When that rabblerousing friar Savanorola and his Piagnoni began stoking the fires of unrest in Florence, Lorenzo decided to move many of the pieces in his collection to a remote country villa that he owned."

"That was foresight on Lorenzo's part, given that Savonarola eventually came to power," Stefano said, "but now that monk is dead – hanged and then burned by the people of Florence. Surely you can contact one of Lorenzo's sons and ask to see the *scutella.*"

"I grew up in that household and dined with Piero and Giovanni every night. Piero, who has succeeded his father, is an idiot. Those who call him 'the unfortunate' are being kind. Giovanni is another story, He is truly Lorenzo's son in every way. One can only wonder how different things might have been had Piero become the cleric and Giovanni lived a secular life.

"At any rate, that is a splendid idea. I shall contact my old friend and see if he knows the location of the *scutella* and whether I may be permitted to examine it."

"Pay close attention to the layering. You can see that the artist was working with just four layers and yet he managed to create a world in a small libation bowl. Although generally regarded as a cup, the *scutella* is really more a bowl, Michelangelo."

After another swallow of wine, Stefano continued, "It's not very large either, but it is breathtaking. After you see it, please let me know if you are as taken with it as I am."

"I promise that I will," Michelangelo said, and then he became very serious.

"Stefano, you are the only person I am telling about this project. For your sake – and mine – I beg you, speak of this to no one. Our safety and our lives may well depend upon your silence."

"You make it all sound so ominous, Michelangelo. We are artists; the world pays little attention to us. They care only for our creations. But since you are being so mysterious, and since this Chianti is so good, you have my word. No one shall learn of this from me."

"And if I need your help, can I call upon you?"

"Only if you bring another wineskin," laughed Stefano. "This one is just about empty."

Michelangelo laughed and said, "Have you drunk it all already?"

"Just about," replied Stefano as he poured the last of the wine into his cup.

Michelangelo pondered his next move and decided that he would contact Giovanni and inquire about the *scutella.*

After that he would see about procuring some agate so that he might practice. At that moment, a sudden bolt of inspiration struck the artist.

Rising, he said, "Stefano, I will be in touch. Be well, my friend, and do stay away from the married ladies. It might be worth your life."

Stefano laughed, "If I had your talent, I would sculpt them all – in the nude, of course."

Michelangelo laughed again, and set out to put the first part of his plan into play.

Chapter Seven – Rome, 1901

After I had splashed some cold water on my face and grabbed my coat, Holmes and I left the convent by the way we had entered. As we made our way across St. Peter's Square that evening, I asked Holmes what had happened.

"I was going to wake you for dinner, but upon looking in, I saw that you were fast asleep and decided that you needed rest more than food."

"I returned to my room and was thinking things through when I received a note from Cardinal Oreglia in which he said that the pope wished to see us as soon as possible. So I woke you and we are on our way."

As we entered the square, Holmes continued walking straight ahead rather than turning toward the basilica and the balcony from which the pope often addressed the faithful who had gathered in the square.

"Aren't you going the wrong way?" I asked.

"Not at all," said Holmes, as we passed near the obelisk in the center. "Might I ask a small favor, Watson?"

"Of course," I answered. Despite the onset of evening, there were still a fair number of people milling about the square. I supposed the pleasant weather served as invitation to stay out late.

"If possible, try to look like a tourist."

"I shall do my best, but it would help if I knew where we were going," I said, as Holmes continued walking in the general direction of the Tiber.

"We are going to the Castle Sant'Angelo, which is on the other side of the square and much closer to the river."

"Is the pope going to meet us there?" I asked.

"Not exactly," laughed Holmes. "Do you know anything about Castle Sant'Angelo, Watson?"

"I must confess my ignorance."

"Given your love of opera, I must say that I am rather shocked. That being said, if you'd like, I will be more than happy to serve as your tour guide, signore," said Holmes adopting what I considered a passable Italian accent.

"The building has a long and varied history," he began. "It was constructed as a mausoleum for the Emperor Hadrian in the second century. Eventually, it was turned into a fortress to help defend the papacy, and several popes have lived there as well. I am told the décor of those apartments is quite grand."

"Moreover, it has also served as a prison, housing such notables as the mathematician and philosopher Giovanni Bruno, who was burned there during the Inquisition; the sculptor and goldsmith Benvenuto Cellini also spent some time there, having been imprisoned by Pope Paul III, before he managed to escape"

"You mentioned opera, Holmes," I asked, "How does that figure in?"

"I apologize, Watson. I had quite forgotten that you didn't accompany me when I attended a performance of Puccini's 'Tosca' last year at Covent Garden. The third act takes place in the courtyard of the castle, where after her lover, Cavaradossi is killed, Tosca flings herself from the ramparts.

While you could make a case for 'La Boheme,' I think it may be Puccini's best work yet."

As we neared the castle, Cardinal Oreglia appeared from the shadows. "Good evening, gentlemen," he said, "I cannot express my gratitude for your promptness."

As we approached a massive wooden door protected by two members of the Swiss Guard in full regalia, halberds gleaming wickedly in the torchlight, the cardinal produced an enormous ring of keys. After exchanging pleasantries with the guards, he opened a large padlock and led us inside.

"I have just been giving Dr. Watson a brief history of the castle," said Holmes.

"Well, you might be interested to learn this building is about to undergo another change," the cardinal explained. "We are planning to turn it into a museum. However, that work will take several years. In the meantime, we keep it guarded at all times."

"If there's nothing here at the moment," I asked, "why would you do that?"

The cardinal was about to speak, when Holmes interrupted him, asking, "May I? I have promised to serve as Watson's docent tonight, Your Eminence."

"By all means," said the cardinal. "I have a suspicion that you know almost as much about the Vatican as I do, perhaps even more, Mr. Holmes."

Holmes smiled, "You flatter me, Your Eminence, but my knowledge is confined to the aspects that interest me such as *il passetto Borgo.*"

"The Borgias, again?" I asked Holmes.

"No, Watson, *borgo*, not Borgia. The word *borgo* is almost a cognate for our English borough or the German word *burg*. In the past, it was used to refer to the newer city that often grew up outside the boundaries of the older city.

"There is a secret passage that connects the Castle Sant'Angelo to the Vatican. Hence the *passetto Borgo*. As we walked across the square, I hope you noticed the large wall to your left."

"It is impossible to miss," I replied.

"Inside that wall is the secret passage. The soul of discretion, Pope Leo suggested that we enter the Vatican through the passage, hoping to escape the prying eyes of those who may be monitoring visitors to His Holiness."

Holmes looked at the cardinal, "Am I on the right track?"
"You might as well have read Pope Leo's mind," exclaimed the prelate.

"May I tell Watson the history of *il passetto*?" Holmes asked.

"Please do, Mr. Holmes. I may learn a thing or two from you about the secrets of the Eternal City."

As we entered a narrow walkway, Holmes began, "I believe it was Pope Nicholas III who had the walkway built in the 13th century. In the late 14th century, Pope Alexander VI – who was a Borgia, had a footway built above the existing walkway, and this passage we are in now did double duty, serving also as a gallery."

At that point, Holmes pointed to a slab that had bas relief images of crossed keys, a stole and an elaborate papal tiara that looked more like a helmet than a miter and said, "There you can see Alexander's coat of arms."

He continued, "As you might expect, Watson, there were more than a few impious popes, and if rumor is to be believed, a number made use of this passage to carry out assignations with their mistresses. Also, it did actually provide a means of escape for Pope Alexander, who put it to good use when the French King Charles VIII invaded the city in the late 15th century. Although Charles was known as 'the Affable,' I am certain that the pope would not have enjoyed his company at that point."

"Just a few decades later, Pope Clement VII also used the passage to escape from the Holy Roman Emperor Charles V, who then proceeded to sack Rome and kill most of the Swiss Guard on the steps of St. Peter's Basilica."

"Mr. Holmes, you amaze me," said the cardinal. "Should you ever decide to give up your career as a consulting detective, be assured that you can always obtain a position in the Vatican Library."

Finally, we came to another large wooden door. Again, two members of the Swiss Guard stood in front of it, the axe heads of their halberds gleaming. Cardinal Oreglia nodded at the men and said, "His Holiness is expecting us."

One of them opened the door, and we stepped into the building housing the papal apartments. We quickly passed through what seemed to be some sort of small wine cellar and then we found ourselves in the kitchen.

There was one man sitting at the table with his back to us. When he heard us enter, he rose and turned to face us. Pope Leo XII was a slight, spare man with sharp eyes and a decided gentleness about him. He was wearing a pure white soutane and a white skullcap.

"Mr. Holmes, it is wonderful to see you again," he said smiling at my friend.

Despite his attempt at geniality, it was easy to ascertain that he was under tremendous pressure, and the strain showed clearly on his face. "I could only wish that the circumstances were different," he added.

Holmes walked to the man, dropped to one knee and kissed the proffered pontifical ring. "As always, I remain Your Holiness' humble servant," said Holmes.

Rising he turned to me and said, "Your Holiness, I would like to introduce you to my dear friend and colleague, Dr. John Watson."

Taking my cue from Holmes, I walked forward, genuflected and kissed the ring of the pope, saying simply, "Your Holiness."

"Ah, Dr. Watson. Your recounting of the exploits of Mr. Holmes has brought me many hours of delight. However, I must beg of you that this adventure never see the light of the day."

Before I could say anything, the pope continued, "Gentlemen, I have taken the liberty of preparing some refreshments. Please join me."

We sat at the table while Cardinal Oreglia poured tea and fetched a small silver salver containing grapes, slices of fresh fruit and pieces of biscotti from a sideboard.

Taking a sip, I was delightfully surprised and said, "Your Holiness. I could be in our rooms in Baker Street right now. This is every bit as good as Mrs. Hudson's."

The pope smiled mischievously. "I remember how disappointed Mr. Holmes was in our attempts at proper English tea on his last visit here. I hope you find this more to your liking, Mr. Holmes."

Holmes tasted the tea and also pronounced it excellent.

The pope's face lit up in pleasure. Pausing, he remarked, "I think this is the first time I have smiled in a week."

"Now, gentlemen, let us enjoy our little *spuntino* before we get to the terrible business at hand."

So we made small talk about opera and classical Italian poetry, and for a few moments, I saw the tension ease on the pontiff's face.

"You know of my love of Virgil and Dante," said the Pope, "but I must confess that the more I read, the more I enjoy the stories of your Chaucer. Although I must admit, translating your Middle English into Italian confounds me at times."

"I am sure that it confounds a great many linguists, Your Holiness," said Holmes. Now, shall, we get to the business at hand?"

The pope looked at Cardinal Oreglia. "Gaetano, I am afraid that I must ask you to excuse us. I would spare you this burden."

The cardinal rose, "I understand Holiness. I shall see you for mass in the morning?"

"God willing," said the pope. We exchanged goodnights, and the cardinal left us in the kitchen with the pontiff.

"I should like to continue our discussion of literature, but I am afraid that procrastination will not help us. Mr. Holmes, you know that Italy is a relatively new nation. To say that my country is experiencing growing pains would be the gravest of understatements."

The pope continued, "We are a nation divided. Unfortunately, our warring factions are more prone to murder than mediation. Earlier this year King Umberto was killed on a visit to Monza by an anarchist, Gaetano Bresci, who shot him four times. While the king and I had our differences, in most cases, I found him to be an enlightened man. A true patriot who always put Italy first. Had he lived, we might have been able to resolve the Roman Question, but now that continues to hang over my head as well."

"If memory serves," said Holmes, "General BavaBeccaris turned his cannons on innocent Italian citizens. It is said Bresci killed the king to avenge the massacre in Milan."

"That is what he claimed," said the pope. "While the king pursued his dreams of expansion in Africa, the Italian economy deteriorated. Prices for everything climbed, and demonstrators took to the streets in many cities. In Milan, things grew so bad that the city was placed under military control. During one demonstration, General Bava-Beccaris ordered his cannons to open fire on the demonstrators. When the smoke had cleared, more than 100 had been killed and about 1,000 had been wounded. Adding insult to injury in the eyes of the people, the king presented the general with a medal in recognition of his service."

"In some quarters, the anger was almost palpable. Bresci's actions may have provided the catalyst to unify Italians of all stripes. Certainly, the liberals and the anarchists have found common cause, and as I am sure you are aware, neither group looks upon the church kindly."

"All my life, Mr. Holmes, I have fought the forces of extremism – from both the left and the right. I have compromised when my conscience allowed and remained obdurate when it did not."

"This latest incident compounds matters in a manner with which I am ill-equipped to deal. My country is in turmoil, and now my church is under siege. With all the different alliances playing out across the continent, it is difficult to tell whether Europe is more unified or divided than it has been in the past."

After pausing, the pope continued, "I am no visionary, Mr. Holmes, but I fear the continent may soon be plunged into an all-encompassing war, and there are those who would like nothing more than to reduce the role of the church in worldly affairs and strip the papacy of what little power it still possesses."

"Before we begin, I feel compelled to warn you, Mr. Holmes, that what I am about to tell you may well determine not only the future of Italy but the future of the Church and the papacy as well."

"I fully understand the gravity of the situation," said Holmes.

The pope looked at my friend and said, "Given the obvious danger involved, shall I continue or must I seek another savior?"

Chapter Eight – Rome, 1501

The stone felt heavy and rough in his hand, but looking at it, Michelangelo could see its potential. Gazing intently at the piece of agate, Michelangelo was dazzled by the array of colors, but the red was outstanding – almost papal – in its brilliance.

As he turned the stone over, examining it from every angle, he began to envision the work ahead. He had turned an enormous piece of Carrera marble into the Pieta – the envy of every sculptor in Italy. Surely, seven small sculptures, admittedly much more delicately detailed, were not something that he would permit to get the better of him.

Michelangelo began by cutting across the stone so that the layers were now parallel with his workbench. Taking a small pointed chisel, he began gently to remove layer after layer until he had reached the white above the red. Referring to the preliminary sketch that he had made the night before, he started at the top. It was painstaking work but after some time, he began to see the outline of a head – white on that brilliant red background.

He was debating whether to eat or keep working when he heard a knock at his door. "Paolo, see who is at the door," he yelled.

He could hear the muffled conversation from below, and then Paolo ascended to the landing and said, "Master, I think you had better speak with this gentleman. He insists upon seeing you.

Descending the stairs, Michelangelo saw a soldier standing in the doorway. "How may I help you, signore?"

"I am Captain Antonio Bari, the head of Cardinal della Rovere's personal guard. His Eminence has instructed me to tell you that he would like you to join him for dinner tonight."

Michelangelo was stunned. He was well aware that there was no love lost between della Rovere and Pope Alexander. In fact, with the backing of the French king, della Rovere had tried to have the pope deposed. He had accused Alexander of simony and striking a deal with Cardinal Sforza, who now served as the pope's vice chancellor, to secure the papacy. Alexander, however, had turned the tables on della Rovere and survived to rule Rome, despite the cardinal's best efforts.

Although there had been no overt signs of the rancor that characterized their relationship, Michelangelo knew that while the rivalry had been reduced to a low simmer for the present, it was never far from boiling over.

With an armed soldier at his door and four others on horse outside, Michelangelo decided that to refuse might not be in his best interest – or that of the pope. "Allow me to clean up and get my coat, and I will happily accompany you."

No one spoke during the ride to Cardinal della Rovere's residence. When they arrived, they were greeted in the courtyard by the cardinal himself. After kneeling to kiss the ring, Michelangelo looked at the cardinal – the proverbial thorn in the side of Pope Alexander.

"This is indeed a pleasure, Michelangelo. I have long dreamed of meeting the man who captured the agony of Our Lord and his mother with such poignancy," the cardinal said, blessing himself. "In your sculpture, it is easy to see both the human suffering and the divine promise of that moment."

"You flatter me, your eminence," said the artist.

"No, Michelangelo, you honor me by gracing my humble home with your presence."

Looking around, Michelangelo thought that there were many words one might use to describe Cardinal della Rovere's residence, but "humble" certainly was not one of them.

"How may I be of service to Your Eminence?" Michelangelo asked.

"Ah, directness. I like that in a man," replied the cardinal. "Come, let us enjoy a small repast while we discuss our business together."

"I didn't know we had any business together," thought Michelangelo.

He followed the cardinal up a flight of steps to a balcony overlooking the courtyard and beyond the wall, the city of Rome.

"I never tire of sitting here and taking in the city," said the cardinal. "And I never tire of hearing what aspiring young artists are up to."

"Now who's being direct?" thought Michelangelo.

As they ate, they talked of various subjects and then suddenly, the cardinal said, "As you know Michelangelo, like our present Holy Father, I too am a patron of the arts. I know that you have received a papal commission."

Michelangelo was taken aback by the cardinal's unexpected revelation.

"Don't look so startled, my son. I wouldn't be much of a diplomat, if I didn't know what was taking place right under my nose, in my own city, now would I?"

"May I ask the nature of your assignment?" the cardinal said.

"The Holy Father and I are still working out the details," said Michelangelo. "However," he added, "it will be a sculpture rather than a painting. Beyond that, I can offer nothing more at this time."

"Cannot? Or will not?" asked the cardinal. "I value a man who can keep a secret, Michelangelo. So I am going to tell you one. And you must guard it as closely as you do the details of Pope Alexander's commission. Do we have an understanding?"

Michelangelo could only nod.

"Good. I do not know how what I am about to tell you will affect your relationship with our Holy Father," Michelangelo could hear the bitterness that had crept into the cardinal's voice as he uttered the last three words, "but you may rest assured, my son, that I am going to be pope someday. And you may be equally certain that once I have been installed on the throne of St. Peter, I shall remember both my friends and my enemies, and I will see that each is rewarded in kind."

The cardinal paused, fixed his gaze on Michelangelo, and then asked in a voice that was almost a whisper, "Are you my friend, Michelangelo?"

"I am, Your Eminence," replied the artist.

"Splendid!" exclaimed the cardinal. "And do *we* have an understanding, my friend?"

"Indeed, Your Eminence," said Michelangelo.

"Excellent. I look forward to hearing from you on a regular basis. You will keep me informed of your progress." "You have my word, Your Eminence."

"Now if you will excuse me, it is almost time for vespers. Unless, of course, you would like to join me?"

"I should very much, Your Eminence, but I have a great many tasks to complete. If you would be so kind, please remember me in your prayers."

"Of course," said the cardinal. "Now, I know you must be about the Holy Father's business, but I do look forward to hearing from you, my friend."

"And, indeed you shall," said the artist.

"Captain, please escort Signore Buonarotti home."

"Oh, one more thing, Michelangelo." The cardinal came to him and pressed a small purse into his hand."

Before he could object, the cardinal whispered, "May not an artist have more than one patron?"

"Goodbye, Michelangelo, until we meet again." The cardinal said then he turned and walked away,

The ride to his home was marked by the same silence that had characterized the journey to Cardinal della Rovere's palace. There was a significant difference though, anticipation and ignorance had been replaced by dread.

Later, sitting in his loft, staring at the cameo that he had begun, Michelangelo had a sudden desire to smash the thing to tiny pieces with his mallet.

"If I leave now and head for Florence, perhaps the Medici will take me in," he thought. Then weighing the obvious, he thought, "Still, the influence – and the reach – of the pope cannot be underestimated."

The stone caught his eye again, and he wanted nothing more than to obliterate it, to reduce it to dust.

Struck once again by the brilliant hues, he thought, "I am an artist. I cannot play these games as well as they, and yet it appears that I must learn."

Taking stock of his situation, Michelangelo began to consider his immediate future. "I am 26 years old," he thought, "but if I make a wrong move, I may not live to be 27."

At that moment, he heard the voice of Paolo from below. "Master, I have finished all my chores. May I leave now?"

"Of course, my child," said Michelangelo.

After the boy had departed, Michelangelo lapsed back into his ruminations. And then it hit him. He was being used as pawn in a game between two bitter rivals.

Although he had learned to play chess at the home of the Medici, he knew that the game itself was currently in a period of transition. He had heard that Isabella, the monarch of Spain, had recently changed the rules so that the queen had become a much more powerful piece. He wondered what other changes might be in the wind.

Michelangelo sat there trying to envision the war that would take place and in which he might be called upon to play an instrumental role. But then he thought, "I am no ordinary pawn. I have talent, and if the Spanish ruler can change the role of the queen, perhaps, I can alter the rules that govern the movement of pawns."

The more he thought about it, the more the idea appealed to him. "If luck is on my side, perhaps I can sneak through the enemy lines and launch an unexpected counterattack from the rear before anyone is the wiser."

With his mind racing, he suddenly found his thoughts turning to the Virgin Mary. He began to pray, "Holy Mother, I am your humble servant. I have tried all my life to bring glory to you and your child. The child you loved…"

And there it was, the answer to at least one part of his problem.

Picking up the piece of agate where he had planned to carve a likeness of Pope Alexander, Michelangelo decided instead to create an entirely different image.

"Thank you, Our Lady," he said. "I knew you would not desert your servant in his hour of need."

Chapter Nine – Rome, 1901

"Your Holiness," said Holmes softly, "I am yours to command. If it is in my power to rectify this situation, I shall do so."

"Thank you, Mr. Holmes," said the pontiff.

"Sometime within the past week, the papal apartments were robbed. What was taken is extremely valuable, but more important is the potential of those items to be used to embarrass the church and the papacy. That is what terrifies me."

"May I ask what was taken?"

"A collection of cameos. Seven in all."

"Where were they kept?" asked Holmes,

"The cameos themselves were kept in velvet bags and they resided in a black wooden box. In turn, the box was hidden in a recess behind one of the paintings in my study. Both the box and the door that covers the recess were locked, and both the box and recess had been relocked after the cameos were stolen."

"Can you tell me the approximate size of the cameos?" asked Holmes.

"I should guess that each, which is housed in a silver frame, is approximately three to four inches wide by three to four inches high by and three or four inches deep."

"Are they all the same shape, Your Holiness?"

"No, Mr. Holmes. There are some that are circular and a few that are elliptical."

"And the weight, Your Holiness?"

"I should guess that each weighs several ounces, with the largest one perhaps weighing close to a pound. Each is mounted in an ornate silver frame that is a few inches deep."

"All told, would you say they weigh about five pounds?" asked Holmes.

"That sounds about right," replied the Pope.

"So, they are fairly small, rather lightweight, and I would guess easily concealed," said Holmes.

"Yes, I guess they are," said the pope with a definite sigh of misery.

"And the size of the box?" asked Holmes.

"I should say it was about a foot wide by six inches high and about five or six inches deep," replied the pontiff.

"One more question, if I may," asked Holmes.

"Of course," said the pope.

"Were they fashioned with pins, so that they might be worn like real cameos, or are they purely artistic endeavors?"

"There are no pins per se attached to the cameos. I suppose if one wanted, the frames could be attached to a chain, but they are not the type of cameos that you see women wearing now. So to answer your question, no. I don't think they could be worn unless they were removed from the silver frames that hold them. However, I cannot for the life of me, imagine anyone but the most depraved soul ever wanting to display these in public," said the pope.

"You said they were valuable in and of themselves," said Holmes. "May I ask what makes them so precious?"

"These cameos were the work of one of the greatest artists ever to live. Michelangelo Buonarotti – the same man who painted the ceiling of the Sistine Chapel and created the Pieta – fashioned them – although why he did so has always puzzled me."

"Michelangelo," mused Holmes, "so these miniatures are the work of an artist who spent years laboring in the service of the Church but also felt the need to create something that could bring shame to the church and the papacy. Interesting."

"How many people know about these cameos?" asked Holmes.

"It is a secret that is passed on to each pope, although rumors about their existence and origin have circulated for centuries, I suppose. I first heard of their existence when I was a seminarian many years ago."

"As you might expect, Mr. Holmes, learning they actually do exist and then seeing them proved rather an unsettling discovery for me. However, to answer your question, as far as I know, I am the only person in the world who knows of their existence with absolute certainty, except of course for yourself and Dr. Watson now."

"Well, we can safely assume that at least one other person knew," said Holmes.

"Yes, but how did that person come by this knowledge?" asked the pope. "As you might suspect, Mr. Holmes, the head of the church is entrusted with a great many secrets. I have taken special pains throughout my reign to make certain that no one has ever learned of these cameos."

"I understand," said Holmes. "I am equally certain that in the course of my investigation, I shall learn how their existence came to light. Now, Your Holiness, may I see the room where the cameos were kept?"

"Of course, Mr. Holmes. Follow me," said Pope Leo.

We left the kitchen and walked up a narrow stairway, which I am guessing was used more often by the servants than the pope. Upon arriving at the second floor, we walked down a wide hall toward the front of the building. We entered a large sitting room and then passed through a door to a much smaller study. "This is where the cameos were kept," said Pope Leo.

"I should like very much to examine this room in detail," said Holmes.

The room contained a large oak desk with one chair behind it and two sitting chairs in front. The walls were covered with bookcases and in between each bookcase hung a painting. Looking at them, I recognized a scene from "The Divine Comedy," which depicted Dante standing between the city of Florence and the mountain of purgatory. I also saw a portrait of St. Michael the Archangel as well as renderings of several other saints and one depiction of Mary, the mother of Christ.

After taking everything in, Holmes looked at the pope and said, "I assume the recess is located behind painting of the the Virgin Mary."

The pope looked totally flummoxed as he stared at Holmes and asked, "But how could you possibly know that?" "I did not know, but I am aware of the high regard with which Your Holiness holds both St. Michael and the Virgin," said Holmes, indicating the artwork. "Given the fact that the portrait of St. Michael is across the room from your desk and appears to be quite heavy while the painting depicting Mary is much closer to your desk and appears to be just wide enough to conceal a recess of the dimensions you described, I deduced that is where the secret compartment must be." "Mr. Holmes, you amaze me," exclaimed the pope.

"May I remove the painting," asked Holmes.

"Of course," said the Pope.

Holmes strode across the room, grasped the frame and lifted. He turned and carefully placed the image on the pope's desk. Taking out his lens, he began to examine the door that concealed the recess. Speaking more to himself than us, he said, "Picking this lock would be child's play for an accomplished thief, but whoever did open this door without the key was no professional. There are a number of small scratches here and there that appear to be quite recent. They are readily visible to the naked eye and indicative of a shaky hand, poor eyesight or both."

Removing a small case from his pocket, Holmes selected a slender pick and had the lock open in about two seconds. He then removed the box, which the pope had described to us earlier. Training his lens upon that lock, he remarked to no one in particular, "There are similar scratch marks on this lock as well."

"I can say with certainty that you were not robbed by a professional thief," said Holmes. "Your Holiness, besides yourself, who else has access to these rooms on a regular basis?"

"Outside of the household staff and my advisors, no one, Mr. Holmes," answered the pope,

"And you're certain of that, Your Holiness?"

"I am."

"Then I am afraid that I must inform you that this robbery was committed by a member of your staff," said Holmes.

"I will not say that's impossible," said the pope. "I have too much respect for your abilities. But I do hope, at least in this instance, that you are wrong, Mr. Holmes."

Softening, Holmes said quietly, "I hope for your sake that I am as well, Your Holiness, but I rather doubt that I am."

"Would it be possible to get a list of the staff and then for you to schedule meetings for us?" asked Holmes.

"I shall have Cardinal Oreglia prepare the list, which I shall send to you in the morning. Also, I shall arrange to have the entire staff here tomorrow afternoon."

"If Your Holiness has no objections, I should like to conduct my interviews in this room," said Holmes.

"Not at all, Mr. Holmes."

"We can do no more tonight," said Holmes. "Would Your Holiness like us to return to the convent through *il passetto*?" asked Holmes.

"If you wouldn't mind, Mr. Holmes."

"Then we will take our leave," said Holmes. "And we will meet you back here tomorrow at …" Holmes let the sentence trail off.

"Does two o'clock suit you, Mr. Holmes?" asked the pope. "I am hoping that you can finish early enough to enjoy your tea at its proper time."

"Until then," said Holmes.

The pope walked us downstairs and back to the entrance of the passageway. "Good night and God bless you, gentlemen, and may I say, I feel much better already, Mr. Holmes."

"Hopefully, we can put this unpleasantness behind us before too long," replied Holmes.

As we walked through the passage toward the Castle Sant'Angelo, I asked Holmes, "Do you really think you can wrap this up that quickly, Holmes?"

"No," said Holmes, "I am afraid that we have taken just the first few steps on what may prove to be a very long and very dark journey, Watson."

"Then why did you tell the pope that?"

"With everything Pope Leo has on his mind, I thought a little white lie might serve him far better than the unvarnished truth at this point."

"Holmes, you are incorrigible!"

"Perhaps, Watson. Perhaps, I am. Now, tell me what you learned from this evening. You saw everything I saw. What struck you?"

"Well, I agree that the locks were picked by an amateur. That much is obvious."

"And how did they get the cameos out of the Vatican?"

"I assume they just put them in their pocket and left," I answered. "I think there's a bit more to it than that," said Holmes. "I think that the woman who took them pinned the bags to the inside of her garment in different places to avoid any telltale, jangling noises as well as to avoid damaging the cameos. After all, Watson, they were created by Michelangelo."

"A woman, you say?"

"Yes, I am quite certain of that. And I am equally certain of how she committed the theft. The only thing that puzzles me is the why, and once we know that we will also know in which direction we must proceed."

We traversed the rest of the passage in silence, nodded at the Swiss Guards and entered St. Peter's Square. Despite the late hour, there were still a few people strolling about. As we passed the obelisk, Holmes said, "I hope you brought your key, Watson. I should hate to disturb any of the sisters at this time of night."

"I have it here," I said.

As we neared the convent, I noticed the entire building was dark, save for the lights in the small chapel.

"Someone is late at her prayers," I remarked to Holmes.

"Perhaps someone has a reason to be," the detective remarked enigmatically.

As we reached the rear door, Holmes turned to me and said very softly, "Give me your key, old man. I am going to smoke a pipe in the courtyard. I rather doubt the nuns would enjoy the aroma of my shag, and I have the feeling that this may turn out to be a two- or three-pipe problem."

I opened the door, handed him my key and headed upstairs while Holmes proceeded into the courtyard. After changing for bed, I looked out the window. Although I couldn't see my friend in the darkness, if I strained my eyes, I thought I could just discern the soft glow of the embers in his pipe.

As I drifted into a well-deserved sleep, I thought I heard the sound of voices and promptly decided that I was dreaming, without giving it a second thought.

Chapter Ten – Rome, 1501

Energized, Michelangelo rose at dawn. After making himself breakfast, he returned to the loft, where he began sketching the new likeness. In an hour, he had a fairly complete drawing. When Paolo arrived, Michelangelo was stunned to discover that it was already past nine.

After hiding the sketch, Michelangelo left the house and set out on foot for the residence of his old friend and schoolmate Cardinal Giovanni di Lorenzo de'Medici. He knew that Giovanni had returned to Rome a year ago and that the pope had received him warmly – at least on the surface. How deep that affection really ran was a mystery, given that Giovanni and Cardinal della Rovere had campaigned against Alexander's ascension to the papacy.

He also knew that Giovanni, always of a scholarly nature, since returning to Rome, had immersed himself in studying art and literature. Perhaps he had tired of the politicking of the Curia or perhaps he simply wished to live in peace, maintaining a strict neutrality that showed he was not a threat to the House of Borgia.

Since the day promised fair weather and plenty of sunshine, Michelangelo decided to walk to the home of Cardinal de'Medici. After about 30 minutes, he arrived at the palace and told the servant who he was and that he wished to see the cardinal. He was ushered into a sitting room. The walls and ceilings were all frescoes and no expense had been spared in the décor.

"Did none of them take a vow of poverty?" Michelangelo wondered.

At that point, Giovanni entered, dressed in the red cassock and biretta of a cardinal, and rushed across the room, his arms open, to embrace Michelangelo. "And how is my old friend?" Giovanni asked, pulling Michelangelo to him. "It's been so long."

"It has been far too long," Michelangelo replied. "I often thought of you while you were abroad."

"A rather necessary sojourn," Giovanni laughed, "but an educational one as well. I spent much of my time studying German and Dutch artwork. And now that I am returned, I must say their best are not nearly as good as ours."

Both men laughed heartily. "I hear you have been busy, Michelangelo. Would you like to kiss my ring and add it to your collection?"

"Is there anyone in Rome, who doesn't know my business?" asked the artist in exasperation.

"Outside of the Curia, I should say a great many people are unaware of your comings and goings. Within the Curia, that is another matter altogether," he laughed.

"It's just as a simple matter of preservation. We all keep a servant fee'd in the houses of our rivals. My chambermaid reports my activities to della Rovere, my groom reports to the pope, and my cook's helper receives a regular stipend from the vice chancellor, Cardinal Sforza. Shall I continue?" he laughed.

"And you have spies in their homes as well?" asked Michelangelo.

"Spies has such a sinister sound to it. I rather prefer to think of them as 'friends,' who keep me up to date on the latest news and gossip and any and all misbehavior," he said, laughing again.

"And am I the subject of such gossip?" asked Michelangelo.

"Indeed, you are. I know that you met with the pope, from whom you received a commission, though exactly what the project is, no one seems quite certain. Then the next day you had dinner with della Rovere, who gave you a purse filled with gold florins. I assume that was for you to keep him informed. You see how it works Michelangelo?"

"And now you are here. Were we not such good friends, I might take umbrage at finishing third."

"I need a small favor," admitted Michelangelo.

"If you are trying to play Pope Alexander against Cardinal della Rovere, you are engaging in a very dangerous game, my friend. Are you certain that a 'small favor' will suffice?"

"I am not playing anyone against anyone," Michelangelo replied. "I am a simple artist trying to eke out a living."

"Artist, indeed! I have seen your Pieta. It is a masterpiece! Simple – not at all."

"You flatter me," said Michelangelo.

The cardinal brushed aside the last remark. "How may I help you my friend?"

"Do you know where the *scutella de calcedonio* is?"

"Of course, why?"

"I should like very much to see it," Michelangelo said.

"Is that your papal commission?" Giovanni asked.

"Not exactly," said Michelangelo.

"But there is a connection?"

"Of sorts. And that is all I will say until I see it," Michelangelo said.

"Then follow me," Giovanni said.

"It's here?" Michelangelo asked.

"Indeed it is. I couldn't trust Piero with such a piece," Giovanni explained.

The cardinal then led Michelangelo up a flight of stairs to the second floor of his palace. There was artwork everywhere. Michelangelo stopped at a small portrait. After examining it carefully, he asked, "Who painted this?"

"A fellow by the name of Raffaello Sanzio, who goes by the name of Raphael. He's quite young, but I think he shows great promise. He rather reminds me of another young artist, I knew some years ago," said Giovanni pointedly.

Michelangelo said, "I see a rival. You must do everything you can to discourage this Raphael."

"You are not serious?" asked Giovanni.

"About discouraging him, no! About a rival, absolutely!"

They entered a large salon filled with statuary, vases and sundry other pieces. Michelangelo tried to take in some of the myriad items that had made up Lorenzo's collection. In the middle, sitting by itself on a beautiful mahogany table covered by a simple white cloth, was the *scutella*.

Michelangelo walked over to it and began to scrutinize it carefully, taking in the different figures. He noticed the careful arrangement as well as the various layers of stone. Looking at Giovanni, he asked, "May I?"

"Indeed. But you must promise to be as careful with this plate as you were with your chisel and the face of the Virgin."

Michelangelo smiled. Holding the bowl in his left hand, he paid careful attention to the each figure. He knew there was widespread disagreement about whom they symbolized, but he didn't care. He examined each carefully, taking in all the minute details.

Then he closed his eyes and ran his fingers over each much as a blind man might study a face. Caressing the images carefully, he could feel where the artist had etched the beard of the figure seated on the left. He felt the delicate work that had gone into the two airborne figures, the hair and the face of the male standing in the center. He had no idea how long he traced the figures before his reverie was interrupted by Giovanni, who said quietly, "You must also look at the reverse?"

Turning the scutella over, Michelangelo was stunned to see the face of a gorgon – perhaps Medusa herself – glaring ominously at him. Again he studied the horrific image in detail, committing every aspect to memory. Then, as he had with the figures on the obverse, he closed his eyes and let his fingers explore the surface, noting the few rough spots, the overall smoothness and the swirling lines that made up the snake-like tentacles of the gorgon's hair,

After he had finished, he placed the bowl back on the table as gently as possible. "Thank you, Giovanni. You have surrounded yourself with works of genius, and I must say that I am inspired."

"You too are a genius, my friend," said the cardinal. "I am just a humble collector."

"You must preserve these things for future generations," said Michelangelo.

"That is certainly my intent, but you know the vicissitudes of fortune, my friend."

"Indeed," said the artist.

"Will you stay for a small repast? We have so much catching up to do," asked the cardinal.

"Another time, Your Eminence," said Michelangelo. "I promise to come see you very soon, and we shall talk and laugh and reminisce."

"I will hold you to that Michelangelo. And remember, lying to a prince of the church is one of the surest ways to eternal damnation."

They laughed again, and as Michelangelo hugged his friend good-bye, the cardinal said, "In all seriousness, my friend, be careful. The pope and della Rovere would like nothing more than to attend the other's funeral. I shall do everything in my power to protect you, but we are in Rome not Florence, and the Medici name does not carry the weight here that it does at home."

"I understand," said Michelangelo, "but the most important thing is your friendship."

They embraced again, and as he made his way home, Michelangelo considered everything the cardinal had told him. "At least I have one ally in this war," he thought.

Chapter Eleven – Rome, 1901

The following morning I was awakened from a deep sleep by a gentle rapping on my door. "Watson, they are serving breakfast, and I am absolutely famished," said Holmes.

Pulling on my trousers, I said, "Come in, Holmes. I will need just a few minutes to dress and shave."

Holmes entered and sat on the only chair in the room. He had a smile on his face that I had seen before.

"Looking at you, I can only assume that you received some sort of good news."

"Better than that, Watson. I told you I had a pretty good idea of who had stolen the cameos and how. Now I know why that person stole them as well."

"You do?" I exclaimed.

"I do," he said, "and I am afraid that we are facing an adversary who is totally ruthless. In fact, I am certain that he will stop at nothing to achieve his goal – and that includes murder."

"What on earth happened last night?"

Holmes said, "I thought it odd that when we arrived back here so late that the only room where the lights were burning was the chapel. So, I decided to smoke in the garden in hopes of learning who was at her prayers so late. I had formulated a theory, and I was hoping that the pieces would fall into place."

"I was just beginning my third pipe when my efforts were rewarded. A nun left the chapel, locking the door behind her.

As she passed me, we nodded, and then I proceeded to drop a lock pick on the path."

"The sound of metal hitting stone was rather distinctive, and I am certain that it probably seemed much louder than it actually was, given the stillness that enveloped us."

"I bent over, picked it up, and said, 'Sister, I believe you dropped this as you passed'."

"As I held it up, her eyes told me everything I needed to know. In addition to confusion, I saw recognition. She knew what I was holding. Before she could make any denials, I asked, 'Would you like to tell me about it, Sister? I can assure you that your secret is safe with me'."

"She began to weep softly. 'I had to do it, Mr. Holmes. They threatened to kill my entire family if I didn't do exactly as they said. My mother lives here in Rome with my younger sister and her three children. They told me they would torture them and kill them slowly. They said if I didn't do their bidding, they would make me watch, and then they would rape and kill me."

"They said if I told anyone, I should look for my nieces in the Tiber – with their throats cut. They are just babies, Mr. Holmes."

"I told her, that I suspected it might be something like that," Holmes said.

"I love the church, Mr. Holmes. I have devoted my life to it, but I could not let them slaughter my family."

"They gave me a tool just like that one and showed me how to use it. Then they told me about the hiding place in the Holy Father's office. They said to remove the bags without looking in them and to pin the bags to the inside of my habit." "Do you know why they chose you?" I asked.

Holmes paused and then continued, "She told me that she was one of the sisters responsible for the pope's laundry, As such, they knew she had access to the papal apartments. Moreover, who would ever suspect a nun of stealing from the pope?"

"You did," I exclaimed, as I continued shaving.

"Yes, I'm afraid that is true," said Holmes ruefully. "But then in my own defense, I must admit that I suspect everyone, although I'm not quite certain what that says about my nature either."

Holmes seemed to ponder this sudden moment of selfrevelation before he said, "And now, Watson. Let us eat. I am afraid we have a very busy day in front of us."

A few moments later, we descended to the dining room and found ourselves alone. As we enjoyed a simple breakfast of brioche and tea, Holmes laid out his plans for the day.

"First, we must contact Cardinal Oreglia and cancel this afternoon's meeting with Pope Leo. Now that I know who took the cameos, I need to find out who made her do it."

"Are you going to tell the pope about her?" I asked.

"Absolutely not. I made the good sister a promise that her secret would remain safe with me. Surely, a man who understands the sanctity of the confessional can appreciate a vow of that nature."

"So, what will you be doing?" I asked.

"I shall be making discreet inquiries into the various anarchistic factions in Rome," he replied.

"Not dressed like that, I hope"

"No," laughed Holmes. "I must do some shopping this morning and procure myself the proper clothing and accoutrements. I rather doubt an Italian would be seen smoking my meerschaum."

"And what about me? What shall I be doing?"

"I need you to pose as a researcher, Watson." "And into what field will I be delving?"

"You must pay a visit to the Vatican Library. There, you will present yourself as Dr. James Watson, a faculty member at Oxford, who is doing research into the rebuilding of St. Peter's Basilica under Pope Julius II."

"To what end?" I asked.

"I want to see how thoroughly the Vatican Library officials vet your credentials. In 1881, Pope Leo opened the secret Vatican archives to qualified researchers. In actuality, though, the word 'secret' is probably better translated as 'personal'."

"These archives contain state papers, papal account ledgers and other such daily drivel. By pretending to focus on the rebuilding, I think you should find yourself somewhere near the papers of Pope Alexander VI. Who knows what you may discover there."

"It was a very active period in the papacy, Watson. After Alexander died, he was succeeded by Pope Pius III, by all accounts a compromise candidate whose papacy lasted less than a month. After Pius, Cardinal Giuliano della Rovere, a sworn enemy of the Borgias, was elected pope, taking the name Julius II."

"His reign was marked by massive building projects, including St. Peter's and the painting of the ceiling of the Sistine Chapel by our friend, Michelangelo. It was also memorable for two other reasons."

"Pope Julius was the pope who granted the dispensation that allowed our King Henry VIII to marry Catherine of Aragon, and we all know how that ended up. Julius II is also blamed by many scholars for causing the Protestant Reformation. So desperate was he to raise funds for his various projects that he offered indulgences to those who gave alms. It was that sale of indulgences that so angered Martin Luther that he posted his 95 theses on the door of All Saints Church in Wittenberg."

"So as I say, Watson, you should find yourself in a section of the archives – if you are able to pass muster – that is rife with papal corruption. One can only wonder what you might uncover."

Having finished our breakfast, we agreed to meet at the convent for dinner and then proceeded to go our separate ways.

I decided to do a little research into the popes of the period before trying my luck at the Vatican Library. I found Sister Angelica and asked her where I might locate a library with English volumes in it. She told me that I should try the Rome National Central Library. Ensconced within the Collegio Romano, the library had been created by St. Ignatius Loyola, the founder of the Jesuit order, and was located not too far from the Trevi Fountain.

Walking across St. Peter's Square, I headed down the Via Gregorio VIII, where I promptly found a cab. We soon crossed the Tiber, and moments later, I stood in front of the college. I made my way inside and was directed to a room filled with volumes in English. I found several histories of the papacy and spent the morning reading about the misdeeds and accomplishments of both Alexander and Julius. I focused my attention on the latter and soon I had a pretty firm grasp of the machinations that led to the destruction of the old St. Peter's and the construction of the new.

I had also developed a plan of my own for getting into the Vatican archives, which I thought had more than a passing chance of success.

After leaving the college, I stopped at a café where I ordered a cup of tea and a pastry. I enjoyed watching the people, and at the same time, I was fine-tuning my scheme in my mind.

After several slight revisions, I found a hansom cab and headed back to the Vatican. After leaving the cab, I walked along the Via Sant'Anna and then turned into the Belvedere Courtyard. I had learned that morning that Pope Julius had used the garden to showcase his sculpture collection, including the statue of Laocoon and his sons. Shortly after it was unearthed, Julius acquired the life-sized statue of the Trojan priest, described so vividly in "The Aeneid," and his boys being attacked by sea serpents and set it up for public display in a niche in his Belvedere Garden. After being taken from Rome during the French conquest of Italy in 1798, the statue had been returned and now resided in the Vatican Museum.

I had made my way to the front door of the Vatican Library. Upon entering, I was greeted by a receptionist who asked my business.

I said that I was a writer doing research for my next book, and I explained that the reconstruction of St. Peter's under Pope Julius would figure prominently in the plot. He seemed quite amenable to my request and offered to show me to that section of the archives himself.

"We do not receive too many requests from writers, signore. Most of those seeking such access are either academics or historians."

"Interesting," I remarked.

"Has anyone else been to the section recently?" I asked innocently.

"Last month, we had a researcher from northern Italy spend some days back there. Aside from you two, I don't think anyone has sought access to those documents for at least a year."

I had to fight to restrain myself from peppering the man with questions about the so-called "researcher." Instead, adopting the most innocent of tones, I asked casually, "It wasn't Dr. Fabonaci from Milan, was it?"

"No signore. It was a Dr. Raffaelo Sanzio from Urbino. Do you know him?"

"No. But I have heard of him," I lied. All the while I was thinking that I couldn't wait to tell Holmes the news.

We were just about to enter the archives when I heard a stern voice behind me say, "Excuse me, Dottore Watson, before you enter the archives, I should very much like a word with you."

Turning, I saw a rather fierce-looking member of the *carabinieri* staring at me with his hand on a pistol at his hip.

Chapter Twelve – Rome, 1501

For the next three days, Michelangelo had no visitors. His life had returned to normal – with one exception. He discovered that the cameo on which he was working demanded an inordinate amount of attention, perhaps even more, than any of his earlier works. Still, the hours passed quickly as he carved, made slight corrections and alterations and polished.

Late one night, he looked at the cameo objectively and pronounced it finished. "I think His Holiness will be pleasantly surprised," he said aloud.

On the fourth day, there was a knock at the door in the early afternoon. He heard Paolo in conversation below, and wondered with whom the boy might be speaking.

He hadn't long to wait to find out. Paolo bounded up the stairs, stood on the landing, his head poking above the floor and said, "Master, Pope Alexander would like you to join him for dinner."

Michelangelo heaved a sigh of relief, and was glad that it was the pope rather than Cardinal della Rovere.

"What shall I tell the messenger?" asked the boy.

"Did he give you a time?"

"Yes master, seven o'clock."

"Tell the messenger that I am the pope's humble servant. I shall be at the papal palace at the appointed time." After Paolo scrambled downstairs, he suddenly yelled up, "The pope says he will send a carriage for you at 6:30." With that distraction behind him, Michelangelo picked up the cameo again and thought, "You are beautiful. Now, let us hope my new master shares my vision."

He spent the rest of the afternoon, checking and rechecking his work, smoothing and polishing and searching for the tiniest imperfection. Finally, finding none, he thought, "If nothing else, this should buy me the pope's good will – for now."

Around six o'clock, Michelangelo began to dress. Putting on his best doublet, he hoped to make a slightly more favorable impression on those surrounding the pope than he had previously.

When the carriage arrived, he carefully wrapped the cameo in a piece of red velvet purchased just for the occasion and put it into his purse.

During the ride, he tried to anticipate Pope Alexander's reaction, and in turn, his own.

Upon arriving at the papal palace, he was greeted once again by Father Ferrante. After exchanging pleasantries, the priest escorted Michelangelo into the papal apartments.

"His Holiness will be with you shortly," Father Ferrante said. "In the meantime, you are to make yourself at home."

Left to his own devices, Michelangelo admired the frescoes and other artwork that adorned the room. His reveries were interrupted by the entrance of Pope Alexander. Once again, he was wearing a white soutane. He was also wearing a red cloak secured at the throat by an ornate gold pin in the shape of a love knot and a red *camauro* trimmed with ermine.

"So good to see you again, my friend," said the pope warmly. "And how are you proceeding in your artistic endeavors?"

"Things are moving apace, Your Holiness," said Michelangelo. "In the wake of our last conversation, I have been practicing."

"Have you, my boy? And are you pleased with the results? I realize that I have set you a difficult task."

Reaching for his purse, Michelangelo said, "I shall let Your Holiness judge the success of my efforts, and if you are pleased, then we can continue. If, however, you should find fault with my humble labors, then you may feel free to search for another artist."

Michelangelo handed the pope the red velvet containing the cameo and said, "I hope this brings Your Holiness some small measure of joy."

The pope pulled back the cloth, turned the cameo over and then stared at it without saying a word. After what seemed an eternity, he pulled his gaze from the stone, looked at Michelangelo, and said simply, "Magnificent!"

Michelangelo felt himself tossed by a sea of emotions, all fighting for supremacy. Eventually, joy emerged triumphant as Michelangelo was glad that he had pleased the pope.

"How did you get her to sit for you?" the pontiff asked.

"She didn't," replied the artist. "In fact, we have never formally met."

"But you have captured her perfectly. I can see the determination in the set of her jaw while the slight tilt of her head conveys the quizzical quality that she so often displays. And her beauty shines through in every detail, and yet you say that you have never met my daughter. How is this possible?"

"I have been gifted with a memory that allows me to retain images, even after seeing something just once," explained Michelangelo.

"I have encountered your daughter at several functions at Cardinal Riario's palace, and I must confess that I was struck by her beauty. I hope that I have done her justice."

"That is a precious gift, indeed," said the pope. Looking at the cameo once again, he said, "I knew I had made the right choice when I asked you to undertake this commission."

"Michelangelo, I must tell you that you have made your pope extremely happy. More importantly, perhaps, you have brought such joy to a father that now it is I who am in your debt."

"You praise is payment enough," said the artist.

"I shall think of something, I promise you," said the pope, "and perhaps I will be able to surprise you as you have me."

"Now, let us enjoy our dinner," said the pontiff.

Michelangelo followed the Pope Alexander into a small dining room, where a lavish table had been set.

The napkins were snowy white, the plates trimmed with gold and the silverware had a substantial heft. The golden goblets all sparkled in the candlelight.

The pope proved a gracious host once again, regaling the artist with stories about monarchs who had misbehaved and cardinals who had strayed.

Michelangelo was quite enjoying himself when the pope asked, "And how are my good friends Cardinal della Rovere and Cardinal de'Medici?"

Although he had expected the topic to arise at some point in the evening, the blasé manner in which the pope had introduced it still managed to take Michelangelo by surprise. Searching for words, he decided to tell the truth. "Cardinal de'Medici is well. He busies himself with his artwork and books."

"And the nature of your visit?" the pope asked innocently.

"The Medici family possesses an ancient cameo that I wanted to study before I attempted the likeness of Lucrezia."

"Oh yes, the scutella," said the pope. "Well, then that was a visit worth making," said the pontiff as he looked again at the engraved image of his daughter. "And His Eminence, Cardinal della Rovere?"

"He summoned me and asked me exactly what I might be doing for Your Holiness. Rest assured, I told him nothing."

"And did he give you anything?"

"A purse with 30 florins," answered Michelangelo.

"Christ was betrayed for 30 pieces of silver," remarked the pope. "I wonder if he is trying to send me a message," he mused aloud.

"I am loyal to Your Holiness," said Michelangelo.

"Would that you were a member of the Curia," laughed the pope. "Now to business, shall we?"

"The date of the banquet has been set. It will take place on October 30 here in the papal palace. Many members of the Curia will be present as will various other dignitaries," said the pope.

"Would you prefer to meet your subjects beforehand? Because I can arrange that, or do you think that marvelous memory of yours will hold you in good stead, given the diverse tasks?"

"I hope that seeing them that night will suffice," said the artist.

"Wonderful. I have secured a number of pieces of stone that I will have delivered to your home, or you may work here. It is your choice."

"I think I should prefer my loft," said the artist. "The light is constant, all my tools are there and it is a bit more private."

"As you wish," said the pope agreeably.

"I have taken the liberty of making a list of the different subjects and the deadly sin that should be assigned to each," said the pope, reaching inside his cloak to hand Michelangelo a scroll.

"I have included some other information there that I think you may find useful," he added.

"Your Holiness is too kind," said the artist.

Unrolling the parchment, Michelangelo looked at the names on the list.

"Is there anyone there with whom you are not familiar?" asked the Pope.

"No, Your Holiness. I have seen all of these men at least once and can recall their visages in detail."

"Splendid," said the pontiff.

"Holiness?"

"Yes."

"How I am to execute these? Surely, none of these men will want to be captured by me."

"No, my son," laughed the pope. "They certainly will not. During the banquet, you will be hidden behind a screen. I'm afraid it is the only method my poor intellect could devise to bring everyone together in the same place at the same time."

"I think that will work," said Michelangelo, "as long as there is sufficient light."

"There will certainly be light at the start of the ball," the pope promised. "However, I cannot say for certainty that the illumination will be to your liking as the evening proceeds. Still, if you should desire to get closer, I will make certain that the robe of a Franciscan friar – complete with hood – is left for you. Should you wear it, don't forget to don the sandals."

"I think that if you time your forays properly, no one will even notice your presence."

"Indeed?" said Michelangelo, "How can you be so certain?"

At that, the pope laughed heartily and said simply, "I am fairly certain this ball will be unlike any other that you may have attended. I will provide you with more details as we get closer to the date."

"As you wish, Your Holiness."

"Now, Michelangelo. I have something for you," said the pope. "This is not the surprise of which I spoke of earlier, but something I should have given you at our last meeting."

The pope rose and walked to a side table. Opening a drawer, he withdrew a small chest. Returning to the dinner table, he placed the chest in front of Michelangelo. "Think of this as a small retainer," he said.

"This is not necessary, Your Holiness."

"I insist," said the pope. "Thus far, you have proven a loyal servant, Michelangelo. I am of the belief that fidelity should be rewarded."

"Thank you," said the artist.

"It does come with one small caveat," said the pope. "Next time you see della Rovere – and I have no doubt that after our dinner tonight, you shall be hearing from him shortly – you must endeavor to persuade him to attend my ball. I am certain that an invitation from me would simply be ignored, but accompanied by some encouragement from you, it might pique his curiosity."

"I shall do my best," said the artist.

"Tell me, Michelangelo. Given his machinations, is he not the personification of pride, or have I missed the mark?"

"No, Holiness, I should consider your assessment impeccable. Were your words an arrow, I am certain they would have hit the bulls-eye dead center."

"And with that complexion, I am equally certain that violet is a color that suits him. Do you agree?" "Again, Holiness. Your arrow flies true."

"Michelangelo, be well," said the Pope.

During the ride home, Michelangelo opened the chest and without counting, he guessed that it contained at least 200 gold pieces.

"I may only be a pawn," he thought, "but at least I am a well-paid one."

He spent the rest of the ride, thinking back over everything the pope had said and he kept repeating the words in his mind, "I am fairly certain this ball will be unlike any other that you have attended," and wondering what exactly the pontiff had planned for that night.

Chapter Thirteen – Rome, 1901

Looking at the *carabinieri*, I felt slightly unnerved. Summoning up my courage, I tried to sound casual as I asked, "How may I help you, signore?"

He strode toward me, stopping about a foot away. "You are Dottore John Watson from England, are you not?" he demanded.

"I am indeed," I replied.

"Are you the same Dottore John Watson, who chronicles the exploits of Sherlock Holmes?"

"Guilty as charged," I answered.

Breaking into a smile, he said, "It is such a pleasure to meet you dottore. I have long been a fan of yours. What brings you to Rome, may I ask?"

"I am researching a book." I said.

"A Holmes' mystery?" he inquired.

"Not exactly," I replied. "I am trying to expand my breadth as a writer."

"I see," he replied. "Is Mr. Holmes with you? I should like very much to meet him."

"He is in Rome," I said, "but where he is right now, I cannot say."

"Well, my name is Captain Tritini, Angelo Tritini. Here is my card. If I may be of assistance to you in any way, please do not hesitate to contact me. And if you could arrange a meeting with Mr. Holmes, I should be eternally grateful."

"I shall do my best," I replied. We shook hands and he left. I was thinking to myself that the day could not have gone any better. I had gained entrance to the archives and made an ally at the same time. Holmes will be pleased, I thought to myself.

My escort said, "Dottore Watson, if you are ready. You may bring paper and writing implements into the archives, but nothing else."

I showed him the pad I had purchased, and followed him down a long hall to the back of the building. We entered a room that was filled from floor to ceiling and side to side with bookshelves, groaning under the weight of hundreds of oversized bound volumes, almost all of which were covered with a thick layer of dust.

"I see what you mean about having few visitors to this section," I remarked.

He nodded, "As you might expect, dottore, most of these volumes are in Latin. A language so few people find accessible these days. Should you wish, I can provide you with a Latin dictionary."

"That would be wonderful. I fear my vocabulary may be a bit rusty."

"I shall be right back. As for the books you are looking for, the volumes containing the correspondence and expenditures of Pope Julius II are right there," he said, pointing to a shelf to my immediate right.

"Since there may be some carryover, how are the volumes arranged?" I asked.

"They are in chronological order. To the left of Pope Julius is a single volume containing materials dealing with the brief reign of Pius III. To the left of that are the volumes that date from Pope Alexander VI, and to the right of the Julian tomes are those dealing with his successor, Pope Leo III. Now, let me get you that dictionary."

He returned a few minutes later as I pretended to peruse the first volume dealing with the expenditures of Pope Julius. After he had left, I replaced it and took out the first ledger dealing with the papacy of Alexander. As I had expected, the Alexandrian tomes had far less dust than their counterparts on either side.

As I stared at the page in handwritten Latin, I began to wish that I had applied myself more diligently to my studies. With no idea exactly what I was looking for, I began casually to turn the pages, hoping to find something, anything that might give me a clue. I started to wonder if the mysterious Dr. Sanzio had found what he was looking for here, and then decided that since the papal apartments had been robbed that he had.

There were thirteen volumes – one for each year of his reign – dealing with the papacy of Pope Alexander VI. I knew that he had been elected pope in 1492 and had died in 1503. Stepping back, it struck me that by far the largest volume was that for the year 1501.

Deciding that it was as valid an approach as any other, I took it down and brought it to a desk. Looking at my watch, I saw that it was just after two o'clock. That gave me three hours, since the archives closed at five. Deciding that I probably had a few minutes less, I began to turn the pages, looking for words that I recognized and any expenditures that might be tied to them.

It was tiresome work and although I saw a few items such as the purchase of a *vestis talaris* or cassock in February and an *equo* or horse in May, there was nothing there that seemed to warrant any special attention.

I began to think that this was a fool's errand, but I decided that I would at least finish this book, and see if Holmes wanted me to return tomorrow. I proceeded through the summer months and saw that a *novum raeda* or new carriage had been purchased in September.

I leafed through the pages covering September and as I started October, I noticed a slight discrepancy. The journal jumped from October third to the fifth. Examining the volume very carefully, I noticed that a page had been carefully removed. Whoever had done it had cut the page as close to the binding as possible. It had been removed quite skillfully and might have gone unnoticed for years. Had the jump in days not caught my attention, I am certain that it would have escaped my attention entirely.

Energized by my discovery, I began to examine the volume far more closely, and I found that three different entries from October were missing, including those for the last two days of the month.

I jotted the dates on my pad – Oct. 3, Oct. 30 and Oct. 31 – and wondered if they might have any significance. I continued my examination and decided that no other pages were missing.

I was just about to begin my examination of the volume for 1502 when the docent appeared and told me that the archives would be closing in 10 minutes. He also informed me that I could leave the dictionary on the desk in case I decided to return.

"I may be back," I said, "I'm not certain."

"Oh," he inquired, "Did your labors bear fruit, then?"

"In a manner of speaking. I must consult with my colleague and see if he wishes me to pursue this line of inquiry."

"Well, it has been a pleasure having you here, dottore, and I do hope that I shall see you tomorrow."

I left the archives and headed toward St. Peter's Square. I was feeling reinvigorated, and I couldn't wait to inform Holmes about my discovery.

As I neared the convent, I saw an old priest and I was certain it was Holmes in disguise. I recalled how he had dressed up as a clergyman once before as we tried to escape Moriarty's henchmen in London.

I was just about to tap the clergyman on the shoulder and tell him, "Fool me once, shame on you; fool me twice, shame on me," when a hand grasped my wrist and I turned to see my friend, looking at me, with the slightest hint of a grin.

"I know you thought that was me, but as you can see, it's not," he said. "And I do thank you for that Watson, it is the only moment of mirth in an otherwise singularly gloomy day."

"What's wrong?" I asked.

"The pope has heard from the thieves," he told me. "I found a message from Cardinal Oreglia waiting for me when I returned to the convent. The pontiff has asked us to meet with him tonight at eight o'clock. Of course, I told him, we would be there.'

"I should think that's a good thing, "I remarked. "We may be able to glean certain information from the communique that will lead us to the thieves."

"True enough," Holmes remarked.

I was just about to give him my news when he looked at me and said, "I am afraid, things have taken a rather sinister turn. Without going into specifics, Cardinal Oreglia informed me that the letter contained certain demands of His Holiness."

"Unless, I am sadly mistaken, it is as we feared," he continued, "Our simple burglary has just become a case of blackmail."

Chapter Fourteen – Rome, 1501

Reflecting on the task given him by Pope Alexander, Michelangelo had to admire the pontiff's ingenuity.

Thinking back to his school days, the artist recalled how often he had been threatened by Father Lawrence, perhaps the most sanctimonious man Michelangelo had ever met, with eternal damnation if he failed to memorize the mnemonic acronym *SALIGIA*. Anyone who could remember the word could easily recall its components:

Superbia, avaritia, luxuria, invidia, gulam, ira, and *acedia.* And if you could recall their names that was the first step in avoiding the pitfalls posed by the Seven Deadly Sins.

For perhaps the first time in his life, the artist found himself thinking of the good father in a kindly manner.

Working from the list provided by Pope Alexander, he had made a number of preliminary drawings, but they were all only half-complete.

On the sketch of Cardinal della Rovere, he had also added notes on the side to help him visualize the elements he would have to address before he could even begin working on the cameo.

Despite some serious misgivings about the power of della Rovere – after all, the man had boasted to him that he would be pope someday – he thought that depicting the prelate as the embodiment of pride seemed somehow appropriate.

After all, hadn't theologians come to regard pride as the most serious sin and thus the source of all other forms of iniquity?

He recalled that Father Lawrence certainly had.

He considered della Rovere's bitter accusations that Pope Alexander had secured his position by means of simony and decided that they smacked of both anger and jealousy, and his attempt years later to convene a conclave for the sole purpose of deposing the pope showed a man consumed by greed and ambition. Add in Cardinal della Rovere's own illegitimate daughter, and suddenly lust made its presence known in his personality. In short, Michelangelo decided that just as Lucifer had been blinded by pride so too had della Rovere fallen victim to hubris or *superbia*.

After some careful consideration, Michelangelo knew exactly how he would incorporate the other elements to complete the portrait.

Next he looked at his drawing of Cardinal Ascanio Sforza.

Long before he had come to Rome, Michelangelo had heard of the cardinal's reputation as a skilled diplomat, and he also knew that Sforza, when he saw that he could not win the papacy for himself, had thrown his support behind Cardinal Borgia. In return, the new pope had named him vice chancellor. To further strengthen that alliance, Sforza had subsequently arranged for his cousin, Giovanni, to marry the pope's only daughter, Lucrezia.

Given that the marriage had been annulled a few years later on the grounds of non-consummation, Michelangelo suspected there was a degree of rancor that existed between the pope and his ever-envious prime minister.

In his depiction of Sforza, he could discern a certain canine-like quality in the shape of the head, and the cardinal's bulging snout, perhaps his most prominent feature, only aided in the comparison. With just a little bit of work, Michelangelo decided that he could transform the cardinal into his bestial counterpart and set it against a background of brilliant green. So much for the sin of *invidia,* he thought.

Michelangelo continued working his way through the pope's list. He was surprised to see that the pontiff had included Cardinal Bartolomeo Marti. After all, the pope had named him majordomo of the apostolic palace and then he had named him camerlengo – a post he had held for less than a year.

Certainly he had done little to distinguish himself, which made him a perfect candidate for *acedia.* The old goat probably deserves it, Michelangelo thought, chuckling at his own cleverness. For he realized that the goat was the animal most associated with sloth.

Cardinal Guillaume Briconnet was next. Having betrayed the pope, the people of Pisa and the city of Milan, all in attempts to advance his own career as well as those of his children, the good cardinal had always acted in the interest of self-preservation. He was, Michelangelo decided, an absolute swine, and depicting him as the personification of gluttony was something that the artist decided would bring him great pleasure.

He continued through the list, considering the various names and weighing the artistic possibilities of the possible associations. All things considered, the pope had been as good as his word. While there were some things the pontiff had insisted upon, he had still left Michelangelo with plenty of room to bring his own artistic vision to bear on the various creations. For the first time, Michelangelo thought this was a project that he might actually enjoy. He even allowed himself to consider that he might have entered a partnership that could last.

After carefully concealing the sketches in the special hiding place in his easel, Michelangelo prepared to go shopping. Since Paolo had the day off, the artist realized that he would have to fend for himself.

As he weighed what he might enjoy for dinner, he was surprised by a knock on the door. As he was deciding whether to answer, the tapping was suddenly repeated – this time with more urgency – and he heard a woman's voice say, "Signore Buonarotti, are you in there?"

He replied, "Un momento, signora."

Descending the stairs, he opened the door and was stunned to find Lucrezia Borgia standing there.

Before he could say anything, she leaned forward and kissed him gently on the mouth. Ending the rather awkward embrace, she said, "I simply had to come and thank you. I have had my portrait painted by three different artists, but none has even come close to capturing me as you have signore."

Stepping back, Michelangelo studied her. He was struck by the flawless complexion and the flowing blonde hair. Although she had turned 21 earlier that year, she exuded a confidence that belied her age – an attribute he believed he had captured in the cameo.

"If you are unhappy with your portraits, perhaps I can remedy that. I should love to have you sit for me," said Michelangelo.

"That would be wonderful," she said. "But I know that you have some work to do for my father, and I am afraid that his task trumps my vanity," she said laughing.

"May I offer you something, signora?"

"Oh please, call me Lucrezia," she said.

"Lucrezia," he let the name roll off his lips, and he liked the sound of it. "Would you like a glass of wine?"

"I should like that very much," she replied.

Michelangelo showed her to his table, and said, "Please sit. I shall be back forthwith."

As he walked into the kitchen to fetch cups and a wineskin, he wondered if gratitude were the only motivation for the visit. He knew that Lucrezia had been married twice. Her first marriage had been annulled, and her second husband had been murdered little more than a year before. Given her pleasant disposition, Michelangelo guessed that she had managed to come to terms with her grief.

Returning with the wine, Michelangelo handed her a cup and then fetched a tray with dates and cheese. As they sat there, he found himself taking full stock of her – the lustrous hazel eyes, the sparkling white teeth and the ample bosom.

Lost in thought, Michelangelo suddenly heard her say, "Signore, I hope my appearance does not displease you. I feel as though you are painting me in your mind."

"I apologize Lucrezia, but you are truly a beautiful woman. And you are correct. I was envisioning how I might pose you, what I might try to capture, and which features to emphasize, were you ever to pose for me."

"You flatter me, Michelangelo."

"My humble home has never been graced by anyone as lovely as you," he replied.

"I find that hard to believe," she laughed. "Do not forget, I have had firsthand experience with three of Italy's leading artists. Still, I must admit that it is quite nice to receive a compliment from a man not wearing clerical robes or seeking some sort of preferment."

They both laughed at her remark.

"Is life at the papal palace so difficult?" he teased her.

"It can be," she replied. "I love my father, and I would do anything for him, but I would also like to live my life. I have been twice married, you know, and I did not love either man."

"Then why wed?" he asked.

"The marriages were arranged in order that my father might forge a new alliance or strengthen an existing one. Having said that, signore, I hope that I can depend upon you to be discreet."

"Your secrets are safe with me," he said.

"I like you Michelangelo. You are not like the men with whom I normally associate," she said.

"And I like you as well," he replied.

Their eyes met, and Michelangelo wasn't certain what he saw there. Triumph? Relief? He found it impossible to discern the emotions she was feeling.

"Well then, since we are friends, there is something that I must tell you. Be very careful when you come to the palace. There are many there who wish my father ill."

"I am well aware of that," the artist replied.

"His enemies will become your enemies. And his allies will become your allies."

She looked at him carefully, paused, and then in a very quiet voice, almost a whisper, she asked, "Are you loyal to my father, Michelangelo?"

Chapter Fifteen – Rome, 1901

That evening as we retraced our steps across the plaza, heading toward the Castle Sant'Anna and the *passetto*, I wondered what kinds of demands had been made of the pope. I asked myself, "Would anyone have the audacity to demand money from the pope? And if they didn't want money, what could they possibly want?"

Holmes seemed preoccupied in thought, and I had learned it was best to leave him to his musings. When he was ready to speak, he would.

As we approached the castle, I saw Cardinal Oreglia waiting for us. "Gentlemen, thank you for coming so quickly," he said. "His Holiness received a letter a few hours ago. As soon as he read it, he became frightfully angry. He looked at me and said, 'The thieves now have the audacity to make demands of the papacy.' And then he asked me to summon you immediately."

As we made our way through the castle and the *passetto*, Holmes asked the cardinal, "How was the letter received?"

"Apparently, it came through the regular post. It was addressed to Pope Leo and marked 'Personal and Confidential.' As you might expect, His Holiness receives a great deal of correspondence, but anything marked in such a manner goes immediately to his personal secretary, who then makes a decision as to its disposition."

"In this case, the secretary opened a large envelope and found a smaller one inside. That too was addressed to Pope Leo, but also written on the envelope were the words *per il papa solo* – for the pope only. At that point, the secretary brought it to the attention of the Pope Leo. His Holiness then summoned me and said, 'I have just received a very mysterious communication. He opened it, read it and became very angry, as I have said, and instructed me to summon you posthaste."

"It must be a matter of grave urgency," said Holmes. "Beyond that, I will not speculate until I have spoken with His Holiness."

We quickly made our way through the passage and emerged into the papal palace to find Pope Leo waiting for us.

"Mr. Holmes, thank you again for coming so quickly. I am sure that Cardinal Oreglia has told you about the letter."

"He has," said Holmes. "Now may I ask what exactly the letter says?"

Cardinal Oreglia turned to leave as he had at our other meeting. The pope stopped him this time, saying, "Stay, Gaetano. I think I should like to hear your point of view on this."

"As you wish, Your Holiness," Oreglia said.

Reaching inside his cassock, the pope produced a brown envelope. "As I am sure Cardinal Oreglia has told you, this was contained in a larger manila envelope."

"Yes," replied Holmes, "and do you have that other envelope as well?"

"I do," said the pope, "Would you like to see it?"

"Very much," said Holmes.

"Gaetano, it is on my desk in my study. Would you get it for me?" asked the pope.

"Certainly, Your Holiness," said Oreglia who then left the room to retrieve the envelope.

Holmes pulled his lens from his pocket and began to examine the smaller envelope. I knew that Holmes needed just a small sample of handwriting, from which he could divine an amazing array of information about the person whose script it was.

After he had looked at the envelope, Holmes said to the pope, "May I see the letter?"

"Of course, Mr. Holmes."

The pope reached inside his cassock again and handed Holmes a single sheet of paper. Holmes began reading, and then he applied his lens to the handwriting.

Impatient at being kept in the dark, I asked Holmes, "What does it say?"

He replied, "I can translate the first part without any difficulty: *Risolvere la questione romana* – Resolve the Roman question."

He continued, "Would Your Holiness please translate the rest of this for me? My Italian is not what it should be."

"Of course, Mister Holmes," said the pope. He read aloud:

"You have one thing that we want, and we have seven things that you desire. You will give your blessing to the Italian government, and you will remove yourself from the battle or you will suffer the consequences. When we have received a sign of good faith on your part, we will return the items. This demand is not negotiable. Do not involve the police.'

It's signed, Culto dei Tre Martiri or the Cult of the Three Martyrs."

"They are asking me to do the impossible," said the pope.

"No," said Holmes. "What they are asking is not impossible, it is just something that Your Holiness finds morally reprehensible. There is a tremendous difference."

"What do you know about this 'Cult of the Three Martyrs'?" asked Holmes

"It had its origins in the late 15th century with a Dominican friar named Savonarola," said the pope.

"He claimed to have seen visions and preached against despotic rule. He proved so popular that the people of Florence eventually established a republic and expelled the powerful Medici family."

"Oddly enough, Savonarola ran afoul of Pope Alexander – the same pope who created the cameos. Eventually, he was tortured and recanted. He was hanged and then burned in the central square of Florence along with two other friars."

"I fail to see how a 15th century priest could be influential today," I interjected.

Pope Leo looked at me and smiled, "You might say the same thing about a humble carpenter from Bethlehem who lived more than 1900 years ago and just look at how wrong you would be."

I felt my face redden with embarrassment and stammered out an apology.

"There is no need to apologize Dr. Watson, I understand what you mean."

"At any rate, Savonarola had his followers, and they were called the *Piagnoni* or 'wailers.' After Savonarola's death, they were hunted down and executed by the papacy and the Medici, effectively bringing the movement to an end. However, during the *Risorgimento*, those pushing for Italian unification discovered a certain national fervor in the friar's writings and sermons, and the new *Piagnoni* were born. They transformed a religious zealot into a political harbinger of change."

"So, we may well be up against a group of fanatics," Holmes mused.

"Fanatics indeed," said the pope, "What they are asking is not just morally reprehensible, Mister Holmes. It runs counter to everything that I believe in – both as a Catholic and as pope. As you know, the Roman Question has vexed the nation of Italy since 1862. The dispute began when Rome was declared the undivided capital of Italy. Prior to that, my predecessors had, for many years, considered themselves prisoners in the Vatican. Many Italians find themselves torn between realizing their long-held dream of Italy as a sovereign nation – with Rome as its capital – and their allegiance to the Catholic Church. As pope, I cannot simply endorse a government that would then hold sway over the millions of Catholics who make their home here. As far as the church's power abroad, I cannot even begin to imagine the consequences of granting such legitimacy to the *de facto* secular rulers of Italy."

"That I might be confronted with such a demand was my greatest fear when the cameos were stolen, and that is why I sent for you immediately, Mr. Holmes. You must recover them before they can be used to embarrass the church and weaken its position in this dispute even further."

At that point, Cardinal Oreglia returned with the envelope, which he handed to Holmes, who immediately trained his lens on the address and then proceeded to examine the entire envelope in painstaking detail.

"This was mailed from the main post office," Holmes began. "The writing is distinctly masculine. I should say the man who penned this is right-handed and quite tall – at least six feet. His choice of words and phrases and the fact that all of the words, as far as I can tell, are spelled correctly lead me to believe that he is quite well-educated.

"The tone of the command to Your Holiness – Resolve the Roman Question – along with the lack of any sort of salutation smacks of a certain imperiousness that leads me to believe that he is in a position of authority and used to being obeyed. That in turn makes me think that he is very self-aware and extremely self-confident.

"Both the paper and the envelopes are of the highest quality. Sadly, the watermark is a common one. As for the ink, it appears to be of the type used by only the newest fountain pens. If I were pressed, I should say a Waterman rather than a Wirt, although I should need a larger sample before I would be willing to place a significant wager on that deduction."

"All of which leads me to the conclusion that we are dealing with a rather well-to-do individual, who will brook little in the way of insubordination on your part, Your Holiness."

"Mr. Holmes, you sound as though you know the man," exclaimed Cardinal Oreglia.

Holmes smiled at the cardinal. "I do not know him – yet," he said pointedly, "However, I am all too familiar with his type, unfortunately."

Turning to the pope, Holmes said, "Unless I miss my guess, I am fairly certain that I have just described any number of different men with whom Your Holiness has debated the Roman Question."

"Well put, Mr. Holmes. So how do we go about finding the right one?"

"Do not fear, Your Holiness. I have my methods, but I am going to need your cooperation if we are to catch the thieves."

"I shall do everything within reason, Mr. Holmes," said Pope Leo. "May I ask exactly what you have in mind?"

"They want a show of good faith from you. I think I know how we may accomplish that and perhaps gain a slight advantage at the same time." Holmes then proceeded to outline his plan.

When he had finished, the pope looked at him and said, "I am placing my trust in you Mr. Holmes. I will do as you ask. So we shall meet at least one more time, then?"

"Yes, Your Holiness," said Holmes. "I think that would be best."

"Gaetano," said the pope, "Will you escort our guests back through *il passetto?*"

"Of course, Holiness," said Cardinal Ortega.

"Be well, gentlemen," said the pope. "I am going to thank God for sending you to me, and I am going to pray to the Blessed Virgin for the success of your plan."

We exchanged goodnights, and as we made our way through the passage, Cardinal Oreglia broke the silence when he said, "I think your plan is brilliant, Mr. Holmes."

"Thank you," said Holmes, "but let's not get ahead of ourselves. We still have a great deal of work to do."

We bade the cardinal farewell at the castle door and as we walked across the plaza in the moonlight, I said to Holmes, "You know, I'm inclined to agree with Cardinal Oreglia. That is a stroke of genius on your part."

"Watson, I must admit that I had some reserve as to whether Pope Leo would agree to go along with it. But with his cooperation, I think we stand a fighting chance of recovering the cameos before they can do any damage."

"I see how the first part of your plan will work out, but I'm in the dark as to how one will lead us to the other."

"I didn't tell the pope everything," Holmes confided. "You see, it is imperative that he appear optimistic and confident. After all, he has a fairly important role to play, and he must be convincing. As for the connection between the two, I thought it fairly obvious."

"Well, it escapes me," I admitted.

Holmes then proceeded to outline the entire scheme, and when he had finished, I found myself admiring not only my friend's genius, but his daring as well.

Chapter Sixteen – Rome, 1501

Long after she had left, Michelangelo could still smell her scent in the room. They had talked and laughed for hours, and he recalled every word that she had uttered and every expression that had manifested itself on her beautiful face.

He supposed that they had flirted a bit, but he had always managed to deftly steer the conversation in a different direction.

Although he certainly found her attractive, even desirable, he was not going to allow himself to be smitten by the daughter of the pope – his primary patron at the moment. And if worrying about the pope weren't enough, he also knew that her older brother, Cesare, was fiercely protective of his younger sister.

An intriguing figure, Cesare had been made a cardinal by his father and then made history several years later when he became the first person ever to resign a cardinalate. There were also whispers that Cesare had been involved in the murder of his older brother, Giovanni, and if the worst were to be believed, Cesare had killed Giovanni himself. Although he doubted their veracity, there were even whisperings that Cesare had bedded his own sister. Whether the rumors were true or just vicious gossip, Michelangelo had already decided that Cesare was not a man to be trifled with.

Turning his thoughts back to Lucrezia, he mused that had he been so disposed, the afternoon might have passed in a very different fashion. The thought of making love to Lucrezia intrigued him more than it pleased him, and if truth be told, to a certain degree it terrified him as well.

Turning his mind to the task at hand, Michelangelo headed upstairs and examined the stones that the pope had sent him. The colors radiated from the different surfaces and he carefully examined each, imagining how deep he would have to scrape to arrive at the desired layer in each.

The pope had supplied him with two dozen samples, and some, he had immediately decided, simply would not do.

By the time he had finished examining each one, he had discarded eight, which left him 16 stones for seven cameos. He then proceeded to consider the colors in each. While the blues, reds and yellows dominated, he had only one sample that he found acceptable for green, violet and orange.

He thought, "I must be at my best on those or else I must ask the pope for additional samples." Opting for the path of least resistance, he decided he would mention it to the pontiff at their next meeting.

Feeling that he had done enough one for one day, he was surprised to see how dark it had grown outside. Standing up, he stretched and all of a sudden was overcome by a great weariness. He fell into bed fully clothed, boots and all.

He slept restlessly, tossing and turning, and when sleep finally did come, his dreams were dominated by grotesque caricatures of the faces of those who had turned his oncesimple world upside-down in just a week.

When he woke in the morning, he was drenched in sweat, and Michelangelo suddenly realized that he was terrified.

The thought of being murdered by the pope in a fit of pique flashed across his mind, as did the possibility of being waylaid and ending up in an alley or the Tiber with his throat slit on the orders of Cardinal della Rovere. Throw in the possible machinations of Lucrezia – whatever her motives might be – and it suddenly hit Michelangelo that he would be lucky to survive, no matter how talented a pawn he might be.

Since backing out of the papal assignment was no longer an option, he decided that his only recourse was to amass an army of unseen allies. Although the pope was on his side at the moment, Michelangelo knew how quickly the winds of war could shift and how rapidly allies could find themselves squaring off against each other.

He sat down and began to make a list of friends whose loyalty was unquestioned. When he had finished, he looked at the names and laughed. He realized that none of them would be able to protect him from the pope, although he thought Giovanni de Medici might be able to exercise some small degree of influence – if for no other reason than the weight his family name carried.

Still, Pope Alexander was an absolute, a force of nature, and Michelangelo was struck by the fact that keeping the pope as a friend must be his paramount concern.

With that thought foremost in his mind, he discovered that he was able to relax a bit. As he set about making breakfast for himself, the fear that had gripped him slowly began to subside.

"I am a pawn," he said, "but even a pawn may capture a bishop or a queen and help to checkmate a king."

As he mulled the possible moves that he could make, he decided that an unannounced visit to Cardinal della Rovere could work to his advantage in two ways. His presence might serve to reassure the cardinal of his loyalty, a perception he could enhance by supplying his eminence with some rather innocuous information.

At the same time, he might discover something that could strengthen his position or perhaps improve his bond with the pope.

After borrowing a horse in exchange for one of the gold pieces that della Rovere had given him, he rode to the cardinal's palace.

Captain Bari met him at the gate. "Is His Eminence expecting you?" the captain asked.

"No," Michelangelo replied, "but I do have information that I think he might find of interest."

The captain asked him to wait and then disappeared into the palace. A few minutes later, he returned and said simply, "Follow me."

Michelangelo walked behind the soldier and was led to the balcony where he and the cardinal had dined at his last visit.

"Good morning, Michelangelo," boomed Cardinal della Rovere. "It is so very good to see you again, and to have you come of your own volition is even more welcome."

Michelangelo knelt and kissed the ring. Rising, he smiled at the cardinal and said, "I wanted to thank Your Eminence for taking the time to see me."

"Nonsense. I will always make time for you. This afternoon the Curia is going to consider how to deal with the Cult of the Three Martyrs that persists in Florence and how best to quash what remains of Savonarola's influence there, but this morning I am free to do as I please."

"Coffee, Michelangelo?" asked the cardinal.

"Coffee would be wonderful."

While they waited for the servant to return, the cardinal looked at Michelangelo and said, "Captain Bari tells me you have information that I might find of interest."

"I believe so," he replied. Having rehearsed the scene in his mind during the ride, Michelangelo said, "I recently carved a cameo of Lucrezia Borgia."

"Did you?" inquired the cardinal, and from his tone, Michelangelo could tell that this was not news to the prelate.

"She is rather an embarrassment to the church," the cardinal said. "Twice-married, divorced and widowed – all by the age of 20. She has been a busy young woman. Her situation is made even worse by the fact that she is the pope's daughter. She should get herself to a nunnery, take the veil and repent her sins."

"She also visited me," Michelangelo said.

"Did she?" the cardinal asked, and Michelangelo knew that was something the cardinal had not known.

"Yes, she came to thank me for the cameo," he explained.

"Do you think her father sent her?" asked della Rovere.

"No. I think she simply wanted to express her gratitude." "With the Borgias, nothing is *ever* simple, Michelangelo," the cardinal said. "Have you any other information for me?"

Choosing his words carefully, Michelangelo replied, "I do, your eminence. As you know, Pope Alexander has given me a commission. I am wondering whether I should refuse it."

"Why would you do that?" the cardinal asked.

"I do not know what the task involves, nor do I know if I can carry it out."

"Michelangelo, to refuse a request from the pope would certainly not be in your best interests."

"I understand that, Your Eminence. That is why I consulted you. I am uncertain as to what course of action I should pursue."

"If I may make a suggestion, my son."

"Please do, Eminence."

"Before you refuse the pope's request, find out exactly what it entails. If you feel that you can share those details with me, then I may be able to suggest a course of action that would imperil neither your body nor your soul."

"Thank you, Your Eminence. I feel so much better now. Although there is one other thing I need mention."

"What is that my son?"

"The pope is planning a ball, and he would like you to attend. Why, I do not know."

"I have heard of this ball," della Rovere said, "And I would say the chances of my attending are about as great as those of Alexander being canonized."

They both laughed heartily. At that point the coffee arrived, and while they drank, they talked about art and the future of the church.

When it was time to leave, Michelangelo said, "I cannot thank you enough. You have relieved my fears."

"Be well, Michelangelo. And remember, my door is always open for you."

"Thank you, Your Eminence."

As he rode home, Michelangelo considered what punishment he might merit for lying to a cardinal. If Dante is to be believed, I shall find myself in the ninth circle of the Inferno. I have been hypocritical and I have broken the bond of hospitality.

He mused about the afterlife and wondered if the praise he had rendered God in the Pieta and his other works might not in some way atone for his sins here on Earth.

After returning the horse, he walked home and saw from a distance that a black stallion had been tethered outside his home. "I have a visitor," he thought. And then he wondered whether his guest were friend or foe.

Chapter Seventeen – Rome, 1901

The next morning, Holmes had departed before I awoke. As I ate a solitary breakfast, I reviewed his plan in my mind. The odds for success, it seemed to me, were about even.

After a second cup of tea, I headed out in search of the local *carabinieri* station. I had thought of sending a messenger to Captain Tritini to make an appointment, but I decided that an unexpected visitor might prove a welcome diversion – if he were not busy.

I headed back to the Piazza del Collegio Romano where the headquarters of the *carabineri* was located. Upon arriving, I asked for Tritini, and a young officer told me that he was in a meeting, and I would have to wait.

After about 15 minutes, Tritini appeared and said, "Dottore Watson, so good to see you again. How may I be of assistance?"

"Is there someplace we can talk?" I asked.

"Let us go to my office."

After a short walk down a hallway, we entered the captain's office. The room itself was neat and tidy, and everything about it smacked of the professional soldier. Two of the walls were covered with maps, while one wall had been reserved for photographs and awards. Judging by the framed proclamations, Tritini had enjoyed a stellar career thus far, and given his age – he couldn't have been more than 40 – seemed destined for greater things.

After we had been seated, the captain looked at me and asked, "How may I be of service?"

"I am here on behalf of Mr. Holmes," I began.

The captain's face immediately showed his pleasure.

I continued, "Mr. Holmes is working on behalf of the pope."

No sooner had I finished the sentence than the expression on the captain's face changed dramatically. The smile had been replaced by a look of apprehension and his entire body had tensed. As he raised his finger to his lips, he rose and walked to the door. Opening it, he looked around, up and down the hallway. Returning to his desk, he picked up a pencil and paper. He wrote and handed me the paper, which contained the words – "Obelisk in 30 minutes."

"I am sorry dottore but my schedule is such that I cannot take on any additional cases right now. May I suggest that you bring any concerns about the pope to the local polizia."

I nodded to convey that I understood and said, "I shall take your advice, and I am so sorry to have troubled you."

I left the station and headed toward the obelisk in the center of St. Peter's Square. As I made my way through the streets, I tried to ascertain whether I was being followed. Knowing that I had a few extra moments, I doubled back on two different occasions, but saw no familiar faces as I retraced my steps.

I entered the square and tried to blend in with the crowds and look like a sightseer. I was about 50 feet from the obelisk when I spotted Tritini. As I approached, he saw me and gestured for me to follow him.

We walked across the square to an open area, and then he turned to me and said, "I must apologize for the histrionics dottore, but the ranks of the *carabinieri* are a house divided.

There are those who believe the pope should bow to the king, and others who maintain just the opposite. At any rate, careers have been lost because of minor indiscretions in conversation."

"May I ask where you stand?"

"I must admit, dottore, I am conflicted. Like all Italians I long to live in a unified country, but I am a devout Catholic, and I believe that the Holy Father should answer only to God. I know that is not the answer that you are looking for, but it is the truth."

"Well, the fact that we are talking here rather than your office tells me a great deal," I said.

There was a long pause, before I broke it by asking, "Shall I continue?"

"Please do, dottore. If I cannot or will not help you, I shall walk away, and it will be as if this conversation had never occurred."

I then explained without going into any detail that the pope was being blackmailed and that Holmes had been brought in because the pope believed that he could learn the identity of the person or persons behind the extortion.

"And what is it that you wish me to do?"

I then explained exactly what Holmes had in mind.

Taking a moment to mull things over, he finally said, "So, let me see if I understand you correctly."

He then looked at me and winked, "You have learned that a group of anarchists is planning to assassinate the pope by sending him a parcel that contains some sort of bomb. And starting Monday, you would like members of the *carabinieri* to be a visible presence in all of Rome's major post offices near the Vatican, checking anything and everything that might be addressed to the Holy Father. And if I understand you fully, the more people who know why they are there the better. Is that it in essence?"

Smiling at the good captain, all I could say was "Exactly!"

He looked at me and said, "Consider it done. Just remember dottore, when all this is behind us, I would still very much like to meet Mister Holmes."

Looking at him, I used the same phrase, "Consider it done."

I spent the rest of the day carrying out Holmes' other assignment.

Returning to the convent, I learned that Holmes still had not returned. I began my meal alone, although a nun named Sister Carmelita entered midway through and kept me company as I finished. We talked about a variety of topics, and eventually the subject turned to art. I told her how impressed I was with the Trevi Fountain and the statuary that surrounded St. Peter's Square.

She then asked me my impression of the Pieta. Somewhat embarrassed, I confessed that I had not yet been to see it.

"You cannot leave Roma without seeing it," she admonished me. "It is my favorite," she added. "And it's right here in St. Peter's Basilica."

"I shall make it a point to see it before I leave," I promised her.

After my tea, I wandered into the garden and lit my pipe. Reflecting on the day's events, I was just preparing to head inside when I heard Holmes' voice say, "Mind if I join you, old fellow?"

"Holmes," I exclaimed, "Will you never tire of sneaking up on me?"

"You looked like a man pondering something intently, and I didn't want to interrupt your train of thought."

"How do you know you didn't?" I asked.

"You have just finished your second pipe – your normal limit before retiring. You weren't preparing to light a third, and you had just shifted and stretched, prior to your arising."

I was always amazed at how silent Holmes could be when he wished. "How long have you been standing here?"

"Only about five minutes. Long enough to see what I needed. I gather from the smile on your face that your day went well?"

"Indeed," I replied. I then filled him in on my meeting with Captain Tritini.

"And the other matter? How did you fare with that?"

"Pretty well, I think. From what I can tell, we need only worry about two locations."

"Splendid!"

"My turn," I said. "Should I begin with: How was your day? Or, where were you all day?"

"First things first then," Holmes replied. "My day went quite well. I spent much of it with Pope Leo. While he understands the necessity of the plan, he has a few moral quibbles about it. As a result, we devoted a great deal of time to discussing the finer points of mendacity and prevarication."

"Once I convinced him that he would be telling no lies, but simply avoiding revealing the absolute truth, and how that course of action would, in the final analysis, serve the greater good, I was able to win him over."

"The pope is an incredibly honest and spiritual man, Watson. I can see that he feels the pressure from both sides. He would prefer a third choice, which then led us to a discussion of dilemmas."

"After that was finally concluded, we set about writing. The proper wording is absolutely essential. Every phrase was carefully weighed and considered, both in terms of denotation as well as connotation. Every sentence was parsed and re-parsed, and every possibility explored."

"When the message was finally composed, he set about rehearsing. With just a little coaching from myself and a few suggestions from Cardinal Oreglia, the pontiff's delivery proved impeccable.

"Now, we must wait for the performance and the reaction of the critics," Holmes said. "And on that note Watson, there is nothing further to be done today. Let us get some sleep and prepare for tomorrow's performance and the reaction it generates."

Chapter Eighteen – Rome, 1501

Michelangelo looked at the strange stallion and then he examined the saddle. "This cost a great deal of money," he mused.

"Are you going to look at the horse all night or are you going to come in?" said a voice from inside his home.

Entering, he saw a man sitting at his table. The stranger was tall, slim and quite handsome. He rose as Michelangelo entered.

"So at last we meet, Signore Scultore," said the man. "It seems that everywhere I go lately, I hear your name. My father constantly marvels at your skill, and now my sister is also quite taken with you."

Michelangelo knew immediately that his guest was Cesare Borgia, by all accounts one of the most dangerous men in Rome.

"That you should grace my humble home is an honor I cannot hope to repay," replied Michelangelo.

"Flattery is not necessary," replied Cesare. "I decided that I simply had to meet the man who is causing such a stir in the papal palace. I hope you do not think me rude for arriving uninvited and unannounced and letting myself in."

"Not at all, signore."

"Call me Cesare, please. And by means of amends, I did bring you two wineskins of sherry from the Jerez region of my country. Now that the Moors have been driven from Spain, the vineyards are finally returning to normal."

"You do drink, signore?" asked Cesare.

"Yes. Of course. Let me get some cups," said Michelangelo.

When he returned, Cesare filled both with the fortified wine. "To the success of your project, whatever it may be," said Cesare.

Michelangelo thought the question posed a test. Say too much, and he might be regarded as a man with a loose tongue, yet to say nothing might be considered rude. As he sipped the sherry, he formulated an answer that he thought might suffice. "Thank you, Cesare, but I am merely an instrument in the hands of Our Father and your father."

Cesare laughed out loud. "Well played, Michelangelo. You say nothing but appear to the casual observer to utter a great deal. You give nothing away, yet suggest that that is because there is nothing to reveal. Again, well played."

"Thank you," was all that Michelangelo could think to respond. "This is a chess game," he thought. "He knows where he wants to steer this conversation, and I must try to ascertain where we are headed and arrive there two moves before he does."

"You know about the upcoming ball?" asked Cesare in a move that Michelangelo had not anticipated.

"Yes."

"And will you be attending?"

"I have been invited," said Michelangelo.

"Excellent," said Cesare. "Had my father not done so, I was going to invite you myself. It promises to be quite the evening."

"So His Holiness has suggested," replied the artist, feeling the verbal landscape shifting once again beneath his feet. Looking at Cesare, it was easy to understand why he was both feared and respected.

"Shall I be blunt, Michelangelo?" asked Cesare.

Again, the artist found himself taken off guard by the question. "By all means," he replied.

"In my world, nothing is more important than my family. I am fiercely protective of those I love. When something or someone new enters their sphere, I always try to make certain that there is no threat present. You know the way my family is regarded here. We are Spaniards. We are the outliers. Many in Italy believe that only an Italian should sit on the Throne of Saint Peter. As a result, there are constant plots against my father."

"I pride myself as a judge of character," said Cesare. "I believe that I can trust you. I believe that you are loyal. Should you need my help in dealing with someone like Cardinal della Rovere, you have but to ask."

"The only thing I require in return Michelangelo is that you not be two-faced when it comes to me or my family."

"I don't think I need warn you of the consequences should I ever discover that you have betrayed us." That said, Cesare smiled a dazzling smile and said, "Drink up. We have plenty of sherry left.

Having delivered his warning, Cesare proved a boon companion. They talked for at least two hours about all kinds of topics, from swordplay to the threat posed by the French. The entire time, Michelangelo kept trying to focus on something that Cesare had said, but try as he might, he couldn't quite shift the remark from Cesare's context to his own.

As he lay in bed, thinking back on the evening, Michelangelo kept trying to recall the phrase that had long eluded him. Finally, it came to him, and it was as though a veil had been lifted. He saw quite clearly how he must proceed and how everything would fall into place if he could but turn one old enemy into an ally.

"The only thing I ask, Michelangelo, is that you not be twofaced when it comes to me or my family," thinking back on Cesare's warning, Michelangelo realized that in that caution was perhaps the key to his safety.

In the morning, he rose and dressed quickly. When Paolo arrived, he told the youngster, "I must journey to Naples. I need to procure some special tools for my work. I shall be gone for at least a week. Keep the place clean, and if anyone asks, tell them where I have gone and why and when I shall return. Do you understand?"

"Yes master," said the boy.

Heading to the stable, Michelangelo said, "I will need your best horse for about 10 days. I must journey to Naples."

After some haggling, he found himself astride a big roan stallion that seemed strong and tireless. When he had crossed the Tiber, Michelangelo paused, looked around and seeing that he was alone, pulled on the reins and the horse headed north – for Florence.

* * *

"And so, Cesare, what do you make of young Michelangelo?" asked Pope Alexander.

"I like him," Cesare answered. "Perhaps not as much as you do, and certainly not as much as Lucrezia. But to be fair, I've only just met him, although she has only met him but once herself, if I'm not mistaken."

The pope laughed, and Lucrezia said, "Oh Cesare, must you always tease me?"

"More to the point," interrupted the pope, "do you think him trustworthy?"

"As much as any man can be trusted. I think that given the right incentive – although I have no idea what that is at the moment – Michelangelo could be induced to betray you."

"So then we must make certain that he remains on our side. I see a very bright future for him, both as an artist and a loyal son of the Church, and I would go to great lengths to make certain that he realizes his proper destiny."

He continued, "Now, if we might discuss another subject near and dear to my heart. You both know that we now have less than a month until the ball. How far along are we with the planning?"

Lucrezia said, "So far I have secured the services of 30 courtesans. You would be stunned to learn how many unattractive women are earning their livelihoods on their backs in Rome."

"Well, you have more than three weeks to find the other 20," said the pope.

"I told you that I would find 50, and I will," Lucrezia replied.

"And the guest list, Cesare?"

"All of our friends and almost as many of our enemies will be in attendance," he said.

"Splendid. Just splendid," said the pope. "And the chestnuts?"

"I have arranged for their delivery the last week of the month," Cesare replied.

"Fifty bags?" asked the pope?

"Fifty bags," he answered.

"Won't you tell us why you need the chestnuts, papa? Please?" asked Lucrezia?

"And divulge my best surprise? I think not," laughed the pope. "And now children, to bed. The hour has grown late, and I have a visitor."

"Is Giulia here?" asked Lucrezia.

"Get along," said the pope, "I have kept her waiting long enough."

They both said, "Good night, papa" and departed.

Sitting on the papal throne, Alexander reflected on his life and his transgressions against both God and man. Looking to heaven, he whispered, "Everything I have done, I have done *ad maiorem gloriam Dei*."

From his chamber, he heard a voice say, "Alexander, are you ever coming to bed?"

"Right now Giulia," he answered, as he stepped down from the Throne of Peter and headed for his bed and her arms.

Chapter Nineteen – Rome, 1901

There are five doors by which one may gain access to St. Peter's Basilica.

Holmes and I entered Christendom's most sacred shrine through the front door, directly from the square. Although St. Peter's can lay claim to being the largest church in the world, it is not the mother church of Rome. During our train ride through France, Cardinal Oreglia had informed me that distinction belongs to the Basilica of St. John Lateran.

Immediately upon entering the church, one cannot help but be overwhelmed. Everything about the basilica is enormous, and as you stand inside and watch visitors walk toward the various statues along the walls, the people seem to shrink before your eyes, dwarfed by the sheer magnitude of the stone renderings.

I had always been impressed by the majesty of Westminster Abbey. As you might have surmised, I am particularly fond of the Poet's Corner. By comparison though, St. Peter's is far more impressive. The basilica covers nearly six acres and can accommodate some 60,000 people. It is also believed to house the tomb of St. Peter, the first pope, and a number of other pontiffs have been interred there as well.

Holmes is not particularly religious, nor am I, but I think we were both taken aback by the magnificence of the structure. With sculptures by Michelangelo and Bernini and an array of lesser known artists, the church is also a popular tourist destination.

We had arrived very early for the noon mass, and I kept my promise to Sister Carmelita and paid a visit to the Pieta, which can be found in the first chapel on the right side of the transept.

I can say only that I was awestruck, and vowed that I would make a small pilgrimage to the basilica on my own.

After we were seated, I looked at Holmes and said, "Before we leave Rome, we must revisit this place. There is simply too much to take in during an abbreviated visit." Looking around, I saw what seemed to be hundreds of statues of saints, bronze doors, mosaics, thrones —all constructed in praise of an unseen god.

"Agreed," said Holmes. "A visit to St. Peter's certainly does give one pause."

At that moment, the bell rang to signal the start of mass. The pope entered and the congregation stood as one. Standing under the elaborate bronze *Baldacchino di San Pietro*, another work by Bernini erected to mark the location of the tomb of St. Peter, the pope began by intoning, "*In nomine Patris, et Filii, et Spiritus Sancti.*"

Still in awe of the building and all it contained, I suddenly realized that despite the thousands of people in attendance, there was absolute silence, except for the voice of Pope Leo. Gazing around the massive structure, I was struck not only by the number of people that had managed to make their way into the church but by the look of absolute devotion on their faces as well.

Surrounded by priests concelebrating the mass and a veritable army of acolytes, the pope proceeded with the opening prayers.

After Pope Leo had read the Gospel, we all sat, and he began his sermon.

What follows is a rather loose, but fairly accurate, translation, which Holmes provided me.

"In a world marked by constant flux and uncertainty, we are all plagued by endless doubts. While some of the questions that disturb us can be answered quite easily, others will require time if we are to resolve them properly."

"While there is something to be said for acting precipitously upon occasion, we must remember that the problems that give us pause are perhaps best addressed after prayer and reflection."

"Like you, I too have issues that beg for a quick resolution; however, I have learned that sudden reversals can lead to even greater difficulties than might have been imagined."

Speaking deliberately and occasionally emphasizing individual words, the pope continued:

"Although the journey we are on can prove arduous, if we persevere and maintain our faith in Our Lord, there is no problem that we cannot solve."

"The temptation on our part is always to ask God for a sign that we are making the correct choice. However, Our Lord did not give us free will so that we could turn to Him in times of turmoil. Rather, he endowed us with that most precious gift so that we might resolve our own problems, and by exercising reason and judgment show Him the glory of his creation."

"Remember, resolving our problems is never easy, but it may be imperative. As a result, we may be forced to make choices that we find personally abhorrent but which are, nevertheless, necessary."

"So, I ask you to pray for me as I grapple with my own temptations and difficulties, and know that I will keep you in my prayers as you deal with yours."

The pope then finished celebrating mass, and as Holmes and I left, the church, I said, "I heard the word 'resolve' several times during the sermon. Did you and the pope use it to send a message to the blackmailers?"

"I am afraid that is exactly what we did, Watson. I have no doubt that if the extortionist were present in church, he heard what he wanted to hear. And if he did not attend, I am equally certain that one of his minions will make certain that he receives the news."

"But why?" I asked. "Why the sermon?"

"The pope wants the cameos back in his possession as soon as possible. The thieves have been fairly slow in communicating with His Holiness. I think they understand that a sudden pronouncement – one way or the other – with regard to the Roman Question might give the appearance that His Holiness was coerced."

Holmes continued, "Both Pope Leo and I agree that we must carry the fight to them. Thus far the pope has been allowed only to react. We believe that they must understand that making demands of the Holy See is something that should not be done cavalierly – if at all. They must also understand that by making such demands, they are opening themselves up to certain consequences."

"The only way to do that is by establishing a line of communication in which both parties are equal partners."

"And you expect them to try to contact the pope in the near future?" I asked.

"I would think they will be penning their next missive by day's end, so that it can be posted tomorrow."

"So that is why you had me involve Captain Tritini. You want eyes in the post offices to see who sends a letter to the pope so that you can follow them and learn their identity."

"Would that it were that simple," Holmes said. "No. I need Captain Tritini's men in the post offices so that they do not mail a letter to His Holiness. From what you have told me, Tritini works in an office where loyalty is suspect. Perhaps it is even a commodity. Also, Watson, do you think I would turn over the most crucial portion of this investigation to someone that I have never met, and that you cannot vouch for totally? No, my friend. I have taken certain steps to assure that we will know of any communication to Pope Leo."

"So then, how will this play out?"

Holmes then proceeded to explain what he expected to happen the next morning.

He finished by saying, "I may be wrong about the chain of events, but I pray that I am not."

Chapter Twenty – Florence, 1501

After four days of hard riding through the rugged Italian countryside, in weather that ranged from brilliant sunshine to a torrential downpour and unbearable humidity, Michelangelo found himself approaching the outskirts of Florence. He had not been home in more than a year. Reflecting, he realized that he had not set eyes upon the Old Man in more than five years.

Although their relationship, if you could call it that, had always been contentious at best, Michelangelo knew that he needed help and the Old Man was one of the few people in Italy who could accomplish what Michelangelo wanted done.

Michelangelo also knew that he had something to offer. All he had to do now was convince the old bastard to agree to the trade.

It was after dark, when he finally arrived at the palazzo on the outskirts of Florence. After he had knocked, Salai, who had caused the Old Man more grief than any one individual deserved, greeted him at the door.

"Michelangelo! Welcome!" he exclaimed hugging him, "Have you come to free me from the clutches of that tyrant?"

Salai, whose real name was Gian Giacomo, had been with the "tyrant" for more than a decade. During that time he had stolen from and lied to the Old Man on countless occasions, thus earning the sobriquet *il Salaino* or the little devil.

"No, my friend. I am not your savior. Besides, I would never tolerate your antics. Why he has put up with you all these years is beyond me. Is he at home?"

"He's in his workshop," Salai replied, "Shall I announce you?"

"I'd rather surprise him," Michelangelo answered. Walking down the hall, he knocked on the door.

"Come in," bade a sonorous voice from within.

Opening the door, Michelangelo saw the familiar figure hunched over his workbench "Hello, Leonardo," he said.

The Old Man turned, appraised Michelangelo, and said, "So it is you. What do you want?" With that, he turned his back on Michelangelo and resumed his labors at the bench.

The hair was longer and a bit whiter than Michelangelo remembered, but the piercing blue eyes were still sparkling with an uncanny intelligence – and did he detect a hint of malevolence?

Deciding that directness would be the best course of action, Michelangelo replied, "I need your help."

Leonardo turned to face him and said, "And why on Earth would I want to help you, you arrogant little shit?"

"You are right. I was an overbearing ass, but I would like to think that I have changed. I am older now, and I regret everything that transpired between us."

"Well, that's a start," Leonardo said.

"I am truly sorry, for everything that happened and everything I said, and I was also hoping that we might put the past behind us. Besides, I think I may have something to offer in return that might interest you."

"I don't believe that you have anything I want," said Leonardo.

"I have an important papal commission and the implied promise of others if I am able to execute this one successfully. Given the current state of affairs in Italy, I see a way that we might turn that situation to both our advantages."

When Leonardo didn't respond, Michelangelo could see that he was on the right track.

The silence continued for nearly a minute. All the while Leonardo, who had turned to face Michelngelo, was looking hard at him. Finally, he said simply, "Continue."

"I have been asked to fashion seven cameos for His Holiness, Pope Alexander. Each of the cameos is to depict one of the Seven Deadly Sins."

"Go on. I still don't see why you need my assistance. Surely the artist who created the Pieta can carve cameos for the Borgia Pope."

"I can, but I want these cameos to be very special. I also want to build in a degree of protection for myself, and that is where I need your help."

Michelangelo then proceeded to outline his vision for the cameos, telling Leonardo only what he needed to know. He also emphasized his fear of retribution should Cardinal della Rovere or anyone else outside the papal family discover the plan.

When he had finished, he looked at Leonardo and said, "I know you *can* do it, but *will* you?"

"With the right materials and a proper forge that would be child's play. I could also do the construction in such a way that no one would even suspect. Still, the more important question is: Why should I?"

"As I said, this could work to both our advantages." Michelangelo knew the next part would be tricky and his entire plan could collapse were he to use the wrong word or utter a phrase that might offend.

"Your name will live forever because of your many accomplishments," said Michelangelo.

"Flattery will get you nowhere," snapped Leonardo. "Get to the point."

"'The Last Supper,' the silver lyre in the shape of a horse's head, 'The Virgin of the Rocks' all stand as testament to your genius, but I think even you would agree that had you finished *le Gran Cavallo*, that would be considered your crowning achievement. That would be your artistic legacy."

"Damn that horse," exclaimed Leonardo. "I wish Ludovico Sforza had never asked me to sculpt it. Honor his father, indeed! I should never have ventured to Milan."

Deciding a little white lie might go a long way, Michelangelo said, "I saw the model before the French soldiers destroyed it. I must tell you it was magnificent." "Did you know those French barbarians used my horse for target practice? Target practice!! Day after day, they fired arrows at a clay horse 24 feet tall – until it just collapsed. Bastards!! It was rather hard to miss," he added.

"Would you like to rebuild it?'

"Not for the Sforzas," Leonardo said bitterly, "And certainly not in Milan."

"How about for Pope Alexander?In Rome?" Michelangelo asked.

"Leonardo's eyes flashed, and Michelangelo knew that he was close to securing the old man's assistance.

"I think Pope Alexander might be interested. He does have a rather sizable ego, after all, and you know that he bears little love for the Sforza family – especially after that disastrous marriage to his daughter," said Michelangelo.

"And you would help me?" inquired Leonardo.

"If you will assist me," Michelangelo said, "One hand washes the other, and both hands the face. Not only will I plead your case to His Holiness, but I will be your silent assistant on the project – if you would like."

"I must admit, you have piqued my interest, Michelangelo. May I sleep on it?"

"Of course. I am rather tired, myself. Can you suggest an inn close by?"

"An inn? Nonsense! You must stay here. After all, we might be working together in the very near future."

"Salai," yelled Leonardo, "I know you are listening at the door. Now, bring us some wine, and if you are smart, you will forget everything you have just heard. Do you understand me, you devil?"

"From the hall, Salai answered, "Yes master. Would you prefer red or white?"

"Red," yelled Leonardo.

"If we do this, you must impress upon him the importance of silence," Michelangelo said.

"If we reach an agreement, I shall," said Leonardo.

"A few moments later, Salai entered, carrying a tray with two cups of wine.'

Leonardo handed Michelangelo a cup and taking the other, looked at him and said simply, "To possibilities."

"To His Holiness," said Michelangelo, "who makes all things possible."

"To His Holiness," added Leonardo.

"Now, let me get back to my work, and we can finish our discussion in the morning. Salai, help Michelangelo get settled in the guest room and then come back here."

As he tried to fall asleep, Michelangelo thought back on the day and decided that it had gone pretty well.

If Leonardo could work his magic on the cameos, that would certainly afford me a layer of protection that I do not have at the moment, he thought. And if unexpected visitors should arrive at my home, hopefully, there would be nothing to see.

The last thing Michelangelo saw before sleep overtook him were the faces of Cesare and Lucrezia Borgia kissing passionately.

Chapter Twenty-one – Rome, 1901

Holmes was in a rather pensive mood that Monday morning. He ate little and barely touched his tea. I had learned over the years that while he could be absolutely still for hours when stalking his prey, when things were out of his hands, he would often become engrossed in thought as he tried to envision a way by which he might gain control.

My few desultory attempts at conversation were rebuffed, and we sat there in silence over a breakfast that became less appetizing by the moment.

Finally, in exasperation, I blurted out, "Shouldn't we be doing something?"

"What would you have us do, Watson?"

"Can we not keep watch at the various postboxes?"

"Watson, I hardly think that an Englishman loitering by a mailbox in the middle of Rome could ever be construed as inconspicuous. Besides, I have eyes on the post, although I do not think that is how the message will be delivered."

"You have what?" I exclaimed.

"I have a street urchin stationed at every mailbox within a two-block radius of each post office within a mile of the Vatican. At the same time, I have my most trusted lookouts stationed near the post offices themselves as well as at each of the three telegraph offices that I think could come into play."

"I am hoping that the thief will spot Tritini's man in whatever post office he chooses. If he mails it despite the presence of the *carabinieri*, we will know. If he leaves the post office and decides to drop it in a box, we will know. And, if as I suspect, he decides to send a telegraph to the Vatican, rest assured, we will know."

"How can you be sure?" I asked.

"Quite frankly, I cannot be absolutely certain, and that is what disturbs me. However, people tend to be predictable. In fact, they can be predictable to a fault, which is why so many ne'er-do-wells end up in front of a magistrate. Most criminals imagine themselves as far more intelligent and cunning than everyone around them. The thought that anyone could tumble to the brilliance of their scheme never crosses their mind."

"So, when they meet up with someone of equal or greater acumen, they are often undone because the idea of being bested and taking extra precautions has never even occurred to them."

Thinking back on the way in which Holmes had matched wits with and defeated some of the greatest criminal minds in Europe – Professor James Moriarty, Col. Sebastian Moran, Charles Augustus Milverton – I knew that his assessment was valid.

"I have begun constructing a maze, Watson, through which our thief must navigate if he is to accomplish his goal. I know where the false turns and dead ends are, he does not. If he takes the bait and enters my maze, his path can lead only to an encounter with me."

"I do not see the criminal genius of a Moriarty here; rather, I sense a political idealist, hoping to carve out his legacy as the man who forced the Roman Question to a resolution.

Offer men of that ilk the right type of inducement, and they are easily manipulated."

I could see that Holmes had given this far more thought than I had. And now I understood why the only person I had ever seen Holmes play chess with was his brother, Mycroft.

I went out into the garden to light my pipe, and I was reflecting upon the constantly shifting nature of the case, when a young lad, about 17 or 18, entered the courtyard and knocked on the convent door. When Sister Carmelita answered, I decided to forgo the pipe and followed him inside, instead.

The nun took us both to the dining room, where Holmes was engrossed in a newspaper.

Sister Carmelita said, "Mr. Holmes, you have a visitor."

Holmes peered over the top of the paper and saw the youth standing in the doorway. "Lucca, what have you to tell me?"

"I did exactly as you said, signore. I watched everyone who came in, and the man, he had the envelope you described, and when he saw the *carabinieri* and heard the officer asking about letters to the pope, he left immediately.'

"Which post office?" asked Holmes.

"He was in the Vatican Post Office on the Via di Porta Angelica," replied the boy.

"Then where did he go?"

"He left the Vatican and took a cab to the train station. I followed him on my bicycle. He went into the post office there as well, but again, as soon as he saw the *carabinieri*, he left.

"Finally, he went to a telegraph office and sent a cable. Then he took another cab to the Via Veneto."

"And he never saw you following him?" asked Holmes.

"I do not think so, but I cannot say for certain, signore."

"But you took the precaution?" asked Holmes.

"Yes, signore."

"Excellent," exclaimed Holmes. "Continue, Lucca."

"After he left the cab, he went inside the Church of Santa Maria Concezione del Cappucci. It is not a popular church like St. Peter's but some tourists go there because of the crypts below. I waited outside for a while, but he never came out. So after I hid my bicycle, I entered the church. When I did not see him inside, I climbed to the bell tower. About ten minutes, later I saw him leave through another door. Although he had changed his clothes and altered his appearance, I recognized him because he was still using the same walking stick. After leaving the church, he climbed into a cab and departed. After descending from the tower, I came straight here."

"You did well, Lucca. Now, can you describe this man for me?" asked Holmes.

"I can do better than that Signore Holmes. I know who he is. His name is Giovanni Gilotti. He used to be the prime minister."

Holmes looked at me knowingly. Then he said, "Lucca, you have done better than I could have hoped for." Reaching into his pocket, Holmes produced some money. Counting off the notes, he handed them to the boy and said, "Here is double what we agreed upon, plus a little something extra for you."

"Molte grazie, Signore Holmes," the boy said.

"Distribute the money to your comrades, and tell them to stay alert. I will see you out, Lucca."

As they left, I could hear Holmes giving the boy instructions, although it was impossible to ascertain exactly what he was saying.

When he returned, I looked at Holmes and said, "A Roman contingent of Baker Street Irregulars. How on Earth did you manage it?"

"I had the good sisters recruit some of their former students for me, and yes, I trust the youngsters far more than I trust the Roman police. Can you imagine if one of Tritini's less noble officers had spotted a former prime minister trying to mail the demand? I think we might still be looking for our man, and I am certain the prime minister would have gladly handed over a fistful of lire to buy the officer's silence."

At that moment, Cardinal Oreglia entered the room. He seemed quite breathless. "Good morning, gentlemen. His Holiness received a telegram this morning just as you predicted he would, Mr. Holmes, but there is a slight twist." "Do tell," said Holmes.

"The communication was addressed to me rather than Pope Leo," said the cardinal.

"That was a last-minute improvisation of the part of the blackmailer," said Holmes. "Do you have the telegraph?" "I brought it with me," he said, reaching inside his cassock to produce a paper neatly folded in half.

Holmes opened it, looked at the cardinal and said, "May I?"

"Of course," replied.

Holmes read, "*Per dare il leone*. Stop. Message received. Stop. Call off the dogs. Stop. When the question has been resolved, the curios will be delivered. Stop. *Tempus fugit*. Stop."

"How did His Holiness react?" asked Holmes.

"He remained impassive and then instructed me to bring you the telegram right away."

"Very good. Very good," said Holmes. Then, focusing his attention on the cable, he remarked, "I can only gather from the mix of Latin and Italian – 'Give to the lion' or Leo and then at the end 'time flies' – that our blackmailer not only wants to impress us with his intelligence but to underscore the fact that has a deadline," said Holmes. "His 'Call off the dogs' suggests that he may indeed have spotted Lucca or at the very least that he sees someone providing aid and counsel to his Holiness."

"Cardinal Oreglia, I should very much like to see His Holiness this evening. There is much that I can share with him, and you may tell him, there is most definitely a light at the end of the tunnel."

"That is the best news, Mr. Holmes. His Holiness has tried to keep up a brave front, but he is not a young man, and this is taking a terrible toll on him. He has done so much good as pope that I would hate to think this shame on the Church might be the thing people remember him for," said the cardinal.

"You asked me here to help you. I am quite fond of His Holiness, and I will do everything in my power to make certain that his reputation remains untarnished."

"Thank you, Mr. Holmes. I shall pass along your request to Pope Leo, and unless you hear differently from me, I shall meet you tonight at nine at the entrance to *il passeto.*"

After the cardinal had departed, Holmes looked at me and said simply, "We have much to do and not much time in which to do it, Watson."

He then proceeded to outline exactly what he expected from me.

"And while I am busy doing that, what will you be doing?"

"I shall be stalking our quarry, among other things," he replied and then he was gone.

Chapter Twenty-two – Florence, 1501

Michelangelo awoke, washed his face and headed downstairs, where he found Leonardo sitting at his dining room table, drawing. Passing several pages to Michelangelo, he asked, "Is this close to what you had in mind?"

Looking at the various sketches on the pages, Michelangelo said, "That's not what I envisioned at all."

"Really?" asked Leonardo, a slight hint of disappointment in his voice.

"No, these are so much better," said Michelangelo.

The old man smiled. "I told you, there is no need for flattery," he said. "I will work with you – if for no other reason than the challenge you have posed interests me."

"Thank you, Leonardo. I just hope that you don't regret your decision."

"Now," Leonardo said, "let us have some breakfast, and consider how to secure the materials we need and a good forge. Salai, bring us something to eat, you rascal."

After outlining their plans in broad strokes, they revised and reworked them for several hours until they believed that they had taken every last detail into consideration.

"So, I will leave for Rome today. I am certain that my absence has given rise to fear in some quarters and raised eyebrows in others," said Michelangelo.

"I will leave tomorrow," Leonardo said, "I have a few things I must attend to here; otherwise, I would accompany you."

"Given the eyes that may be watching me, I think it best that we travel separately. By the time you arrive, I hope to have everything in place. I shall meet you at Piero's house six days from now."

"Agreed," said Leonardo. "I have had Salai pack a meal that you can eat as you travel. Be safe, Michelangelo."

They embraced, and bid each other farewell. As he mounted his horse and turned to head for Rome, he saw Leonardo standing in the door, smiling broadly and waving to him.

Even as he returned the gesture, he found himself thinking, "I hope that I have made the right choice."

The ride back to Rome seemed a blur. As Michelangelo revised and reworked his own plans, the hours and the days passed very quickly.

He arrived home in the evening on the fifth day. After returning the horse, he headed straight for Piero's house.

Fortunately, the blacksmith was home.

"Michelangelo, it's been too long," said Piero. "What brings you to my house at this hour?"

"Several things," said Michelangelo. "I could use your help, my friend."

Without hesitating, Piero said simply, "Ask."

"I need to install two guests at your home for a period of time. One of them is going to want to use your forge," he added.

"That's not so much to ask," Piero said, "Anything else?"

"Just one thing, and I say this for your own good." "I'm listening," said Piero.

"No questions," replied Michelangelo. "I will explain all in due time. In the interim, here are 50 gold pieces to cover the cost of their lodging and to pay for the use of the forge."

"That's too much," protested Piero.

"No questions *and* no arguments," laughed Michelangelo.

"We go back a long way," Piero said. "You have done me many favors and given me much work. When my wife passed, I thought you were my only friend."

"Thank you, Piero," said Michelangelo. "Now, no more discussion. They will arrive tomorrow night."

"Do I know these people?" asked Piero.

"I believe that you do. I hope you will be pleasantly surprised, and I shall return tomorrow after dark."

"Thank you, Michelangelo. Anything you need, just ask."

As he walked through the darkened streets toward his home, Michelangelo wondered who was more on edge over his prolonged absence – the pope or della Rovere. "I shall find out soon enough," he thought.

As he turned onto his street, he saw a familiar horse in front of his house, and his downstairs rooms were all aglow. I guess I'll find out momentarily, he thought.

As he entered, he heard a voice say, "Where have you been, you bastard?"

Looking, he saw Cesare Borgia rising to his feet.

"I am just back from Naples," replied Michelangelo. "I went there to get some special tools and to examine some granite for a future project."

"What tools?" asked Cesare.

Michelangelo unfolded his bedroll and showed Cesare a gleaming assortment of chisels and gravers that Leonardo had given him. "These are made of the finest steel in all of Italy," he explained. "In order to execute the papal commission, I must have these."

"We could have sent someone to get them for you," said Cesare.

"I don't think so," explained Michelangelo, "You see, these were made expressly for my hands. See how the knobs fit exactly into my palm. See how the length of the chisel is in direct proportion? Look at the teeth on these chisels. See how they vary ever so slightly in width? I helped the artisan design these, and unfortunately, I had to be there to oversee their production myself."

"My father has been worried about you," said Cesare.

"Again, I apologize for any concern that I may have caused His Holiness. Did not my houseboy tell you where I went and why and when I would return?"

"He did, but there are bandits on the roads and accidents do happen," said Cesare pointedly.

"Well, I am back in one piece. I have my new tools, and I am ready to go to work for His Holiness."

"Excellent," said Cesare. "We have only one week until the ball, so I am sure that you can understand my father's apprehension."

"Of course, of course," said Michelangelo.

"The festivities are scheduled to begin Wednesday night with a dinner for all the guests. I imagine my father would like to meet with you at least one more time before then."

"I am His Holiness' to command," said Michelangelo.

"Excellent," said Cesare. "I expect you will hear from me in the next day or two."

"I am at your disposal as well," said the artist.

Michelangelo watched as Cesare thre his cloak over his shoulders and headed for the door. As he opened it, he turned to Michelangelo and said, "If I may, signore, just one more question."

"Of course."

"You just made a cameo of my sister. It is a beautiful piece. So why did you need new tools?"

Michelangelo looked at Cesare and saw just a hint of suspicion in his eyes. "Follow me, please." With that Michelangelo turned and headed upstairs to his studio with Cesare at his heels.

Going to his workbench, he showed Cesare two broken chisels and several others with dulled blades that he had arranged before he left.

"As you might expect, carving in stone is painstaking work with little room for error. In producing a cameo such as the likeness of your sister, I may go through several blades. As you know, I generally work on larger commissions, so I was able to get through the one cameo with the tools at hand, but I knew to carry out your father's commission, I was going to need a complete set of new tools for carving miniatures, and the only place to secure the implements that I wanted was to go to Benito, toolmaker to the great Bellini."

Cesare seemed satisfied with Michelangelo's tale. As they descended the stairs, he smiled and said, "I apologize if I seem overly suspicious. My only excuse is that my years as a cardinal have prepared me for intrigues of every possible nature."

"I understand," said Michelangelo.

"I must confess, signore, I have killed men because they posed a threat or proved untrue to my family. Let us hope it does not come to that with you. I should hate to end such a promising career so prematurely." And with that, he mounted his horse and rode down the darkened street in the direction of the Vatican.

Chapter Twenty-three – Rome, 1901

Giovanni Giolitti was a man who was not easily surprised. However, the last two days had been filled with a number of unexpected twists and turns.

Sitting in his office, he decided that he deserved a drink. Although it was not yet noon, he opened his liquor cabinet and gazed upon the array of different-colored bottles before selecting a single-malt scotch. Pouring himself a glass of Aberfeldy, a relatively new brand that he had received as a gift, he sat back and tried to make sense of where things were going, and how he might stay one step ahead of his opponent.

He had suspected that the pope might reference the Roman Question in his Sunday homily, but to have the pontiff devote his entire sermon to it had been more than he might have hoped.

Buoyed with excitement, he had donned his disguise and gone to the post office the next morning to mail his next missive to the pontiff. The sight of a *carabinieri*, whom he did not know, asking for anyone mailing anything to *il papa* had unnerved him slightly.

Exiting the Vatican post office, he had taken a cab to another post office, farther from St. Peter's Square, where the scene had been repeated.

Deciding that they were looking for a mailing, he had opted to send a carefully worded telegram to Cardinal Oreglia. Fortunately, there were no uniforms present in the cable office, just the usual group of boys on bicycles loitering outside, looking to deliver messages for gratuities.

As he climbed into a cab, he mused on the morning's events. Surely, there was an unseen hand at work here. Pope Leo is clever, he thought, but he is not devious enough to develop a plan such as this.

Looking out the cab window, he noticed a young boy on a bicycle about a block behind pedaling furiously. "Did I see him at the first post office?" he asked himself. Looking again, he thought he recalled the youngster's red shirt. He told the driver to stop at a tobacco shop and wait while he went in. After purchasing several cigars, he returned to the cab. A glance up the street revealed that the boy was not there.

Feeling slightly relieved, Giolitti told the driver to take him to the Church of Santa Maria della Concezione dei Cappuccini on the Via Veneto.

When he arrived, he took his time paying the driver. Before entering the church, he glanced back up the street and saw two nuns walking on one side of the street. On the other, he spotted a youngster with a bicycle, who appeared to be fixing his tire, However this one was wearing a black shirt and a cap.

Giolitti entered the church and knelt down as if in prayer. He waited for a few moments. When the boy did not enter, he descended to the crypts below and made his way to the inner sanctum. When he was alone, he removed the wig and dark glasses. He put the jacket and cap that he had worn into his briefcase and replaced them with a proper suit jacket.

He thought about checking on the cameos and then decided against it. He had taken few precautions and had just changed his clothes, and if those reasons weren't enough to dissuade him, it was broad daylight and he had neglected to put the sign in place.

He then left the church through a different door and, after scouring the streets looking for boys on bicycles and finding none, he took a cab back to his office. Had he gazed up, he might have seen a youngster watching him intently from the heights of the bell tower.

Upon arriving, he had told his secretary to hold all his calls and then he locked himself in his office.

Sitting in his chair now, he looked at his office and thought about his career. He told himself, "I am a survivor. I eluded prosecution in the Banca Romana scandal, and I would have made a handsome profit but for that fool Tanlongo."

"I have served as prime minister, and I am now the minister of the interior. Zanardelli may be the Prime Minister of Italy, but I am the kingmaker. If I can resolve the Roman Question on the side of the government, my power base will be complete."

However, there was a nagging doubt deep in the back of his mind. He had an uneasy feeling that he had overlooked something. That somehow, inexplicably, he had missed something that morning.

So he sat there, sipping the scotch, and examining each move that he had made that morning and then reconsidering each future move for the slightest flaw.

"I have so many layers of protection that no one will be able to trace this to me, unless I wish them to." And then it hit him. Going to the post himself could have proved his undoing had the boy recognized him. He found comfort in the fact that he had been disguised and the youngster was certainly gone when he left the church.

He thought about the boy. What if the red shirt were merely a clever distraction to catch his attention when he saw it and allay his fears when he noticed that it was gone?

Perhaps the youngster had changed the shirt just as he had altered his appearance. Deciding to redouble his efforts at anonymity, Giolitti determined to make better use of the other *Piagnoni* in carrying out the more routine tasks. He had learned a hard lesson about trust when he was ushered from office, and it was about to pay dividends.

Deciding that the initiative was there to be grasped, he began to compose another letter to the pontiff.

It took him a long time to get it just right. When he had finished, he read it over several times and decided that it struck a nice balance between imperiousness and impatience.

Realizing that everything had come full circle, he focused on devising a method by which the message might be delivered safely but without any risk of having the messenger compromised.

After he had walked each step through in his mind, he chided himself, "Why didn't I think of this sooner!"

But then he smiled, and said, "But you did think of it now!" Deciding that his cleverness merited a small celebration, Giolitti poured himself another glass of the Aberfeldy.

"It is almost checkmate, Pope Leo," he thought as he savored the aroma of the scotch before sipping it and relishing the subtle hints of honey and heather.

Chapter Twenty-four – Rome, 1501

Michelangelo rose very early the next day and spent the entire morning working on the stones for the cameos. Now that he had a plan and the pieces were falling into place, the work seemed easier.

Having already selected the pieces he would use, he attacked them with a passion born of confidence. His hands felt steady and his eyes remained clear and focused despite the dust that his tools raised from the stones.

As he moved from one piece to the next and from color to color, he could see the images clearly in his mind. All that was missing were the figures that he had been told would be supplied at the ball. He could have told the pope that he didn't really need to attend the ball, but His Holiness had insisted. "I know you are familiar with the cardinals' countenances, but there are faces at the ball that will be new to you," the pope had said, "and they are every bit as important as the prelates when it comes to preserving them for posterity. Perhaps they will inspire you."

Following the natural inclination of the rock, he spent the hours shaping each stone into either a circle or an oval and then beginning to scrape away the unneeded layers until he had reached those colors that offered the most striking contrast. He needed to have a white or pale "canvas" on which he would carve, sitting against a variant background.

The work went smoothly and surprisingly quickly, and by lunchtime, he had shaped and polished three stones to his liking. The stark contrast in hues appealed to his sensibility and the thickness was just about what he and Leonardo has discussed.

After a short break, he returned to the work – scraping, cutting, chiseling – and by early evening he had completed rough outlines for all seven.

All of a sudden, it hit him that he was famished, and he decided to eat before proceeding any further. After rummaging through his kitchen, he realized there was nothing in the house. Paolo had purchased no provisions while he was had been away, and he had not taken the time to restock his cupboard after returning from Florence.

Deciding that he needed to get away from the work, he thought he might purchase something in the nearby tavern.

As he entered, he saw a few familiar faces and they nodded at him in recognition. After ordering, he sat alone and watched as men and women flirted, and he found himself laughing out loud when an old drunkard leaned too far back on his stool and fell over.

He wondered if he might have been happier as a stablehand or a soldier and then decided that he liked his life. God had blessed him with a gift, and who was he to question the Creator?

After leaving the tavern, he returned home, gathered up the stones, wrapping each one carefully in a piece of red velvet and carefully placing them in a saddlebag. He then began the walk to Piero's house.

The sun had set hours earlier and the cooler air was refreshing. The thought that he had but a few days until this mysterious ball quickened his pace.

Long before he reached Piero's house, he knew that Leonardo and Salai had arrived. He could hear Piero bellowing, and as he drew closer, he could hear Leonardo trying to act as a mediator.

Michelangelo knocked loudly on the door and entered. The yelling ceased momentarily, and Leonardo said, "Thank God, you are here. We arrived about an hour ago, and they have been at each other's throats ever since."

Leonardo turned to Piero and Salai and said in a stern voice, "Kill each other if you must, but do it quietly. Michelangelo and I have work to do."

With that Leonardo reached into his pocket, fished out two gold coins and said, "Go! Eat! Drink! Fornicate! Fornicate with each other, I do not care, but leave us be. We need to focus, and tomorrow you will both earn your keep."

Piero gave Michelangelo an apologetic look and then said to Salai, "Follow me. I will show you how to get the most for that florin."

When they were gone, Leonardo looked at Michelangelo and said, "Did you bring the stones?"

Michelangelo put his bag on the table and began to remove the stones, one by one. As he did, Leonardo unwrapped and examined each one carefully. "You have done well, Michelangelo. I have but two suggestions." Picking up one, he advised, "I think this could be thinner yet." Selecting another, he said, "I hope this holds up. It seems to me, almost too thin. Have you other stones prepared in the event of an accident?"

"I have," said Michelangelo, "but they are not nearly as finished as these. I am hoping they shan't be needed."

"Let us hope so," said Leonardo, "but I would prepare one or two more just in case." With that, he began measuring the stones and writing down the dimensions of each. When he had finished, he took a small balance scale and weights from his bag and began weighing each.

After he had finished, he turned to Michelangelo and said, "You have done well. They are all quite close. There are just a few grams difference between each."

"And the cases?" asked Michelangelo.

"Now that I have the measurements, I can start tomorrow. If anything changes, if a stone should break, you must let me know immediately."

"Tomorrow?" asked Michelangelo incredulously.

"After you left, I happened to remember that I had some extra silver lying about from the lyre that I made for Il Moro Sforza. I suppose I should have returned it, but there was something about that man that I found positively odious."

Michelangelo laughed, "I met him but once, yet I know exactly what you mean."

"Do you have enough to create all seven cases?" asked Michelangelo.

"If I am careful," said Leonardo, "and we make certain that Salai doesn't steal any."

They laughed and then Michelangelo said, "You have been kinder to me than I deserve."

"We all make mistakes, my son," said Leonardo. "You were young and impetuous, and I took things more personally than perhaps I should have, At any rate, we have put all that unpleasantness in the past."

"Now, how low long do you think it will take you to finish the first part?" asked Leonardo.

"That all depends upon the detail work. If I keep it relatively simple, I should have all of them completed by Wednesday morning – the day of this mysterious ball I told you about."

"Leave two here tonight, if you can. That way I can start work first thing in the morning. Remember, though, the length and the width cannot change unless you tell me."

"I understand," said Michelangelo. "I shall leave you the largest circle and the largest ellipse. Will that help?"

"Enormously," said Leonardo.

"And you're sure silver, rather than gold?"

"I believe so. Silver is somewhat harder than gold, which means it will wear better, but it also makes intricate carvings that much more difficult. In this case, though, we want the focus to be on your images rather than the cases holding them – for obvious reasons. I will fashion ornate cases for you with some filigree work, but they will not be so beautiful that they detract from the cameos. After all, this is your commission, Michelangelo, not mine."

"Still, if you wish gold, I will work in that medium. But that may take longer, as I will have to acquire it, and it will be far more expensive, obviously. The choice is yours," added Leonardo.

"I will be guided by you" said Michelangelo.

"You really have grown up," remarked Leonardo with a slight smile.

"Thank you," said Michelangelo.

"Don't thank me yet. And don't think we won't be trying to kill each other before this is over," said Leonardo.

Michelangelo laughed, "Here are your stones, old man. Good luck trying to get Piero and Salai out of bed tomorrow morning."

"I have my ways," said Leonardo. "I shall see you tomorrow night, about this time?"

"Yes."

"And you will have one or two finished stones for me to work with?"

"I shall try," said Michelangelo.

"Safe home, my son," said Leonardo. "I'm to bed, and if this weren't Piero's house, I would lock the door and leave them to fend for themselves."

"Someday, you and I must have a discussion about Salai," said Michelangelo.

"There is nothing to discuss," said Leonardo.

From the tone in his voice, Michelangelo was certain that was a conversation that would never take place.

Deciding to subjugate his pride once more, Michelangelo said simply, "As you wish, maestro. Now sleep well."

Chapter Twenty-five – Rome, 1901

Holmes returned to the convent early in the evening.

"Has your day been productive?" I asked.

"Somewhat," he said rather ambiguously. "Are you ready to go? It's almost time for our meeting with Pope Leo."

We crossed the square in silence. I knew better than to try to engage Holmes in conversation when he was feeling reticent.

We met Cardinal Oreglia and walked through the *passetto* in silence. As we exited into the papal residence, Pope Leo was waiting at the table for us as he had been on our first visit.

"Cardinal Oreglia tells me that you have news, Mr. Holmes."

"I do, indeed, Your Holiness," replied my friend. "And I am hoping that after we talk, I will have a better idea of how to bring your travails to an end."

"Praise be to God," said Pope Leo.

"I believe that the man responsible for the theft is known to you," began Holmes. "In fact, I would be willing to bet on it."

"Who is this man?" asked Pope Leo.

"How well do you know Giovanni Giolitti?" asked Holmes.

"All too well," sighed the pontiff. "And if you are going to tell me that he is the one behind for the theft, I will tell you that I am hardly surprised. I have been mulling things over since our last conversation, and Giolitti was one of the few names that I had not eliminated."

"I know a little bit about him," said Holmes, "I am hoping that you can add details so that I have a more complete picture of him."

The pope began, "I believe that he is an evil, unprincipled man, Mr. Holmes. He is the worst kind of hypocrite. During his tenure as prime minister, the Roman Question was a constant bone of contention between us."

The pontiff continued, "He is a student of Machiavelli and a practitioner of realpolitik. You are familiar with the term?"

"Yes, Your Holiness. I too have read von Rochau's *'Grunsatze der Realpolitik',*" said Holmes, "and while I can see the appeal of his ideas to some minds, I personally find them to be more enslaving than enlightening."

"Giovanni Giolitti is a Roman Catholic in name only. In actuality, he worships at the altars of mammon and political expediency. He is a brilliant man, having earned his law degree when he was but 18. He is especially adept at finances. With his gift for numbers, he can add two and two and come up with six different answers and make each sound as though it is the only correct one.

"After being elected to our Chamber of Deputies, a body akin to your own House of Commons, he launched a series of attacks on Agostino Magliani, who was the incumbent treasury minister. When the cabinet of Prime Minister Rudini fell from power, due no doubt in part to the machinations of Giolitti, it was he who ascended to the post of prime minister."
"However, Giolitti's administration was characterized by both scandal and corruption. While all of the state banks were in dire

straits, the Banca Romana had loaned enormous sums to property developers. When the real estate market collapsed, it came to light that Prime Minister Francesco Crispi and thenTreasury Minister Giolitti were both aware of a damning report by government inspectors which they had decided to suppress because they feared its release might undermine the bank even further."

"Having managed to ascend to the position of prime minister in the midst of the scandal, Giolitti attempted to make Bernardo Tanlongo, who had served as the bank's governor, a senator. He believed that would prevent Tanlongo, a former farm hand who, like Giolitti, possesses a certain genius for numbers, from having to testify against himself and by extension, Giolitti. However, the senate resisted Giolitti and refused to admit Tanlongo.

"Forced to arrest his friend, it is generally believed that Giolitti then abused his position by destroying certain documents that would have been used as evidence against Tanlongo. Caught up in the maelstrom, Giolitti was forced to resign, leaving the country on the verge of insolvency and relations with France – a group of Gallic investors had teamed with a consortium of Belgian financiers to found the Banca Romana – strained to the breaking point.

"For the past several years, Signore Giolitti has kept a low profile, speaking occasionally in public, but slowly and stealthily assembling a power base. Now, he is back in the government, serving as minister of the interior. If he can bring the Roman Question to a resolution that favors the government rather than the church, his comeback will be complete, and he will once again be Italy's prime minister. "As I said, Mr. Holmes, he is a devious man, and if I am reading this situation correctly, a desperate one as well."

"Thank you, Your Holiness," said Holmes. "If this were a game, he would be a worthy opponent, but there is far too much at stake to look upon the situation lightly. All I can tell Your Holiness is that I have dealt with men of his ilk – and his intelligence – in the past, and not one has ever bested me. I intend to make certain that Mr. Giolitti is not the first."

The pope smiled, and Holmes continued, "Now, Holiness, there are other things that we must discuss. I should like to know how you as pope learned about the cameos, and I should also like to know how you think Giolitti may have discovered their existence."

The Pope looked at Holmes with pleading eyes and said, "As I told you earlier, Mr. Holmes, when one assumes the papacy, he is entrusted with a great many secrets." He looked at Cardinal Oreglia and said, "Gaetano, will you excuse us once again? I am so sorry."

"No need to apologize," said Oreglia, who then rose and left Holmes and me with Pope Leo sitting at the table.

Speaking softly, Pope Leo began. "As you may imagine, this office is filled with trials and tribulations, many of which are unique to the papacy. After being invested, each pope is given the combination to the papal safe by the camerlengo of his predecessor. The safe is filled with documents, some of which are hundreds of years old. While most are concerned with various aspects of dogma, there are a few that deal with more worldly things."

"Among the latter is a letter from Pope Alexander VI that details the origins of the cameos. Written in Latin on a piece of parchment that has grown yellow and brittle with age, the letter also touches their possible use."

"I should like very much to see that letter," said

Holmes, "but I will understand if Your Holiness is reluctant."

"Allow me to get it, Mr. Holmes. Now that the existence of the cameos is known to others, I see little point in hampering your investigation with a secret that is no longer a secret."

After the pontiff had left us, Holmes looked at me and said, "This is a bad business, Watson. However, if Giolitti has kept the secret to himself and not explained the significance of the theft to his underlings, I think we may be in luck."

"I think that's rather much to hope for," I replied. "Sounds to me as though you are hoping for a miracle," I snorted.

"Not really," said Holmes. "I believe Giolitti may be the only one who can fully appreciate the leverage over the pontiff that the cameos provide the person who possesses them. I'm rather hoping that whoever carried the pieces from the nun to Giolitti – and perhaps it was the bounder himself who took them from the sister – failed to realize the value of the cargo."

At that moment, the pope rejoined us, carrying the letter. He removed a silver chain with small, almost circular medallions at either end that had been wrapped around it and placed it on the side of the table. Then the pontiff unrolled it very carefully and placed a fruit bowl at the top and a wine decanter on the bottom in order to prevent it from rolling up.

The three of us stood there, gazing at the words penned by a notorious pope some 400 years ago. Although it had faded to a degree, the neat script was still quite legible.

The pope looked at us and asked, "Shall I translate gentlemen?"

"Please, Your Holiness," said Holmes.

"To my esteemed successors,

If you are reading this, it means that you have ascended to the Throne of Peter. I pray that your reign is far more tranquil than mine. Having been surrounded by a Curia composed of vipers and other serpents, I decided to bring them to heel.

Assisted by one Michelangelo Buonarotti, a promising artist who had achieved some small degree of fame by creating a piece that was known as the Pieta, I embarked upon a plan to bring the cardinals in line.

I commissioned the artist to create seven cameos, each one depicting a member of the Curia actively engaged in one of the Seven Deadly Sins. In order to inspire and assist the artist, I determined to hold a special ball, and I invited him to find his muse in the behavior of the guests at the party.

If you have gazed upon his creations, I think you will agree that he succeeded admirably. Should you find the cameos abhorrent to your sensibilities, you will find little solace in the fact that I believe that once seen, the images are seared into your brain and create an indelible impression that will never leave you.

I know that they have never left mine.

Given the rather obvious duality of our existence – body and soul, heaven and hell, angels and demons -- it seems as though like so many other things, vice and virtue are always but one turn removed from each other.

If the fruits of my labors have made you uncomfortable, I do extend my sincerest apologies and suggest that you focus on the virtues that accompany each vice rather than the sinful acts engendered by each human failing.

Yours in Christ,

Rodrigo Borgia,

Pope Alexander VI,

6, November, 1501"

After he had finished reading, the pope looked at Holmes and asked, "Well, Mr. Holmes, did you find the letter enlightening?'

"If my suspicions are correct, there is far more to these cameos than you know. If you don't mind, I should like very much to copy the last few paragraphs of this letter."

"As you wish, Mr. Holmes. Am I missing something?"

"I believe that you may be," replied my friend, and with that he set about putting pen to ink. When he had finished, he said to the pope, "May I see the chain that secured the parchment?"

The pope handed it to him and Holmes examined it carefully. Looking at the tiny silver charms, Holmes muttered, "*Virtutes* and *vitium* – virtues and vices – one inscribed on each side of the amulet; I should have expected as much."

Looking up, Holmes asked the pope, "This chain has always been here?"

"To best of my knowledge, both the chain and the letter were fashioned at the behest of Pope Alexander," replied Pope Leo.

"It certainly follows the pattern of duality outlined in his letter, with each of the medallions bearing the words 'virtues' and 'vices.' Can your Holiness tell me why these circles have these tiny projections at each end?"

"I am afraid that I cannot Mr. Holmes. I must confess that I have never given it much thought. I suppose that they may have been joined at one time and broken apart. If that is not the case, then I can only surmise that they are slight flaws in the workmanship."

"Yes, perhaps you are right, Your Holiness. It is getting late, and I believe that I have everything I need now. Tomorrow, I shall pay a call on Signore Giolitti and see whether I can persuade him to return the cameos. Perhaps, I can convince him to see the error of his ways."

"I shall pray that your labors are successful," said the pope, "but having dealt with Giolitti on many occasions, I am not expecting an answer to my prayers."

We took our leave of the pope after he had made Holmes promise to report to him the next day.

As we walked across St. Peter's Square in the moonlight, Holmes looked at me and smiled, "You know," he said, "I was almost tempted to quote Scripture to His Holiness, but given the strain that he is under, I forced myself to refrain."

"And what would you have said to him?"

"When he said that he doubted that his prayers would be answered, I thought about quoting Christ himself – 'Why are you fearful? Oh ye of little faith.' – but I must confess modesty forbade me."

"Are you that confident?" I asked.

"I am, and after I spend some time with a Latin dictionary, I suspect that I may know even more," he replied. "There are some rather provocative phrases in that letter that intrigue me and they will bear further scrutiny."

He continued, "And that chain is also most telling, is it not?"

" 'Flaws in the workmanship,' indeed," he snorted.

Chapter Twenty-six– Rome, 1501

For the next two days, Michelangelo worked on the cameos incessantly, stopping only when he was famished or the dust parched his throat. After nightfall, he would carry the products of his labors to Piero's house. There Leonardo would meticulously measure and weigh and make slight adjustments as he tried to fit the stones into the cases he had constructed for the frames.

Tuesday night, the night before the ball, Michelangelo made the trek to Piero's and when he arrived he found Leonardo, Salai and Piero sitting around the table, laughing and drinking.

"Ah, you are just in time, Michelangelo. Join us, won't you?" asked Salai, as he fetched another cup.

"We have so little time," said Michelangelo. "The ball is tomorrow night."

"But I am finished," said Leonardo. With a flourish, he pulled a cloth from the table and there gleaming in the candlelight, Michelangelo saw the seven silver cases, all of which had been polished to a brilliant sheen. "How is this possible?" he asked.

Leonardo said, "I have not stopped working since we arrived. Unfortunately, Piero hasn't slept much either, and Salai has proven his worth once again. Look at his filigree work."

Michelangelo inspected each, admiring the intricate carvings that Salai had executed under daunting time constraints. "They are stunning," he said to them. "Simple, yet elegant. I should think His Holiness will be well pleased." Rubbing his thumb and forefinger together, Salai said, "Let us hope he shows his appreciation in a tangible way."

Leonardo looked at him reprovingly and said, "Sometimes the work is its own reward. In this case, we have helped a friend. That should be payment enough for you." Then, reaching into his pocket, he produced two more gold florins. "Here is a token of *my* appreciation," he said.

Michelangelo did the same, and said, "Go, enjoy yourselves. Hopefully, this is just the first installment."

After they had left, Michelangelo looked at Leonardo and asked, "And the other pieces?"

"They too are just about finished. Let me get them." He returned carrying the items about which Michelangelo had inquired and put them on the table next to the cases.

"They are so small," exclaimed Michelangelo. Picking one up, he added, "And so light!"

"I have tried each one, Michelangelo. They will work, I promise you. Take them with you to your house tonight. So far, I think I have managed to keep these secret even from Salai, but I cannot say with absolute certainty. The lad has an inquisitive nature. Several times, he nearly caught me working on these, and I would rather they remain our secret."

Picking up a case and one of the cameos, Leonardo demonstrated for Michelangelo, how they would work in tandem. He then showed him the key to the mechanism, and said, "I do not think anyone will suspect."

"Nor I," said Michelangelo, "I am indebted to you forever." "No Michelangelo. It is I who owe you. In calling upon me, you showed me that the quarrel that parted us – bitter as it may have been at the time – is truly insignificant in the grand scheme of things. You have taught me forgiveness."

"How long will you remain in Rome?" asked Michelangelo.

"I shall stay until this commission is finished. If you need my help, I am here for you. And please, make time in the next few days to tell me about the ball."

"I shall spare no details, and if I can manage it, I shall let you see the cameos before I present them to the pope."

"I should like that very much. Good luck, my son, and I will wait to hear from you."

As he walked home, Michelangelo felt more optimistic than he had in weeks.

He slpt well that night, and no one disturbed his dreams. However, a pounding at the door awoke him the next morning. Stumbling downstairs, he shouted, "Who is it?"

A voice from outside that he recognized as Captain Bari's said, "Cardinal della Rovere requests your presence immediately, signore."

"Give me a few minutes to get dressed, I've only just awakened."

"I should hurry, signore," said the captain. "The cardinal is a man who dislikes being kept waiting."

After making himself presentable, Michelangelo opened his door to find the captain and four soldiers waiting for him. Knowing that to ask what the cardinal wanted would be fruitless, Michelangelo mounted the horse they had brought for him, and they set out for the cardinal's palace.

Upon arriving, he was ushered onto the porch where the cardinal sat waiting, "So good of you to come, Michelangelo."

Mulling things over, he decided that humility might be his best course of action, "I had planned to call on Your Eminence this afternoon."

"Yes, yes, I'm certain that you did," said the cardinal. "Let us be brief my son, I know time is of the essence. You are going to the ball tonight." The cardinal said as a statement – rather than a question.

"Yes, Your Eminence. Pope Alexander has requested my presence. Will you be attending?"

"No, my son, but I understand why you must go. I shall expect a full report tomorrow."

"Of course, Your Eminence. I had planned to do as much if there is anything that I feel warrants your attention."

"Let me be the judge of that, Michelangelo. Just be prepared to tell me everything that happens in great detail. Also, has the pope given you any additional the details on your commission?"

"No, Your Eminence. I am to learn everything tonight."

"Then we shall have much to talk about tomorrow? No?"

"It would seem so, Your Eminence."

"Splendid. I shall either send Captain Bari for you, or perhaps I shall visit you myself. I am intrigued by the creative process, and would very much enjoy seeing how an artist like yourself fills his day. Until tomorrow, then?"

"I am your humble servant to command, Your Eminence."

He had reached the top of the staircase when the cardinal said, "Take the horse, Michelangelo. Consider it a gift. Tell whatever hostler you employ to contact me and I will take care of everything."

"I cannot, Your Eminence."

Holding up his hand, the cardinal said, "You can and you shall. And there will be no further discussion about it."

"Does the animal have a name, your eminence?"

"I call him Fedele, for he has always proven true. Now go, enjoy the ball, and we shall talk tomorrow."

Riding home, Michelangelo was hit by the fact that within the next two days, his future and his career would be determined by the whims and opinions of others. For the first time, he felt helpless, powerless. Looking to heaven, he said, "Dear Lord, I do not know what you intend for me, but I am your humble servant first and always."

After stabling the horse, he walked home, and as he turned onto his street, he was greeted by the sight of Cesare Borgia's horse, tethered in front of his house once again.

Entering his home, he again found Cesare seated at his table. Before he could speak, Cesare asked, "And how is the good Cardinal della Rovere this fine morning?"

"How could you possibly know? I've only just returned from his palace."

"On my way here, I saw you ride by with Captain Bari and his men. Ascertaining your destination was not so difficult."

"The cardinal is well," said Michelangelo.

"What *exactly* did His Eminence want?"

"He wanted to know if I planned to attend the ball, and when I told him that I did, he said that he would expect a full report tomorrow."

"Let me remind you, Michelangelo. Cardinal della Rovere is not a man to be trusted – nor is he to be taken lightly. Should you run afoul of him, my father and I will do our best to protect you, but we cannot guarantee your safety forever."

"I understand."

"Good. The final preparations are being made for the ball. My father will send a carriage for you this afternoon." "I shall be ready," said Michelangelo.

"Then I shall see you this evening," said Cesare as he rose.

"Cesare?"

"Yes?"

"Is there nothing you can tell me about this ball? I have heard people speak of it, but no one seems to know the occasion or any of the particulars."

Standing in the doorway, Cesare stopped and thought for a moment, and then choosing his words with extreme care said, "Like all theologians, my father has long been fascinated by the duality of human nature. Tonight, with the help of certain members of the Curia and various others, he intends to explore the contradiction that is man."

Chapter Twenty-seven – Rome, 1901

Over breakfast the next morning, Holmes looked at me and asked, "Now that you have slept on it and had time to mull it over, did anything in Pope Alexander's letter strike you as unusual?"

"I must admit that I am rather curious about that ball that he mentioned. I am also intrigued by the fact that he hired Michelangelo to bring his ideas to fruition."

"And nothing else?" asked Holmes.

"Not offhand," I said. "Although I fail to see the point of his rather mundane discourse on the duality of human nature. Why be obtuse? Just tell us what you mean."

"Ah Watson," laughed Holmes, "You must remember, he wasn't writing for us, but only for future popes. Something tells me the significance of his words has been lost over the centuries."

"And you saw something there?" I sputtered, "To me, Holmes, it was indecipherable nonsense."

Holmes chuckled softly, "Try to imagine yourself a Renaissance pope sitting on the Throne of the Fisherman, rather than a modern medical man. As pope, your world is guided by faith and your knowledge is limited. If you can but put yourself in his shoes, I imagine you will see things rather differently."

"I shall try, but I cannot promise. Now, what are we doing today?" I asked.

"You are going to see Captain Tritini," Holmes said. "I have made a list of points I need you to go over with him." He handed me a sheet of paper, and I glanced at it. "You know he is only a captain. I am not certain that he possesses the power to carry out everything you have written here."

"Just tell him to do the best he can," said Holmes amiably.

"And while I am visiting with Captain Tritini, what will you be doing?"

"I think I shall pay a call on Signore Giolitti," he said smiling.

"Do you think that is wise?" I asked.

"Wise? Perhaps not. However, I can assure you that it is necessary, Watson."

My day passed rather quickly. I met with Tritini and showed him Holmes' list. As I feared, he was able to accommodate several of the requests, while others he admitted were utterly impossible.

After leaving his office, I headed back to St. Peter's Basilica, determined once again to explore that monument to faith in greater detail and at a more leisurely pace.

As wandered through the vast church, I tried to take in all the statues and stained glass as well as the towering bronze *baldacchino*, which I learned was 95 feet tall and made almost entirely of sculpted bronze, I was suddenly struck by the faith of the artisans who crafted these magnificent creations, all to honor an unseen god. I left feeling slightly jealous because I had nothing comparable in my life.

As I returned to the convent, I saw Holmes taking a pipe on the bench in the garden. "How did your meeting with Signore Giolitti go?"

"About as well as can be expected," Holmes replied dryly.

He began by saying, "I called upon him at his office, which is a reflection of the man's enormous ego. The walls are covered with framed Daguerrotypes and photographs of Giolitti with various world leaders. There's even a photograph of him with Pope Leo. The face that graced all those images is that of a man who is used to getting his way. He is rather tall and imposing. He has a thick head of dark hair that is receding rather rapidly, which punctuates his rather pronounced pre-frontal development, and like many Italian men, he affects a full moustache, which is accented by a small goatee.

"What little room remains on the walls is filled with proclamations honoring him as well as his various degrees. It's a far cry from any office that I might ever have envisioned for myself," sniffed Holmes.

"I informed his secretary that I was employed by the British Ministry of the Interior and that a mutual friend, Sir Charles Ritchie, had suggested that I visit Signore Giolitti, should I ever find myself in Rome."

"He kept me waiting for a few moments and then came out and ushered me into his office."

"He is a very sharp customer, Watson. Before I could introduce myself, he turned and said, 'I wasn't aware that you were working for the Home Secretary, Mr. Holmes. I was under the impression that you were still toiling as a consulting detective. Would you care for a cup of tea?' "

196

"I said, 'I won't insult you by asking…,' and he cut me off, saying, 'You have your little spies on bicycles Mr. Holmes, but I have my people everywhere. Something else to drink? Coffee, perhaps?' "

"No thank you, signore," I replied, "I think it best that we get right to business."

" 'I had heard you were a man with little patience for trifles,' he continued, 'How may I be of assistance?'" "I believe you are in possession of several items that do not belong to you,' I said, 'I have come to return them to their rightful owner."

"He smiled at me in a rather condescending manner and said, 'Mr. Holmes, I am afraid that you have me confused with some street brigand. What exactly are these items to which you refer?'"

"Signore Giolitti, let us not play games. You have my word that the law will never hear a word of anything that we say. I understand your position, but do you really think that blackmailing the pope over something he believes is totally beyond his control can in any way justify your actions?"

"'Without admitting anything, please allow me to quote the great Italian writer Nicolo Machiavelli, 'The end justifies the means.' Make of that statement what you will Mr. Holmes."

"'At that point, Watson, I despaired of appealing to his sense of fair play, so I tried another tack. I said, 'Signore, I will tell you this. I told His Holiness that any man with the audacity to rob the papal apartments and then to make demands of the papacy was a man to be both feared and reckoned with.'"

"The self-satisfied smile on his face after I made that statement was an indication that I was plowing fertile ground. So I continued with more blandishments, 'Signore, I have spoken to the pontiff, and I have assured him that such an individual would never compromise.'"

"'Let us say that I knew someone who possessed the items in question. What is your suggestion?' he asked."

"'The pope has asked that one of the cameos be returned as an act of good faith, and then he will meet with you or your representative to discuss resolving the Roman Question. After which, depending upon the outcome of your meeting, you will either return the rest of the cameos or follow a course of your own choosing, which I assume would mean making the existence of the cameos public knowledge.'"

"''That seems like an eminently fair request,' he replied. 'I shall attempt to contact those who may be able to help us and see if they are amenable.'"

"Signore Giolitti, please. Let us drop the charade. You, or someone you know has the cameos. That you have acted as you did, I can understand, although I might have done things differently," I stated.

"'I shall see what I can do, Mr. Holmes.'"

"Before I leave, may I ask a question?"

"'By all means, Mr. Holmes. I am not promising an answer, but nothing ventured, nothing gained.'"

"As far as I understand, the existence of these cameos is a closely guarded secret. I am curious as how you came to learn of them."

"The man actually had the audacity to puff out his chest, Watson, then he looked at me and said, 'Let us venture into the realm of conjecture, shall we, Mr. Holmes? I am certain that you have heard of Leonardo da Vinci. Are you aware that he fashioned the silver cases in which the cameos sit?'

"No," I replied honestly. "This is the first I have heard of that."

"'How much do you know about Leonardo. Mr. Holmes.?'"

"I am aware of his paintings and his drawings that encompass everything from ball bearings to underwater diving suits to various flying machines."

"'Do you know anything about his personal life?'"

"On that matter, I am afraid that I must plead complete ignorance," I admitted.

"'So I can assume that you have never heard of his apprentice, Salai?'"

"'I cannot say that I have,'" I answered truthfully.

"'Salai, whose real name was Gian Giacomo Caprotti di Oreno, was the bane of Leonardo's existence. In fact, the word *salai* can be translated as "little devil." At any rate, Salai entered Leonardo's household as a youth. I believe he was 9 or 10 at the time. He spent most of the rest of his life there, assisting Leonardo and quite often serving as a model. If you should ever see Leonardo's "Bacchus" or "John the Baptist," you will find yourself looking at the face of Salai."

"In fact, there are some who believe that the face of the Mona Lisa bears more than a passing resemblance to Salai.

Curiously, when Leonardo died, he left La Giocanda, several other paintings and half a vineyard to Salai."

"Despite their closeness, Salai and Leonardo often clashed. Salai apparently stole money from his master on several occasions, and was described by Leonardo as stubborn, a liar and a glutton. At the time, there was a great deal of civil unrest in Florence caused by a monk named Savonarola."

"Playing to the masses, Savonarola managed to force the powerful Medici family from the city and create a quasirepublic there – although it was fairly short-lived."

"At any rate, Salai was a follower of Savonarola's. He was what was called a *piagnoni,* which can be translated as a 'weeper' or a 'wailer.'"

"I am reasonably certain that Leonardo knew nothing about Salai's political leanings, just as I am equally certain that he was completely ignorant of the young man's rather detailed diaries.'"

Chapter Twenty-eight – Rome, Oct. 30, 1501

The carriage arrived at exactly 3 p.m. Freshly shorn and shaved and wearing a new doublet that he had purchased for the occasion, Michelangelo had to admit to himself that he was excited. During the ride to St. Peter's he speculated on what kind of ball the pope might possibly be hosting.

Upon arriving, he was escorted by Father Ferrante into the papal chambers. This time, however, they moved deeper into the building. Finally, he found himself in an enormous room where the pontiff was waiting for him.

"It's so good to see you again, my son," exclaimed the pope jovially. "Are you looking forward to this evening? I must admit that that I am."

Looking around, Michelangelo saw that three enormous tables, each capable of seating at least 40 people, had been arranged in a gigantic U in the center of the room. Across the open end of the U was a smaller table at which 10 might be seated comfortably. That table was actually blocking the main doors to the room, and it appeared to sit on a dais that one reached by climbing three steps, so it was somewhat higher than the others.

On each of the tables were several candelabra as well as a glistening display of silverware, cups and plates.

Michelangelo also noticed that various divans and settees had been scattered about the room, as well as what seemed to be hundreds of loose, oversized pillows. He further observed that there were large torches in every possible holder and that several braziers had been placed in various spots throughout the room.

Gazing up, he saw various curtains, all of which were furled at the moment, suspended from the ceiling. Next to each was a rope that when pulled would release it, so that when it fell, the person in that area was assured a modicum of privacy. He also noticed a number of elaborately decorated paper bags hanging by ropes from the ceiling near the table on the dais. Although they were much closer to the floor than the hanging screens, he could not even begin to fathom their purpose.

"What is this room?" he asked the pontiff.

"This is the biggest salon in the papal apartments. Normally, I hold papal audiences here, and meet with ambassadors and the assembled Curia," the pope replied, "but I have cleared my schedule for the next few days so that we might enjoy ourselves, even as we consider the reach of our office. Come, let us have some light refreshments now. Dinner will not be served for several hours and this promises to be a long night."

Turning around, Michelangelo saw that two trifold screens had been set up in the furthest corners of the room. In the center of each of the three sections of the screens were small grilles.

Pointing to them, Michelangelo asked, "What are they, your Holiness?"

Looking, the pope laughed, "They are temporary confessionals, though I rather doubt they will get much use tonight. You will be installed behind the one on the left, and my *ceremoniere,* Johannes Burchard, will be ensconced behind the other. Should anyone desire penance from you, you can either hear their confession and grant them absolution, or you may tell them you are too busy – they will understand, I assure you – and to go see the other priest. If you should choose the former, I only ask that you make certain those confessing are given short shrift."

"Remember, too, there is a Franciscan robe in your confessional; don it before the ball and no one will question your authority. I will make certain that the servants provide you with food, drink and anything else you may require over the course of the night."

At that moment, Lucrezia entered the room. In a gown of royal blue with her hair coiffed, she looked almost ethereal. She kissed her father and then gave Michelangelo a warm smile before she said, "Signore Buonarotti, so good to see you again."

"Have you two met?" the pope asked.

"Oh father! I told you I rode to his house the day after you showed me the cameo. I wanted to thank him in person," she said.

"Did you?" asked the pope. "It must have slipped my mind. We are just going to enjoy a small repast, my dear. Would you care to join us?"

"I would be delighted," she replied.

"As they walked down the hall, behind the pope, Lucrezia winked at Michelangelo and flashed him a knowing smile.

Michelangelo thought, "She is a vixen – best be on my guard."

As they sat at table, chatting about art and sundry other matters, Lucrezia suddenly broke a momentary silence by asking, "Does he know the details of the ball yet, father?" "No, my dear. I want that to be my special surprise. Signore, you have already told me that you are not easily shocked. I hope that is still the case."

"It is, Your Holiness" replied Michelangelo.

"Well, I will tell you this, signore. Tonight, we shall find out just what it takes to unnerve the accomplished Michelangelo. All I ask is that you remain behind your screen for the first few hours. Once the activities begin, if you should desire to participate, feel free. If you opt to refrain, I will understand that as well."

"I understand, Your Holiness," said Michelangelo, "And you have my word that I will abide by your command."

"Excellent. Now you must excuse me, I have some last-minute details to attend to. Lucrezia, will you entertain our guest until for a while? I know you must get ready as well. I shall see where Cesare is and what he is up to; perhaps he will be able to relieve you."

"Thank you, father, but I'm certain that won't be necessary. My dress has been chosen and it will take me but a few minutes to change. I will keep Signore Buonarotti company and then see that he is comfortable in his confessional before I go to get ready."

"I shall meet you and Cesare on the other side of the main doors at 8 and then we shall make our grand entrance." "And promise me that you will not divulge any details? And that means no hints as well," the pope scolded her playfully.

"Not even one?" she pleaded.

The pope looked at Michelangelo and asked, "How could anyone refuse her?" Turning his attention back to Lucrezia, he said, "Here is what you may tell Michelangelo." The pope leaned over and whispered in her ear. Giggling, she said, "Father, you are terrible!"

"Promise me, Lucrezia," he exhorted.

"I promise," she said.

Left alone, Michelangelo looked at Lucrezia and said, "What have I gotten myself into?"

"I promise that no harm will come to you signore artista. After all," she laughed, "if something should happen to you, who would paint the next portrait of me?"

And so they continued with light banter, and then suddenly Lucrezia said, "It is nearly twilight. Let me escort you to your confessional, father."

As they walked in silence, Michelangelo began one final assessment of the situation. He was in the papal palace, there by the invitation of and under the protection of Pope Alexander. He was to be hidden and disguised, for he had already decided to wear the Franciscan robe. Outside of the papal family and his few friends, the only other person who knew he was attending was Cardinal della Rovere. And while that was certainly cause for concern, it seemed as though every precaution had been taken to shield him. What could possibly occur that could place him in danger?

His thoughts were interrupted by Lucrezia, who said, "We are here, Michelangelo. He realized that he must have walked in silence for several minutes and now he was standing before the trifold screen behind which he was to spend the evening.

Walking behind it, Lucrezia emerged from the other side and said, "The robe and sandals are there. It has been stocked with wine and water as well as a selection of dried fruit and cured meats, should you get hungry."

Stepping behind it, Michelangelo saw everything as she had described it. He also noticed a plush chair, paper and charcoals and against the back wall, a small divan.

"I don't think I shall be sleeping," he said to Lucrezia. "Should we move this out into the main room?"

"No," she replied, "Father insisted that it be put there. Anyway, you may get weary."

"I suppose you are right," he said.

When he turned around, he realized that she was kneeling because he could see the outline of her face through one of the grilles. "I should like to make my confession, Father Buonarotti," she said. Before he could speak, she continued, "It has been two days since my last confession, and I regret that I have but one hint to give you, Father."

"I had almost forgotten," he said.

"Are you familiar with Dante?" she asked.

"Somewhat," he replied.

"Consider then the second circle of the 'Inferno,'" and with that she stood and skipped out of the room, laughing.

Michelangelo thought about her words but could find no context for them. He decided that she had either misheard her father or the pope needed to re-read Dante.

After all, the Curia was coming to the papal palace for dinner and a ball, and Dante's second circle contained those who had yielded to the sin of lust.

Chapter Twenty-nine – Rome, 1901

"Are you saying that both Leonardo da Vinci and Michelangelo had a hand in creating the cameos?" I asked.

"Yes, Watson. I must say the involvement of Leonardo came as something of a surprise, but the fact that his assistant apparently detailed everything that he did at least solves one part of the mystery," Holmes said.

"Yes," I added, "but how did he come to learn of their location in the papal apartments?"

"I strongly suspect that Giolitti has a spy in the pope's employ," said Holmes. "Once he learned of the existence of the cameos, he no doubt instructed his spy to be on the lookout for a safe or other hiding place."

"But after he had discovered their location, why not have the spy steal the cameos?" I asked.

"That might have taken his agent off the board; that's why they forced the nun to steal them. That Giolitti knew of our involvement in the case just strengthens my theory."

"Do you have any idea who the spy is?" I asked.

"I have my suspicions," said Holmes, "and we may yet turn his or her presence to our advantage."

"What's our next move?" I asked.

"I have baited the trap," said Holmes, "now we can do little but wait."

From experience, I knew that Holmes possessed the patience of a saint, and then I found myself chuckling at my own cliché. "He may need it," I thought.

I watched as Holmes tried to busy himself, re-reading the English newspapers we had collected over the past few days. This went on for about two hours until one of the nuns entered the sitting room and handed Holmes a note.

Upon reading it, he looked at me and said, "While he is no Moriarty, Giolitti is proving himself a formidable match, indeed. Watson, I must go out for a while."

"Is there anything I can do in the interim?" I asked.

"Check with your friends at the Vatican archives, and see if they can turn up any documents that mention a Salai. He was Leonardo's assistant."

"I shall do my best. Will you be back in time for supper?"

"I cannot say," answered Holmes, "but I will be in touch." Turning on his heel, he strode resolutely out of the room.

* * *

Giovanni Giolitti detested surprises. He had anticipated that Pope Leo would retain Sherlock Holmes to help reacquire the cameos, just as the pontiff had employed the detective to look into the death of Cardinal Tosca a few years earlier.

However, he had been more than a little taken aback when he had opened his door that morning, expecting to find some officious British flunky sitting in his waiting room and had instead cast his gaze upon the aquiline profile of the rather austere-looking detective.

Thinking back over their meeting, Giolitti reasoned that were their places reversed, he might have done much the same as Holmes. However, he was not about to fall for the opening gambit played by the detective.

Gazing out his window, Giolitti scanned the street looking for youngsters lounging about and any other unfamiliar faces. Seeing none, he then tried to put himself in Holmes' shoes and decided that were he the great Sherlock Holmes, he would make every effort to keep his spies wellhidden.

Mulling over the possibilities open to him going forward, he then wondered how many pairs of eyes he would have to elude, and decided that with the Vatican footing the bill, money was no object. As a result, Holmes could hire as many youngsters as he thought he would need. Then he recalled the *carabinieri* in the post offices and decided that even more eyes would have to be taken into account.

Giolitti then made a decision to keep the detective's young assistants busy. Sitting down, he proceeded to write a series of notes and addressed them to friends and colleagues all over the city, including the outer environs. He then had his secretary summon 10 different messengers, who were then dispatched as decoys to locales on both sides of the Tiber. Each courier was instructed to remain at the delivery site until nightfall and then to return home.

An hour later, he wrote 10 more notes and dispatched 10 more messengers with the same directions. After he had repeated the process three more times, Giolitti decided that Holmes and the Vatican would be hard-pressed to find 50 trustworthy youths in Rome.

Heading down to the basement, Giolitti changed his clothes, donned a wig, colored glasses and a hat and left his building, walking with a cane, through the tradesmen's entrance.

The street was totally deserted.

As he rounded the corner of the Palazzo de Quirinale and crossed the square in front of the building, he could see no one following him. Just to be sure, he sat on a bench and leisurely smoked a cigarette. It was a pleasant day, warm and sunny, and the square was largely empty.

After his second cigarette, he was relatively certain that he was not being followed, but just to make certain, he hailed a cab and took it the Trevi Fountain. From there, he walked to the basilica of Santa Maria di Via. He entered the church, lit a candle, said a prayer, waited a few minutes and when no one else entered, he left by a different door.

Finally, feeling somewhat at ease, he walked to the National Gallery of Antique Art, still checking occasionally to see if he were being tailed.

As he strolled through the Barberini Palace, admiring the works of Caravaggio, Tintoretto and his favorite, El Greco, he thought about Holmes and the dangerous game they were playing.

He focused on the detective's request that one of the cameos be returned as a show of good faith. "Well played, Mr. Holmes, but did you really think I would be so stupid as to leave my office and allow you or one of your minions to follow me to their hiding place? I think not.

"You have deployed your forces throughout the city following my diversions. At my leisure, I will retrieve a cameo and then you may present it to the pontiff. The only question, now, is which one to return?"

As he walked the streets, still checking for tails, he slowly made his way to the Via Vittorio Veneto. Looking at his watch as he approached the church of Santa Maria della Concezione dei Cappuccini, he realized that he had been traveling around Rome for nearly two hours.

Entering the church, he saw no one inside – at first. The he caught sight of an old priest, who appeared to be sleeping in one of the pews.

Giolitti decided that caution was paramount; approaching the priest, he said, "Father, would you hear my confession?"
When the priest didn't stir, Giolitti repeated his request a little louder.

As he said it a third time, the priest's eyes began to flutter, and he slowly threw off the chains of Morpheus.

Looking up at Giolotti, the priest asked groggily, "*Stavo dormendo?*"

"Yes, father, you were asleep."

"*Che hora e?*" asked the priest.

Pulling out his pocket watch, Giolitti said, "It is 3 p.m., father."

"*Gesu Christo!*" the priest exclaimed, "*Sono in ritardo!*"

As the portly priest struggled to his feet, Giolitti watched in amusement, before asking, "For what are you late, father?"

"*Un matrimonio*," replied the priest, as he hurried toward the rear of the church, moving quite well for a man of his considerable girth, opened the door and left.

"I hope they will be very happy," yelled Giolitti though he doubted the good father had heard him.

Sitting in the church for 10 more minutes, he waited for someone else to enter. When no one did, he descended into the charnel house below but not before he had placed a "Closed for repairs" sign across the steps.

* * *

Built in the early 17th century, the church had been commissioned by Pope Urban VIII, whose brother, Antonio Barberini, had been a Capuchin friar. As churches in Rome go, Santa Maria della Concezione dei Cappuccini is rather unremarkable. The nave is small, and while one of the side chapels contains the body of St. Felix of Cantalice, the first Capuchin to be canonized, and another boasts a fairly dramatic altar piece depicting Michael the Archangel, there is nothing particularly noteworthy about the structure itself.

However, beneath the church, the remains of nearly 4,000 Capuchin friars had been interred, making Santa Maria perhaps the largest ossuary in the Eternal City.

As far as the public knew, the ossuary was divided up into six small chapels. After descending to the underground level, visitors first enter the Crypt of the Resurrection, Giolitti's favorite chamber and perhaps the least unsettling of them all. On the rear wall, a painting of Jesus raising Lazarus from the dead is surrounded by skulls, leg bones, pelvis bones, arms and other human remains, artistically arranged on the floor, walls and ceiling. Despite its macabre nature, Giolitti still found the artwork, if such it could be called, attractive. Anyone taking the time to really examine the rooms would see hearts, floral designs and even chandeliers cleverly constructed of various human bones, all serving as graphic reminders that life is fleeting.

As he walked along the windowed corridor toward the mass chapel, Giolitti found himself reciting the words of the *memento mori* on the placard that graced the entrance.

Written in five languages, the sign reminds all who enter: "What you are now, we once were; what we are now, you shall be."

He passed the Mass Chapel, the Crypt of the Skulls, the Crypt of the Pelvises, the Crypt of the Leg and Thigh Bones and finally came to the Crypt of the Three Skeletons. Looking up, he saw the skeleton of a child, holding a scythe made of shoulder bones and a pair of scales made from various finger bones. The reminder was anything but subtle: Death has no regard for age.

On the altar itself, two more skeletons, both children, reached toward an adult skull in the middle.

After making certain that he was alone, Giolitti entered the crypt, reached behind the cross the robed skeleton on the left was holding and removed a small key that had been inset in the rear of the crucifix.

He turned to the altar and slid the key into an innocuous looking hole hidden behind the skull in the center.

Kneeling, he pushed back the stone on the left side at the base of the altar; it slid back fairly easily, making only a slight scraping noise, and Giovanni Giolitti, though he thought it profoundly undignified, began to crawl into the seventh chamber – the one the public would never see – the Crypt of the Persecuted.

Chapter Thirty – Rome, 1501, Oct. 30

Michelangelo had settled into the chair and was trying to recall the cantos that made up the second circle of the "Inferno" when he heard footsteps. Peering through the grille, he saw a priest walking behind the other screen.

Considering that they were alone for the moment, Michelangelo whispered, "Do you have any idea how long we must wait?"

A voice answered, "I should think less than an hour. Is that you, Franco?"

"No. My name is Michelangelo. Who are you?"

"I am Johannes Burchard, the papal master of ceremonies."

"I am pleased to meet you, father," said Michelangelo, "Are you not attending the ball?"

"No. His Holiness has asked me to chronicle the evening's events, much as I keep track of the papal expenses. He has also asked me to give absolution to any and all who might request it."

"Have you any idea what to expect?" asked Michelangelo.

"No, but with the Borgias involved, I can only hope for the best."

Michelangelo thought about telling the priest of Lucrezia's hint and then decided against it. Instead, he asked, "Why do you say that?"

"The family is as willful as any on Earth. Alexander appears to have little regard for his priestly vows. Cesare was once a cardinal, but resigned to pursue a career in the military. As for Lucrezia, you know her mother was a courtesan? Well, she is very much her mother's daughter, and what she has of her father is his baser half."

Michelangelo was stunned by the priest's bluntness – especially in the papal apartments – and decided to pursue another line of conversation. "Do you know why I am here, Father?"

"Of course," said the priest. "How are the cameos coming? Those stones cost a fair amount."

"I shall know much better after this ball," he answered.

"I will tell you this, Michelangelo. If the pope is pleased with your labors, you will be handsomely rewarded."

"That is comforting," said the artist.

They lapsed into silence for some time, and then suddenly, voices could be heard in the distance.

"I believe the first guests have arrived," said Father Burchard. "So let us take a vow of silence for the rest of the evening, my son."

"As you wish, Father."

Through the screen, Michelangelo saw that a small group of cardinals, no more than four or five, had entered the room and were beginning to take their places at the various tables.

As they milled around chatting and exchanging pleasantries, Michelangelo wondered what they were looking for and then he discerned that place cards had indicated who should sit where.

Next, Michelangelo saw Cardinal Sforza, the pope's vice chancellor, enter and take his place near the head table, and then he saw Cardinal Piccolomini take a seat at the opposite table. Slowly, the hall began to fill until it seemed a sea of red. Michelangelo thought it odd that they were seated at every other setting, and he wondered what other guests the pope might have invited.

After 20 minutes or so had passed, a bell sounded – almost as though mass were about to begin. The cardinals rose as one and then the main doors were thrown open and Pope Alexander entered the room, followed by Lucrezia and Cesare.

After they had reached their seats at the dais, the pope began to speak. "Welcome, my friends. Tonight, we celebrate the approach of Allhallowttide. But before we remember our saints and the souls of all those seeking a crown in heaven and before we don purple – for Advent is fast approaching – I offer you one special evening of fellowship. I invite you to dine, to drink, to relax and to enjoy yourself without fear of repercussion – in this world or the next."

The pope's remark was greeted by a smattering of polite laughter. Undaunted, he continued, "And for those who may feel the need – either before or after our supper – there are two priests in the rear ready to hear your confessions and absolve you of your sins."

Many of the cardinals glanced at the screens when the pope gestured, but none rose to be shriven.

With that, an army of servants entered the room. Some busied themselves lighting the candelabra on the tables and then extinguishing the torches on the walls. Others carried in enormous trenchers laden with meats, pasta, vegetables, breads and cheeses. Each table was provided with two whole suckling pigs as well as beef and various types of fowl. Still other servants made certain that the cardinals' goblets were never empty.

The members of the Curia were enjoying the lavish meal, and watching them was making Michelangelo hungry.

After some time had passed, Cardinal Sforza rose and called for silence. Looking at the members of the Curia, he said, "I should like to propose a toast to His Holiness, whose largess of spirit is matched only by his purity of soul."

All the cardinals responded, *"Propini tibi salute."* Michelangelo could only suppose that toasting the Pope's good health in Latin was a Vatican tradition.

The pope looked at Cesare first and then at Lucrezia; when both nodded, he turned his gaze on Sforza and said, "Such kind words, Cardinal Sforza, are deserving of a reward. And those of you who have toasted my health shall also be rewarded in equal measure."

He nodded to the servants who began placing a small covered dish in front of each prelate.

When they had finished, the pope picked up a small bell and gently tinkled it. "I have invited a number of guests to dine with us this evening. Please make them feel welcome and tend to their needs, both spiritual – and otherwise. And should you feel the need to wear it, each of you will find a mask under the dish just placed in front of you."

When he had finished speaking, Michelangelo saw that the cardinals were all staring at the rear of the room, but they weren't looking at the confessionals.

Hearing them before he saw them, Michelangelo realized that a large group of women were about to enter the room. He could smell their perfume, and he could hear their gentle laughter. He could also sense their nervousness.

Finally, the women began to come into view, and Michelangelo was shocked to see that they were all stunningly beautiful. Leading them was a woman in a red dress the same color as the cardinals' robes. She was wearing a tall hat that resembled a miter and carried a walking stick that had been shaped like a crozier.

Following her were about 50 women. Many wore dresses that accentuated the sensuousness of their bodies. Michelangelo looked at the cardinals – all of whom were smiling lasciviously – and recalled Lucrezia's hint.

"This cannot be happening," he thought.

The women took their places between the cardinals at the tables, and Michelangelo now understood why they had been seated as they were.

He watched as they ate, drank and laughed, and he noticed that not one cardinal donned the mask. Occasionally, he would look at the pope and his children, smiling as they presided over this affair. At one point, the pope called the woman in red to his side. After a brief conversation, he smiled and nodded.

Tapping his goblet with a knife, the pope managed to get both the cardinals and the courtesans to pay attention. "My brothers," he began, "it troubles me to learn that some of our guests are in distress. They are in danger of losing their home. Can we as good clergymen allow that to happen?"

The answer was a resounding "No!" from prelates and prostitutes alike.

"I have asked Mistress Antonia how we may be of assistance to those in need, and she has proposed an auction. Looking at the woman seated next to Cardinal Urcioli, the pope said, "Marguerite, would you come here?"

A tall brunette wearing a sheer white dress rose and walked to the dais. As she stood next to the pope, Michelangelo saw that she had lovely brown eyes, straight white teeth hidden behind full, sensuous lips, but her enormous breasts were where all eyes were focused.
"Marguerite is in such dire straits that she has offered to sell the only thing she owns – her gown – so that the money can be used to keep the landlord at bay."

"I bid five florins," yelled Cardinal Trombetti.

"Ten florins," countered Cardinal Urcioli.

Then a cardinal whom Michelangelo didn't recognize bid 12 florins for the dress. After the bidding had reached 40 florins, Cardinal Puccini was declared the winner. As he rose to speak to the woman, she slipped the straps over her shoulders and the dress fell to the floor.

The reaction was a gasp – as her obvious charms were displayed for all to see. She bent, picked up the dress and said to Cardinal Puccini, "I should like to tell you about the workmanship that went into this dress," all the while leading him to one of the more secluded divans in a far corner of the room.

The process was repeated with a Nordic-looking woman with long blonde hair and eyes as blue as the Adriatic, selling her gown of silver damask. Cardinal DeLeo claimed her as his prize and they, too, sought out a quiet corner.

At this point, Cesare stood up and before the next auction began, said, "A gentle reminder, my brothers. We have all night and even tomorrow, if need be. Do not exhaust yourselves prematurely, as there are more prizes and surprises on the way."

As the auctions continued, the room became a whirlwind of erotic sights and sounds. Michelangelo heard grunts mixed with higher voices screeching in pleasure. Looking left, he saw Cardinal Sforza being serviced by two women simultaneously. To his right, he saw Cardinal Brunati standing up and thrusting himself deep into a Nubian woman from behind as those nearby cheered him on.

Directly in front of his "confessional," he watched enthralled as a petite redhead knelt – not for forgiveness or in prayer – but to perform fellatio on Cardinal Ferrari.

Everywhere he looked, he saw displays of lust and carnal pleasure. Stunned and uncertain what to do, Michelangelo remembered his purpose and began to sketch. The act of drawing calmed him and suddenly the goings-on around him seemed less sinful and more artistic.

Over the cacophony of pleasure that filled the room, the small bell could be heard tinkling and the unholy exertions slowly abated.

Up on the dais, the woman who had been dressed like a cardinal when the evening began had retained only her hat and crozier-like stick, and it was she who was ringing the bell.

When she had everyone's attention, she spoke, "I sincerely hope that you have heeded Cesare's advice and have not exhausted yourselves. After all, the night is young and the fun is just beginning."

"Ladies," she said, "if you are not busy, please attend to the candles."

With that, the women detached themselves from their partners and moved to the tables where they began to lift the candelabras and place them on the floor.

With an evil smirk, Mistress Antonia said, "Now, for your pleasure, we are going to attempt something that you may not have witnessed before." Calling a buxom brunette to her, she whispered in her ear and the woman laughed.

Turning back to the cardinals, she said, "I have exciting news. Sabrina has agreed to go first."

Chapter Thirty-one – Rome, 1901

Giolitti entered the Crypt of the Persecuted and, as always, was struck by just how small and cramped the room was. When the monks had begun burying friars beneath the church in the 1630s, the Roman Inquisition was scouring the countryside above in search of heretics and anyone else whose opinion dared to differ from the views espoused by Holy Mother Church.

In an effort to protect their members who had run afoul of the Inquisition, the monks had constructed this chamber as a place of last refuge.

If legend were to be believed, Galileo was one of the first to seek shelter there as the monks attempted to arrange safe passage for him from Rome back to Pisa. Giolitti knew that the Inquisition had eventually caught up with the astronomer and after forcing him to denounce his theory of heliocentrism – under the threat of torture – had placed him under house arrest for the remainder of his life.

He thought about others who might have been forced to spend days, weeks, perhaps even months, cowering in silence and seclusion from the henchmen of an angry church. The same church that was still trying to cow the masses into submission today. Obviously, they have learned little from the past, he thought; perhaps a fresh reminder of that bloody time might bring them to heel today.

Looking around, he was struck anew by the spartan conditions. The room contained a small wooden table, two battered stools, a straw mattress and little else. Lighting a few candles, Giolitti pushed the stone back into place, locking it behind him. He then went to the far wall and although he knew the location by heart, he still counted down three bricks from the top left corner and then he counted in three bricks to the right.

Looking at it, he marveled at the fact that to the naked eye it was undetectable. Removing the brick, he then extracted several velvet bags from the crevice. He placed them on the table and then removed each cameo from its bag.

As he arranged them, he found himself admiring the craftsmanship of the two greatest artists of the Renaissance – Michelangelo and Leonardo. "But for your creations and an impious pope, I might have been doomed to spend the rest of my life as minister of the interior, serving at the whims of people who have no idea what is required to run a government," he thought.

As he examined each piece, he was struck anew by the brilliant colors of the stones and the precision of Michelangelo's work. He also admired the craftsmanship of the silver boxes that acted as frames, allowing the cameos to stand freely.

Picking up the last one, he saw a naked Cardinal Giuliano della Rovere, who would become Pope Julius II. As the "warrior pope," it was he who would redesign St. Peter's Basilica and then commission Michelangelo to paint the ceiling of the Sistine Chapel.

None of that grandeur was evident here. Against a background of deep violet, Giolitti saw only a man, his hand wrapped around his engorged penis. From his back sprouted a pair of wings as if to indicate his superiority to ordinary men.

Behind him, partially obscured by his torso and the wings, were sections of a wheel on which he would be broken in hell for his sin of pride. Kneeling before the cardinal were three women, ready to please him, all of whom appeared to be worshipping the prelate while he remained oblivious to their adoration. The artist had certainly captured the man's arrogance, and Giolitti wondered if Michelangelo might have been painting at all had his next patron seen this.

Yes, Giolitti thought, this is the sin of pride captured by an artist. Studying the face more intently, he could see the look of total self-absorption on the cardinal's face, and Giovanni realized that della Rovere truly had considered himself superior to all other men – and women.

"This is the one I will send to Pope Leo with a brief note attached quoting the Book of Proverbs:
'Pride *goeth* before destruction, and an haughty spirit before a fall.'"

"If that doesn't drive home the point, then I have greatly misjudged His Holiness," Giolitti said and then he realized that he was whispering aloud.

He placed the rest of the cameos back in their bags, returned them to the secret compartment and carefully replaced the brick. Then he checked the room, taking great pains to make it look as though nothing had been touched and no one had been there.

Moving to the far end of the room, Giolitti peered out through a peephole to make certain that the hallway was still empty. Again, he found himself admiring the ingenuity of the friars, who had created this tiny aperture that somehow afforded a panoramic view of the entire corridor, despite the fact that it actually looked out through one of the eye sockets of a skull that adorned the Crypt of the Three Skeletons. Satisfied that he was alone, Giolitti undid the lock, pulled the stone toward him and crawled out of the chamber. After rising and carefully dusting himself off, he was glad that he had changed his clothes. He then locked the stone in place, replaced the key and left the Capuchin crypt with the cameo in his pocket.

He tried to imagine Pope Leo's reaction upon seeing it and decided the pontiff would receive it with mixed emotions. His joy at having one of the missing cameos back would certainly be tempered by the realization that six more were still at large and that the depiction of Cardinal della Rovere pleasuring himself was by far the least offensive image of them all.

At the top of the stairs, he removed the "Closed for repairs" sign. Seeing that the church was empty, he exited through the front doors and walked back in the direction of the Barberini Palace before he found a cab.

As had happened once before, it never occurred to Giolitti to look heavenward, or he might have seen the shadowy outline of a figure crouched in the bell tower who appeared to be carefully studying his every move.

* * *

As Holmes had requested, I returned to the Vatican archives and despite several hours of digging and a great deal of help from the librarian, I was unable to locate any references to Leonardo's assistant, Salai.

When I returned to the convent, I learned that Holmes still had not returned. As I dined alone, I wondered what might have become of my friend. While such disappearances were far from unusual, Holmes usually found a way to communicate his whereabouts.

It was a pleasant night, so I decided to talk a walk through the square, enjoy a cigar and admire the statues of the saints.

Although the sun had almost set, there were still traces of light in the western sky and quite a few people in the square.

I began by examining the fountains that graces the square, and throwing a coin into each.

As I wandered along the colonnades, my eyes kept glancing up to the statues high above me. From the ground, it is difficult to tell one saint from another, especially at twilight, although I thought I recognized St. Agnes, the virgin martyr, and one or two others. On one of those occasions when I was looking to heaven instead of in front of me, I bumped soundly into a rotund priest who had been hurrying across the square and nearly sent him sprawling.

As he was adjusting his collar and fixing his hat, I exclaimed, "Father, I am so sorry. I was admiring the statues of the saints and trying to figure out which is which?" *"Perche facevi che?"* he replied.

"Did I hurt your face?" I asked. "I am un dottore."

"Che tipo medico lei fa?" he asked.

I was thumbing furiously through my Italian dictionary hoping to translate his questions, when I heard a familiar voice at my elbow whisper, "He wants to know why you don't look where you are going and what kind of doctor you are?"

I looked for Holmes and then saw only the priest grinning broadly at me.

"Holmes, you rascal," I exclaimed.

He raised his finger to his lips and whispered, "Not here, Watson. I shall meet you back at the convent as soon as I am certain that I am not being followed.

With that he looked at me and in perfect Italian said, *"Sei un medico stupido."* And then he hurried off across the square toward the Via Sant'Anna.

I am not alone in noting Holmes' uncanny acting ability. While we were investigating the case that I have called "The Sign of Four," a wheezing old man doddered into our rooms at Baker Street. Of course it was Holmes, but his performance was so convincing that Inspector Athelney Jones had told my friend, "You'd have made an actor and a rare one." I also recalled to my chagrin that Holmes had fooled me once before when he had dressed as a priest and entered my railway carriage as we were fleeing London in an effort to escape the clutches of Moriarty.

Knowing that my friend was safe put a spring into my step, and I thought we must be nearing some sort of resolution if Holmes were wandering around Rome dressed as a priest.

Little did I know how far off the mark my thoughts would be.

Chapter Thirty-two – Rome, 1501, Oct.30-31

Michelangelo watched spellbound as Mistress Antonia tied a priest's stole around the woman's eyes. "Can you see, my dear?" she asked.
As Sabrina shook her head, her pendulous breasts swayed gently from side to side.

With that, Antonia led Sabrina to one of the bags hanging from the ceiling. After spinning Sabrina three times, much to the delight of the Curia, all of who were watching here, she handed her the walking staff that resembled a crozier, she said, "You know what to do, my dear. Go ahead."

After pausing a moment to regain her equilibrium, Sabrina swung at the bag and missed it entirely. Her momentum caused her to spin in a circle, her breasts swinging provocatively. The cardinals laughed and clapped, urging the girl on. With her second swing, she managed to deal the bag a glancing blow and the spectacle of her breasts swinging freely was repeated for all to enjoy. On her third attempt, she made solid contact and the bag split open releasing a flood of small, brown items that cascaded to the floor and rolled all over the room.

As the cardinals applauded, Antonia said, "Now, comes the real fun. Those are chestnuts scattered about the floor and whoever can pick up the most without using her hands shall win this beautiful azure tunic which Cesare has generously donated."

Immediately, all the women, including Sabrina, began crawling about the floor. As they slithered between the candelabra, some would pause, lower themselves to the floor and then call for a cardinal to bring a cup. Others bent over backwards and gathered the chestnuts by lowering their buttocks to the floor and squeezing them between their nether regions.

Soon, the cardinals had paired off with the prostitutes of their choice and before long, some had eschewed the game entirely in favor of other more readily available pleasures.

Cardinal Sforza was relishing the oral ministrations of a Spanish courtesan, perhaps the most attractive woman of the group. Yet despite her obvious skill and his own pleasure, Michelangelo could see the cardinal's eyes relentlessly wandering about the room, searching to see if any of his comrades had found a woman more beautiful or more talented. Such unease in the midst of such carnal pleasure marked Sforza as a man constantly looking to see if anyone had outstripped him in any respect. "You may not realize it," thought Michelangelo, "but you will never be happy because you are envious."

Of the Seven Deadly Sins, that was the one with which Michelangelo had struggled the most in his youth. Finally, however, he had come to see his talent for what it was – unique but nonetheless, limited. The realization had freed him, but looking at Sforza's face, with the darting eyes and insatiable curiosity, he knew the cardinal was still driven by a desire to possess what others had and to become what others were. "You shall grace the second cameo I carve," thought Michelangelo, "and your jealousy shall run rampant on a background of brilliant green."

Michelangelo then turned his attention to Cardinal Briconnet, who was moving from one courtesan to another, ordering those he considered his underlings to step aside and allowing the different women to pleasure him in different ways. Watching the Frenchman indulging in all the room had to offer with little regard for the feelings of others, Michelangelo knew that Bricconet would be the embodiment of gluttony when it was time to fashion that particular cameo.

Gazing about the room through the grille, he saw the aged Cardinal Marti, reclining on a divan and pointing to various chestnuts on the floor. As the women crawled by, he would grab their private parts and they would squeal with pleasure and laugh and grab him in turn. "So now *acedia* has a face," thought Michelangelo. "Marti is too lazy even to contribute to his own gratification. He shall be depicted as the personification of sloth, and I shall clothe him in the shell of a snail."

Suddenly, Michelangelo heard a voice say, "She's mine, you bastard." He looked to the right and saw Cardinal Fiorza pulling a courtesan from the arms of Cardinal Rispoli.

"Why not ask her whose company she prefers?" replied Rispoli.

Fiorza raised his arm to strike Rispoli when suddenly Cesare intervened. "Brothers, there are more than enough women to go around," he said. Then looking at Rispoli, Cesare continued, "Won't you join me at the dais? I should like a few words with you."

Rispoli smiled at Fiorza and said, "Take her." As Cesare and Rispoli walked off, Michelangelo saw that Fiorza's face was a bright crimson. Suddenly, he began to slap the courtesan on her thighs, asking in a slurred voice, "Do you like pleasure or pain or both, my dear?"

"The pope warned me about you," thought Michelangelo. "And tonight, you have shown your true colors. Your scarlet countenance betrays you, and now I, too, have seen wrath personified."

At that moment, the bell tinkled once again, and Antonia announced, "We have a winner! Anna, will you claim your prize?"

A young woman then stepped forward and Cesare handed her the tunic. "You are the queen of the Ballet of Chestnuts! All hail the queen!"

As the cardinals chanted, "All hail the queen," the girl blushed and then Antonia said, "Our next contest is a rather special one."

Flexing her arms, she said, "It requires strength," and then spreading her hands apart slowly, she said, "as well as length." She continued to spread her hands even further, adding "and even more length."

To those cardinals not otherwise occupied, she said, "This is a chance to prove your virility – and there will be two winners. For the cardinal who can maintain the act the longest, the pope has promised a pair of silken slippers. And for the cardinal who can repeat the act most often, a cask from His Holiness' private cellar."

She continued, "Take a few moments to refresh yourselves, find a partner that pleases you and then we will begin."

Michelangelo asked himself, is there no end to this debauchery? And he wondered how much longer this night – and the cardinals – could continue. He turned to his sketches and looking at the faces and the notes, thought, "Only two sins remain. What shall I do then?"

He heard the bell tinkling and saw that only three cardinals had decided to participate in the latest challenge. He saw that Cardinal Rispoli had taken a slim brunette for his partner while Cardinal Tossi was paired with a Moorishlooking courtesan. The third participant Cardinal Malerba, a giant of a man from Sicily, had selected a rather fleshy, darkhaired beauty as his mate.

When the bell sounded a second time, each man began to thrust into his partner. Both Rispoli and Tossi lay supine and had their women mount them and do the work by controlling the pace, while Malerba had his partner kneel on the divan while he stood, taking her from behind.

After several moments, Rispoli grunted loudly as he spent himself, and despite the tender ministrations of his partner, was unable to resume. Tossi's partner paced herself better but soon he too was done. All the while Malerba kept thrusting as his partner moaned with pleasure. When Tossi's partner was unable to coax his flaccid member back to life, Malberba was declared the winner of both prizes. Upon hearing the proclamation, the cardinal gave a loud grunt and finished by caressing his partner to orgasm. "Thank you, Cardinal Malerba," thought Michelangelo, "in a roomful of lechers, you stand head and shoulders above the rest."

With Malerba chosen to represent lust, the only sin that remained was greed.

"Will you show yourself tonight?" asked Michelangelo. "Or must I improvise?"

As the coupling continued, albeit at a much more subdued pace, Michelangelo heard Cesare say, "Brothers, you may stay the night, if you so desire. But for now, our revels are ended."

Despite the protestation of several members of the Curia and a few of the women, the servants came in and began to light the torches on the walls as they prepared to clean the room.

The cardinals were beginning to depart – some with their companion of the evening and others alone. Many stopped to express their gratitude to His Holiness, Cesare, Lucrezia and Mistress Antonia for an evening they would long remember.

"As long as you enjoyed it," the pope said. "I shall be hearing confessions tomorrow for any and all who may feel the need of forgiveness. After all, better to be absolved of your sin now than to chance the fires of hell," he laughed.

At that moment, inspiration struck and Michelangelo knew whose face would grace the final cameo as the depiction of greed.

Shortly thereafter, Cesare appeared behind the screen and said to Michelangelo, "There is a carriage outside that will take you home. I suggest you keep the robe on with the hood up. The fewer people that know you attended, the better.'

After Michelangelo had collected his sketches, he told Cesare, "Give my best to your father. Tell him it is an evening I shall long remember as well."

"Perhaps next time, you will participate?" asked Cesare.

While he found the thought revolting, he said to Cesare, "Perhaps. One never knows."

"I do not think so," mused Cesare. "You do not have the stomach for it, signore. I can see it in your eyes."

"Perhaps you're right," agreed Michelangelo.

"Just remember, silence is a virtue and one esteemed highly by the pope. We shall be in touch shortly, signore. Good luck in your endeavors."

Feeling used and exhausted, Michelangelo could find comfort only in the fact that his subjects had been chosen, their faces and their acts committed to memory, and the work could begin in earnest in the morning. The thought that it would all soon be over made the burden that much easier to bear.

Chapter Thirty-three – Rome, 1901

I returned to the convent and waited for Holmes. About 30 minutes later, he arrived, looking more like himself.

"Where is your cassock, father?" I asked playfully.

He smiled broadly and said, "When I can deceive my old comrade, I know that my disguise is a success."

"I shouldn't think that I would be a very good barometer," I replied. "After all, you have deceived me far more often than I have seen through your attempts at dissembling."

"Yes, but you have a keen eye, Watson. Speaking of which, have you seen any of the nuns about? I am famished."

I told Holmes that I was rather hungry myself, and we ventured down to the kitchen, where we found Sister Angelica preparing to attack a small mountain of dishes.

"I'd like to make you a proposition, sister," said Holmes, "Watson and I will clean all the dishes and the pans as well if you will make us two omelets."

She laughed, and said, "Mr. Holmes, I don't think I could refuse that offer even if I wanted to, but there is one proviso."

"Yes?" asked Holmes.

"Will you clean up after yourselves? I'd prefer not to come down tomorrow morning to plates and cups in the sink."

"Of course we will," said Holmes.

"Done," she said.

We worked in silence, the nun bustling about the stove while Holmes rolled up his sleeves and began to wash as I dried each piece and put it away.

Suddenly, Sister Angelica broke the silence, "Mr. Holmes, I know you are here at the behest of the Holy Father. And I know what you do. I do not know what you are looking into, but if I may be of any assistance in any way, please do not be afraid to ask."

Holmes told her, "Sister, I appreciate your offer and I am certain that I speak for both Watson and Pope Leo when I say thank you. Your boys have been invaluable, and if I can think of any way that you can help, I will ask, I promise."

We finished with the dishes a few minutes before Sister Angelica, and she told us to go sit in the dining room. Shortly thereafter, she carried in two plates with omelets and brioche. She then brought us a tray with cups, silverware, sugar and cream. On her third trip, she placed a steaming kettle on a trivet and said, "Let the tea steep another minute or two, and don't forget your promise."

We stood as she left, and I said, "You have my word, sister."

Left alone, Holmes and I then ate leisurely, and we both agreed that Sister Angelica's cooking was on a par with that of Mrs. Hudson.

When we had finished, I looked at Holmes and said, "I can tell you have made progress."

"Indeed," said Holmes, "I know where the cameos are, but I'm afraid that obtaining them presents something of a problem."

"How could that be?" I asked. "If you know where they are, just go get them and return them to the pope."

"I know the building they are in," said Holmes," but the fact remains that they could be hidden anywhere. No, I'm afraid Signore Giolitti must lead us to them. Something I am sure that he is loath to do, and now that he knows he is being followed, he is going to be more cautious than ever."

"No, Watson, obtaining them for His Holiness still poses a rather difficult task. Let us do the dishes as we promised, and perhaps a good night's rest will offer us a different viewpoint in the morning."

As we cleaned the few dishes that we had used, I asked Holmes, "Is Giolitti that clever?"

"Yes, Watson, he is. He possesses a certain canniness that complements his own innate intelligence. He would have made an incredible acolyte for the late, unlamented Moriarty."

Then, looking at me, he smiled and said, "But not to worry. Against the two of us, I am certain he will come a cropper."

So we made our way to bed, and I slept well. I thought about everything Holmes had said and then I reflected on some of our more challenging cases, and the next thing I knew Holmes was knocking at my door.

"Come on, Watson. It's past eight, and I don't want to miss breakfast."

"I'll join you downstairs," I replied.

"Do be brisk. I have a plan that I should like to put in motion. I'll tell you about it over biscuits and tea."

When I joined Holmes in the dining room, he informed me that Sister Angelica was so inspired by our labors in the kitchen that she had prepared a special breakfast for us.

"I don't know what it is," said Holmes, "but she insisted that at least once during our stay here, we should have a 'proper Italian breakfast' – whatever that may be."

As Sister Angelica came through the kitchen door, she smiled at me and wished me good morning. Turning to Holmes, she said, "I heard that – and you are about to find out."

She settled a large tray of pastries in front of us.

"Ah, croissants," I exclaimed.

At that the nun made the sign of the cross and exclaimed, "Heaven preserve us. They may resemble that other pastry, but these are *corneti*. I was so pleased with the state of my kitchen this morning that I baked these just for you."

Pointing to the one side of the tray, she explained, "These are *cornetti simplice* or *cornetti vuoto* – there is nothing inside. *Vuoto* means empty." Indicating the remaining pile, she said they were *cornetti alla marmelatta*.

"I have filled some with your marmalade and others with a delicious raspberry jelly," she informed us.

Taking a bite of a marmalade-filled one, I exclaimed, "Sister, this is delicious."

She looked anxiously at Holmes, awaiting his opinion. Holmes had taken one of the *cornetti simplice*, and after tasting it, he looked up at the nun and exclaimed, "Bravo.

Sister, before we leave, you must give me your recipe so that Mrs. Hudson can try her hand at these."

Beaming with pleasure, the nun replied, "Of course; now let me get your coffee."

I looked at Holmes and whispered, "Did she say coffee?"

"I'm afraid she did," he replied.

At that moment, she reappeared carrying a tray with four cups. "I know that you prefer your tea. But no selfrespecting Italian would dine on *cornetti* without either a coffee or a cappuccino. Not knowing your preference, I made both. Enjoy your *colazione*, gentlemen."

I tasted the coffee, which was served in a tiny cup, and found it far too bitter for my taste. The cappuccino, by contrast, was lighter and with a bit of sugar it provided a pleasant substitute for tea. Looking at Holmes, I could see that he found neither as palatable as a cup of Darjeeling, but I knew he was too chivalrous to say anything.

When we were alone, I asked him, "Tell me more about this plan of yours."

"It's still in the preliminary stages, but I was thinking that if we could persuade Giolitti…"

At that moment, Sister Basile entered the dining room and said, "Mr. Holmes, a messenger just delivered a package for you." She handed my friend a small parcel and then left us.

Holmes inspected it carefully, "No return address," he murmured. With his pocketknife he cut the cord and removed the brown paper to reveal a second parcel almost identical to the first. Attached was a tag that Holmes read aloud, "To Pope Leo, care of Signore Sherlock Holmes."

"The man is insufferable, Watson. Now, he tasks me as his messenger."

"Is that the cameo?"

"I'm certain that it is. Allowing for the box and paper, it feels about the same weight. And the box is just the right size."

"It's the sheer effrontery of the man, Watson. Were the stakes not so high, I assure you I should act very differently, but the pope comes first. So let us enjoy the rest of these *cornetti* and then pay a call on Pope Leo. I should imagine he will receive us with mixed emotions, but now at least I shall be able to put one of my theories to the test."

Chapter Thirty-four – Rome, 1501

When Michelangelo awoke the next morning, he hoped for a brief second that everything he had witnessed just a few hours earlier had been nothing more than a bad dream. However, when he saw the robe and sandals on the floor and the pile of sketches on his workbench, he knew that he had indeed been a spectator at some sort of Bacchanalian orgy, one organized by no less a personage than the pope himself.

The thought horrified him, but the possibility of ending up in the Tiber at the hands of Cesare or one of his associates terrified him more. Determined to put this episode behind him, he bolted down breakfast and set to work.

Although he had refused to attend the Pope's ball, Michelangelo nevertheless started with Cardinal della Rovere and began by carving the prelate pleasuring himself as a trio of women looked on. He tried to capture the cardinal's pride while endowing him with an arrogance found in few men.

He had given Paolo the week off, so he labored without interruption all morning and late into the afternoon. The work was tedious but as the cameos took shape before him, it became rewarding as well. When he stopped to eat, he looked at his creation and smiled. The prelate's pride was obvious in the sneering smile and the overbearing attitude. The subtle details – the hint of a satyr suggesting a horse, the demonic smile, the wheel behind him, which he blithely ignored – all served to underscore the image of a man so absorbed with himself that the world held little meaning. "You could be a rival for Lucifer," he thought, and it was at that point that Michelangelo envisioned adding the finishing touch – the wings – thus endowing him with an obvious superiority – all the while underscoring the similarities between this prince of the church and the prince of the devils.

After he had finished the detail work and polished it, he took the cameo and inserted it into the mechanism that Leonardo constructed. Then taking the device he inserted it onto the frame and heard it snap into place. Then he tested it, and to his great joy, he found that it worked splendidly just as the old man had promised it would. Securing it in its place, Michelangelo hid both the cameo in its frame and Leonardo's key.

He then turned his attention to Cardinal Sforza. The green stone, the suggestion that Sforza's countenance was more canine than human, the eyes that looked everywhere at once but never saw happiness, all suggested an unquenchable envy. He posed the cardinal behind a naked Mistress Antonia, his hand cupping her breast, but the cardinal's gaze was on another couple, their backs to him – their happiness evident. Deciding to take a chance, he took his smallest chisel and working very slowly, he scraped carefully all the way down to the intaglio layer so that it seemed as though the cardinal possessed brilliant green eyes. Next, he turned his attention to the mouth, so that Sforza was smiling – but there was no warmth in his face. He completed the image by adding icicles hanging from the top to suggest the coldness of his heart and the complete lack of warmth behind the façade of humanity.

Michelangelo had no idea what time it was, but when he looked at the second cameo, he felt a deep sense of accomplishment. Placing it in its frame, he secured it in place.

Although he felt inspired and considered continuing, he was also exhausted, so once again, he threw himself on his bed fully clothed and was asleep a few minutes later.

When he awoke, sun was streaming through the skylight, and he guessed that it must be close to noon. He sent a boy to the tavern for food and tea and then began work on Cardinal Marti's cameo. Selecting the stone with the light blue intaglio, he began to carve a bed. On the bed he etched the image of a naked Marti, penis engorged, carefully adding the suggestion that he was sporting the horns of a goat. In the distance, he depicted two naked nymphs gesturing for the cardinal to join them. Then surrounding the bed, he carved serpents – all of whom seemed to be threatening the recumbent cardinal, who remained inert – too lazy to move, even to save himself or to join his consorts. Giving it a critical examination, Michelangelo decided there was little he could do to improve it, so he polished it and placed it in its frame.

Choosing the stone with the brilliant red layer, Michelangelo quickly chiseled down to the white above it. He wanted the images to be smaller than the others because he wanted the scarlet to be the most pronounced element of the work. He depicted Cardinal Fiorza with long flowing hair behind him, such as an animal might have. His mouth was open in a roar and he was swinging his crozier like some sort of club. He was the sole figure in the cameo, and it was obvious that his unbridled fury had isolated him because others were afraid to come near him. Looking at it, Michelangelo had definite reservations. It was decidedly different from the others. As he picked up the next stone, he vowed to return to Fiorza, and he did have an extra red stone if it came to that.

For Cardinal Briconnet, who would embody gluttony, Michelangelo had something special in mind. He had deliberately left the stone with the orange intaglio larger than the others. He sat the cardinal on a log and gave him the cloven hooves of a pig for feet. Although Briconnet was not heavy,

Michelangelo depicted him with a gigantic stomach and enormous rolls of fat. Because the body was so different, he spent extra time on the facial features. The thin lips, the Gallic nose and too-close eyes all combined to lend the French cardinal a certain ascetic air that was belied by his body. On the table next to him were plates of rats, toads and snakes – all waiting to be devoured by the ravenous cleric.

Michelangelo was just preparing to etch the various creatures when he heard a knock at his door and a familiar voice called out, "Michelangelo, are you in there?"

He recognized the voice as Cardinal della Rovere. "Uno momento, Your Eminence." Michelangelo quickly hid his sketches in the secret drawer in his workbench and he would have hidden the cameo there had it fit. He checked the finished cameos and picked up the one containing the image of della Rovere. Checking it once more, he covered it with a green cloth. Then he placed it at the rear of his workbench and set his palette on top of it. Going to the window, he peeked into the street below and saw that the cardinal had not come alone.

With della Rovere waiting at the door, he decided there was nothing to be done but to hope for the best. With that he descended the stairs, threw open the door and said, "Your Eminence, I am honored that you should come to my humble abode." As he genuflected, della Rovere extended his hand so that Michelangelo could kiss his ring.

After he had entered and looked around, the cardinal said, "When you didn't visit me yesterday or this morning, I was afraid that you had taken ill, so I decided to check on you myself to see if you needed anything."

"No, my apologies, your Eminence, but I have been working and sometimes, quite honestly, I get so consumed in the project that I lose all track of time."

"Are you working on the cameos for His Holiness?" "I am," said Michelangelo.

"How was the ball? Did you find it inspiring? Do tell me all about it?

"May I offer you something, your eminence?"

"No, not right now. Just tell me everything about the ball. From what I have heard, it was quite the scandalous affair. Have I been misinformed?"

"Not at all," said Michelangelo. And for the next hour, he recounted everything he had seen and heard from behind the grille of the confessional.

The only time della Rovere interrupted him was to say, "The pope had Mistress Antonia oversee the contests?"

"Yes, Your Eminence."

"Well, if nothing else, I must admit he does have excellent taste in whores – for a Spaniard. Continue, my son."

Michelangelo picked up the story where he had left off, and when he finally finished, della Rovere asked, "And you did not participate?"

"No, your eminence."

"I am proud of you for resisting the temptations of the flesh, Michelangelo. Now, may I see the fruits of your labor?"

"I usually prefer that the patron be the first person to see the finished work," said Michelangelo.

"But you are not finished yet, are you?" asked della Rovere. "Besides, Michelangelo, when I am pope, I shall be your patron."

"You flatter me, Your Eminence."

"Then let us have a look, shall we?"

"But…

"You don't have anything to hide, do you Michelangelo?

"Of course not, Your Eminence."

"Then, let us go to your studio." With that the cardinal began to ascend the stairs with Michelangelo in tow.

Della Rovere went directly to the workbench and picked up the cameo of Cardinal Marti. He looked at for a long time, and then he began to laugh. "You have captured him, my son. That lazy bastard wouldn't move to help Christ himself down from the cross."

Next he turned his attention to the cameo with Cardinal Briconnet. Again, he laughed and said, "This is the essence of that French swine. You are truly gifted, my son."

After examining the cameo with the angry Cardinal Fioza, della Rovere opined, "This is quite different from the others, but I think the contrast works here."

Finally, he came to the cameo of Cardinal Sforza. He took it to the window, studying it intently. After several minutes, he turned around and said, "Brilliant! You know I

248

might have been pope had he not sold his vote to Alexander. The detail is stunning and the inclusion of Antonia and the green eyes – we are going to have a long and prosperous relationship when I am on the Throne of Peter."

"I am glad that Your Eminence is pleased."

"And you may rest assured that your secrets are safe with me, Michelangelo. I know how vindictive these men can be,"

As he placed the cameo back on the workbench, the cardinal suddenly caught sight of the palette.

He looked at Michelangelo and said, "Are you still painting as well?"

"I try to paint every day, but lately, there has been so little time."

"I understand completely," said the cardinal sympathetically.

As he picked up the palette, he said, "Perhaps, some day you will paint me."

"That would be my honor," said Michelangelo.

As he turned to replace the palette, della Rovere saw the outline of the box under the cloth. Looking at Michelangelo, he asked, "And what are you hiding here, my son?"

"Nothing, your eminence."

"Then, if you don't mind, I'll take a look at it." And with that he withdrew the box from under the green cloth.

Chapter Thirty-five – Rome, 1901

An hour later, Holmes and I walked across St. Peter's Square and up the stairs into the basilica. Holmes had sent a messenger ahead so we were met at the door by Cardinal Oreglia and a member of the Swiss Guard.

"I'm guessing you have news, Mr. Holmes," said the cardinal.

"Indeed, your eminence. The pace is quickening, and I also have a small package to deliver to His Holiness."

We followed the cardinal into the basilica and turned to our right. After passing two more members of the Swiss Guard, we found ourselves in a long hallway approaching an enormous staircase.

"This is the Scala Regia, sometimes called the royal staircase" explained the cardinal. "It connects the Apostolic Palace with the basilica. The staircase is something of an illusion," he explained. "You see how it appears narrower at the top and thus longer than it actually is. Another of Bernini's little parlor tricks carried out on a grand scale," said the cardinal.

My eyes were drawn to the right and an enormous statue of a man mounted on a horse. "That is the Emperor Constantine," explained Oreglia, and pointing to the window above he indicated a Latin inscription "In Hoc Signo Vinces."

"In this sign you shall conquer," murmured Holmes. "I'm going to take that as an omen."

Pointing to the left, the cardinal said, "And there is the Emperor Charlemagne."

"In years past, the statues imparted a subtle message to all those leaving the Vatican," the cardinal said.

As we ascended the stairs, we found ourselves stopping on a landing about halfway up. Despite the absence of windows, there was plenty of illumination. When I asked the cardinal about the source of the light, he jokingly remarked, "Perhaps it's a miracle."

At the top of the stairs, we entered the papal apartments and Pope Leo was waiting there for us with two more halberd-bearing members of the Swiss Guard, dressed in their blue-and-gold uniforms topped by helmets with large red plumes. They remained at attention, standing a discreet distance from the pope, but close enough to spring into action should a threat arise.

After we had knelt and kissed his ring, Holmes said, "We need to talk Your Holiness."

The pope nodded and said simply, "Follow me."

He led us down a hall decorated with elaborate frescoes and out into a large garden. "I often come here to think," he explained. "Before we begin," he asked, "may I get you anything?"

"No thank you, Your Holiness," Said Holmes.

The pontiff then led us to a small gazebo in the very center of the garden.

"We may speak freely here," said Pope Leo.

"I received a package via messenger this morning," said Holmes. "It was addressed to you in care of me."

"You don't think ..." said the Pope.

"I think that Giolitti has done exactly as we asked," said Holmes. "He has returned one of the cameos as a show of good faith."

"May I see the package?" asked the pope.

Reaching inside his coat pocket, Holmes produced the parcel and handed it to the pontiff.

I could see his hands trembling as he fumbled with the twine, trying to undo the knot. Finally, Holmes produced a small penknife which he handed to the pope. "This may make things easier, Your Excellency."

The pope took the knife, cut the string and pulled out a small box. Opening the top, he pushed aside some paper and gasped.

"Is it a cameo?" asked Holmes.

Without turning his head, the pope just nodded, his eyes remaining fixed on the object inside.

"Your Holiness?" asked Holmes.

"He has sent the cameo of Pope Julius II, the man who commissioned the Sistine Chapel. If the public ever saw this …" and his voice trailed off.

"Well, you have it back, and the public will never set eyes upon it," said Holmes, trying to console the pontiff.

"I think there is a note of some sort here," said Pope Leo. Pulling out a sheet of white paper, he unfolded it and read aloud, "Pride goeth before destruction, and an haughty spirit before a fall."

"It appears that Mr. Giolitti has sent us a nonetoosubtle warning," said Holmes, "and for that bounder to couch it in a quote from the Bible. This is truly outrageous!"

"Still, I must deal with Giolitti, and I cannot in good conscience submit on the Roman Question. Mr. Holmes, I am lost. Do you see any solution to my dilemma?"

"I do," said Holmes, "but first, I have a small request of Your Holiness."

"Anything, Mr. Holmes.

"The other night when you showed us the document that dealt with the cameos, it was wrapped in a silver chain with amulets at either end."

"That was how I found it and that is how I shall leave it for my successor," said the pope.

"May I ask Your Holiness to get the chain for me?"

"It is in a safe in my study," said the pope. "Would you like to examine it there, or shall we remain out here?"

Looking around and seeing no one except the two Swiss Guards off at a distance, Holmes said, "I think we might be better served out here – far from the possibility of prying eyes and eavesdropping ears."

"I shall return momentarily, gentlemen," said the pope as he hurried off down one of the paths.

"You are worried about the spy in the household?" I asked.

"Not worried. I just need to know that Giolitti has not been given any indication of our plans until it is too late for him," he said. "He is a slippery customer, Watson, and I am certain that he has a fallback plan just as I do."

"You have two different plans?"

"I try to consider steps to account for all the possible scenarios," said Holmes placidly. "Fortunately, I have seldom had to resort to my alternative – but it has happened on one or two rare occasions."

"Let us hope that this case is no different from most," I said.

We sat in silence for a few moments, and then I saw the pope hurrying toward us. When he had reached the gazebo, he handed the chain to Holmes. "This is what you wanted, Mr. Holmes?"

"Yes," he replied, "now I need one more indulgence from Your Holiness."

"Anything," replied the pontiff.

"I should like very much to examine the cameo," he said.

Handing my friend the box, he said, "Mr. Holmes for centuries, until they were taken, only the successors of St. Peter have seen this image. However, since Giolitti and Lord only knows how many others have looked upon it, I guess, to use your English euphemism, the cat is out of the poke."

Holmes and I both chuckled, and Pope Leo looked confused. "Is that not right," he asked.

"You were very close, Your Holiness," I said gently, "We generally say that the cat is out of the bag, meaning a secret has been revealed. The other expression is 'to buy a pig in a poke,' which means to purchase something without examining it."

"Ah, Dr. Watson, but I believe that your word poke comes from the French word *poque*, which I believe can be translated as 'sack' or 'bag.'"

I laughed and said, "You win, Your Holiness, but I can guarantee you that you will never hear an Englishman say, 'The cat is out of the poke.'"

"Unless, of course, his mother is French, in which case, he might follow the pontiff's example," Holmes said. He had been standing at the edge of the gazebo, his back to us. I thought he had been examining the cameo in the light of day, and now he had rejoined us and the conversation.

As His Holiness smiled, Holmes returned the cameo to him, and cautioned, "Keep this in a much safer place than you have in the past, your Holiness."

Squeezing it in his hand, the pope said, "It is going into a new safe that I have ordered, never to see the light of day again in my lifetime."

"Your Holiness, don't you think a joint work by Michelangelo and Leonardo belongs in the Vatican Museum rather than being hidden away in a safe?" asked Holmes.

"Under ordinary circumstances, I would agree with you, Mr. Holmes. However, the only thing preventing me from destroying this blasphemous object is the fact that *is* the work of both Michelangelo and Leonardo."

"May I have one more look then?" said Holmes.

As the pope handed the cameo to my friend, he exclaimed, "Mr. Holmes, what have you done?"

Chapter Thirty-six – Rome, 1501

The cardinal stared at the cameo in silence. Then, as he had earlier, he went to the window where he continued his examination.

After several minutes, he broke the silence, saying, "I must admit that you have captured him, Michelangelo, but, honestly my son, did you have to make him appear so saintly? He looks positively angelic!"

"He is my patron, Your Eminence."

"Yes, yes, but take it from one who knows, Pope Alexander and the virtue of humility are scarce acquainted. The likeness is uncanny, but a crown of thorns – really! Isn't the fact that he appears to be praying to a God that I doubt he scarce believes in sufficient flattery?"

After a pause, the cardinal continued, "Still, as you say, he is your patron. I can only hope that should you ever essay my likeness, you will find it in your heart to be just as flattering."

"I shall do my best, Your Eminence."

"I am sure you will. Now, before I leave, who else are you going to depict for the other deadly sins?"

"After what I saw at the ball, I think Cardinal Malerba is the personification of lust while Cardinal Piccolomini might serve as my model for greed."

"Piccomolini's rather a non-entity, but I can see where he might covet what others possess. And whom have you chosen for the greatest sin of all – pride?" asked the cardinal. "I am glad you brought that up, your Eminence. I was thinking that I might reach outside the Curia, and I wanted to get your opinion."

Della Rovere asked, "Did you have anyone special in mind? Not that slinking Machiavelli? That scribbler is not worthy to be included here."

"No, I was thinking of someone who in a sense equated himself with the papacy and by extension God," said Michelangelo.

"Savanarola!" exclaimed the cardinal. "Yes, my son! Perfect! He was the spawn of Cain, I am certain of it. If you can manage that – and I have no doubt you can – you will have won the approval not only of the pope but myself as well. Bravo, Michelangelo. I should very much like to see that one when it is completed."

"As you wish, Your Eminence."

"One final question, my son?"

"Yes, Eminence?"

"You were commissioned to sculpt the Seven Deadly Sins, and yet you have included an eighth cameo, depicting Alexander as the epitome of humility. May I ask why?"

"As you know, being a patron yourself, we artists often include our benefactors in our works. Have you seen Mantegna's painting of Ludovico Gonzaga? Or del Cossa's depiction of Borza d'Este? I could not depict the pope as one of the sinners, so I opted to portray him as an example of humility – the antithesis of pride. Also, just between us, I was afraid that omitting him might cost me part of my commission."

"Although I find the depiction personally offensive, I am sure that you are acting wisely," said the cardinal.

"Now, my son, I must be off. The Curia is meeting this afternoon, but as I said earlier – your secrets are safe with me just as I hope mine are with you."

Pressing a small purse into Michelangelo's hand, the cardinal said, "I will see myself out. Be well, Michelangelo, and should you require anything, always remember that as pope, I will be your next patron."

The cardinal descended the stairs and Michelangelo heard the door open and close. Going to the window, he watched as the cardinal climbed into his coach and headed off down the dusty street.

Alone again, Michelangelo breathed a long sigh of relief and thought, "It's true. A pawn may outmaneuver a bishop – or in this case, a cardinal – every now and then."

Feeling refreshed, Michelangelo set about committing the image of Cardinal Malerba to the cameo. Selecting a stone with a deep-blue layer, he carved down to the white above it. He depicted a naked Malerba enjoying the pleasures of two women. He added the suggestion that a strong wind was buffeting the clergyman and his consorts – insinuating that their pleasure was being greatly diminished by strong gusts of wind.

Finally, he selected the yellow stone and he set about carving the likeness of the renegade monk Savonarola.

Claiming to have seen visions, the Dominican had convinced the people of Florence to expel the powerful Medici family.

Preaching against secular art, sodomy, adultery, drunkenness and other moral transgressions, Fra Giralamo had in effect become the de facto ruler of Florence. When Charles VII of France had crossed the Alps, the rabble had seen the invasion as proof of the friar's gift of prophecy.

Even his railings against a corrupt church had been tolerated by Pope Alexander, but when Florence – at Savonarola's behest – had refused to join the pope's Holy League against the French invader, Alexander summoned the preacher to Rome. Savonarola's refusal was the beginning of his end.

The pope quickly excommunicated the preacher and threatened Florence with an interdict. Facing the threat of censure by Rome and the denial of the sacraments, the citizens began to question the authority of the friar. Challenged to a trial by fire by a rival preacher, Savonarola had stalled, further angering many Florentines.

Eventually, Savonarola and his two top aides were arrested and imprisoned. Under torture, he admitted that his visions were fictions. However, he quickly recanted, but subsequently confessed again.

On the morning of May 23, 1498, the three were led into the Piazza della Signoria, where they were stripped of their Dominican robes and hanged. As their bodies swung, fires were lighted below to consume their carcasses. As a final act of degradation, their ashes were collected and scattered in the Arno to prevent devotees from worshiping any relics.

Michelangelo worked down to the white layer above the yellow. On the right, he carved the coat of arms of Alexander. In the center stood the Dominican, Savonarola, his back to the coat of arms and thus the church. On the left, Michelangelo carved an ornate lily – the symbol of both Florence and France. "That is fortunate," he thought, as he outlined the blossoms.

The punishment for envy is usually freezing rain, but since fire had figured so prominently in the preacher's death, Michelangelo suggested flames at the bottom engulfing the friar's feet while rain fell but failed to extinguish the blaze.

When he had finished, he noticed that it was quite late and he was famished. Placing everything in a hiding place that he had fashioned in the floor, he decided to see if he could still get food and drink at the tavern.

As he walked the darkened street under the moonlit sky, he thought, "We are almost at the endgame.

"All that is needed now is the pope's approbation of the cameos and his approval of the plan that I have had devised to secure my own safety after Alexander passes."

Chapter Thirty-seven – Rome, 1901

Enigmatically, Holmes smiled at the pope, and asked innocently, "Is something wrong, Your Holiness?"

"What have you done?" the pope repeated excitedly. "Where is the image of Pope Julius?"

Holmes chuckled. "As you read Pope Alexander's letter the other day, I was struck by his emphasis on the concept of 'duality.' Then when I saw the chain that bound the letter, I couldn't help but notice the tiny projections. You told me you thought they might have been joined at one time or barring that, that they were imperfections in the work. I found it simply impossible to believe that the man who created the Pieta, working in conjunction with the genius behind the Mona Lisa, would present anything to his most powerful patron in less than perfect condition.

"Obviously, then, those projections served a purpose. I considered your description of the cameos and their cases and determined that Michelangelo had created not seven but 14 cameos. Half of them focused on the Deadly Sins while the remainder dealt with their antithetical counterparts, the Heavenly Virtues.

"Michelangelo carved the cameos on both sides, and the case allows the second image to remain hidden. During one of my early cases, I came across a ring that did the exact same thing, but I digress. It took me a few tries, but if you are looking at the image of a sin or vice, you must insert both projections with the words 'vitium' facing up and then turn them to the left or the 'sinister' side. That opens the mechanism – which I am fairly certain is the brainchild of Leonardo – and allows the cameo to be flipped. Simply turn it over, twist the keys and now it is locked in place.

"If you are looking at the virtuous side, both keys must be inserted with the word 'virtutis' facing up and turned to the right. It is really an ingenious locking mechanism."

"Mr. Holmes, I am stunned," said the pope. "You are right. If the rest of them function as this one does, and if the reverse images do indeed depict virtues rather than vices, then they do belong in the Vatican Museum."

"Holmes," I exclaimed, "You have solved a mystery that has eluded people for 400 years."

"Yes," he said, "I have solved a mystery, but solving the case is far more important."

"Something tells me, I'm not going too far out on a tree here, but I am willing to bet that you have a plan, Mr. Holmes," said the pontiff.

Holmes and I both smiled at the pope's gentle malapropism, before my friend said, "I do, Your Holiness, but, once again, it will require your cooperation."

"Unless it places my immortal soul in danger of damnation, you have it, Mr. Holmes," said the pope.

"Then, here is what must be done," said Holmes, who then proceeded to outline everything in great detail for Pope Leo.

"Having received the cameo as a token of Giolitti's good faith, you must meet with him."

"Yes, I suppose you are right," said the pope.

"I should like you to schedule the meeting for tomorrow night at 7. Can that be done?" asked Holmes.

"I shall rearrange my itinerary," said the pontiff. "I had planned to have dinner with a small group of cardinals from America, but that can always be pushed back a day."

"When Giolitti arrives, you must keep him here for at least an hour."

"Given our history and what is at stake, I should think that also seems quite likely."

"Finally, when Giolitti leaves to retrieve the cameos, you must offer to have two members of the Swiss Guard accompany him if he wishes. If he refuses, as I have no doubt he will, you must try insisting, but ultimately, allow Giolitti to leave here unescorted."

"As you wish," said the pontiff, "But in order for him to agree to return the cameos, I must agree to settle the Roman Question in his favor."

"If you do not settle it, you must at least appear to settle it," said Holmes.

"I'm not certain that I follow you, Mr. Holmes," said Pope Leo.

With that, my friend proceeded to outline several possible approaches that Giolitti might take in an effort to make the pope submit.

He and the pontiff tried to take into account every possible answer and objection that might be raised.

When they had finished, Holmes had me play the role of Giolitti, and the pope and I traded questions and answers, with Holmes constantly interjecting to offer advice to both of us.

It took close to two hours before Holmes was satisfied with the pontiff's responses.

"Do you think I am ready?" asked the pope.

"I shall pray that you are," said Holmes.

"Now, there are several other points on which you must reassure Signore Giolitti." Holmes then proceeded to elucidate them one by one.

Although the pontiff expressed misgivings on one or two occasions, Holmes was eventually able to win him over. Listening to the two of them debate a variety of philosophical topics such as amphibologies and the doctrine of strict mental reservation, I was once again impressed by the breadth of Holmes' knowledge on so many different topics. Holmes then explained the rest of the plan to the pontiff and shortly after, we parted.

As we walked through the square, I made my feelings known to Holmes.

"Watson, you flatter me. Still, while I much prefer the agony columns to the 'City of God' or the 'Summa Theologica,' I am, as you well know, an omnivorous reader with a strangely retentive memory for trifles."

I sniffed, "I don't think His Holiness would appreciate your dismissing the works of St. Augustine and Thomas Aquinas as 'trifles.'"

"Perhaps, you're right," replied Holmes. "At any rate, it's nearing five o'clock, and I am quite hungry. So I thought we might enjoy dinner and then make our way to the Teatro Costanzi, which gave 'Tosca' its world premiere last year. "Tonight, there is a performance of Rossini's 'Semiramide,' which opened the opera house in 1880. I am also told there is a very promising soprano in the lead and an accomplished contralto singing Arsace. Are you interested?"

"Of course," I replied.

"Excellent. Cardinal Oreglia has recommended a little *osteria* on the Via Monte Testaccio. He described it as totally unpretentious, and he said the food is among the best in Rome. I am going to assume that is high praise indeed, coming from such an obvious gourmand."

Looking at my watch, I said, "We should have just enough time to enjoy our dinner and get to the theater before the first act begins."

"Yes," Holmes said, "let us savor this evening because tomorrow promises to be a day of uncertainty and quite possibly danger."

Chapter Thirty-eight – Rome, 1501

The next morning, the first thing that Michelangelo did was to write a note to the pope requesting an appointment at His Holiness' convenience. After sending it with a messenger, he spent the rest of the morning painting and reviewing the plan in his mind.

About an hour later, there was a knock at the door. As he opened it, he was greeted by Cesare Borgia, who said, "My father has been waiting for you to contact him. He would like you to come at once, and he sent me in a carriage to fetch you."

"Just give me a few minutes," Michelangelo said. Going upstairs, he retrieved the cameos from their hiding place, wrapped each in a piece of red velvet and placed them carefully in his bag – arranging them in a very specific order.

As he walked downstairs, he said to Cesare, "I am ready."

"Wonderful," exclaimed Cesare.

They rode to the Vatican in silence, broken occasionally by Cesare's attempts to make conversation.

"You must excuse my reticence, Cesare. It's just that I am very nervous about meeting your father. After all, without his approval, all my work will have been for naught."

"I am certain that my father will appreciate your efforts," said Cesare, who added, "I must confess that I too am quite eager to see your creations. However, my father threatened to excommunicate me if I looked upon them before he did."

The thought of Cesare, once a cardinal and a member of the Curia, being cast out from the Church for looking upon the cameos before his father made Michelangelo chuckle, and before long both men were laughing and the tension had been broken.

When they arrived at the papal palace, Cesare led Michelangelo into a small room off the main hall where the ball had taken place.

"Make yourself comfortable," said Cesare, "I'll tell my father that you have arrived. Should you be hungry or thirsty …" and he pointed to a sideboard laden with food and beverages.

Left alone, Michelangelo decided to sample the grapes. They looked plump and inviting. Popping one into his mouth, he felt the juice cascade across his tongue as he bit it. Taking a bunch, he poured himself water and proceeded to examine the frescoes on the walls.

He was so absorbed in admiring the detail of a work by Bernadino di Betto that he never heard Pope Alexander enter the room.

"Do you like the work of Pinturicchio?" asked the pope, startling Michelangelo.

"I do very much," continued the pope. "Even though he has done work for the della Rovere family, I find his style irresistible."

"He has an eye," admitted Michelangelo, "and he is certainly prolific. But I do think he needs to demand more from his apprentices."

"Oh?" said the pope.

"Consider this seraph," said Michelangelo. "Look at how uneven the brushstrokes are. Fortunately, it's not a focal point, but neither should it be treated as an afterthought."

"As you say, he has an eye," laughed the pope. "Still, he is not half the artist you are. Perhaps his nickname – the little painter – is more apropos than originally thought."

"You flatter me," said Michelangelo.

"Now, I understand that you have something to show me," said the pontiff.

"I hope you like them," said Michelangelo, who began to withdraw the cameos from his bag in the reverse order in which he had deposited them earlier, placing each on a table.

After he had arranged the velvet pouches on the table. He said to the pope, "Please humor me and open them in the order in which I have placed them."

"As you wish, my son." Removing the first cameo from its pouch, the pope began to laugh heartily. As he gazed upon the image of Cardinal Briconnet with the enormous stomach, he said, "Well done, my son, he may be a cardinal, but Briconnet is truly a swine, and you have captured him perfectly."

Next the pope looked at the image of Cardinal Marti. "This is brilliant, Michelangelo. How he ever became a clergyman – much less a cardinal – continues to mystify me." As he opened the velvet that encased the image of Cardinal Malerba, he smiled, turned to Michelangelo, and said, "He was truly a wonder to behold at the ball, was he not?"

Turning his attention to the image of red-faced Cardinal Fiorza next, he said, "Michelangelo, with each cameo you surpass the previous ones. These are better than I might have hoped."

"I can only hope you find the last three as much to your liking as the first four," Michelangelo said.

Picking up the next one, he unwrapped it and looked upon the image of his vice chancellor. The pope turned to Michelangelo and said, "You do know he is the man responsible for my sitting upon the throne of St. Peter?"

"I do, Your Holiness."

"And yet you depict him as jealous? Despite the presence of the comely Mistress Antonia, the eyes are searching, restless – and to make them green – Michelangelo, as I have said, you truly have a gift. You see into the souls of men. I can only hope that you do not look too closely into mine. I think Cardinal Sforza would murder me and my entire family if he thought he could escape punishment. He is a viper, always sneaking about, seeking to undermine me. Considering the power of his family, he would have been my second-in-command if for no other reason than because I needed to keep him close."

"Given the insight these cameos demonstrate, I cannot even imagine what remains." Picking up the next cameo, he looked at Michelangelo and said, "Only two sins remain – greed and pride – and I am guessing that this is greed? Am I right?"

"Indeed, Your Holiness," replied Michelangelo.

Removing the velvet, he looked at Michelangelo, and said, "Maestro. Of all people, that wretch Savonarola. The bane of my existence for many years. Yes, Michelangelo, because he could not enjoy the bounty of God, which manifests itself in so many ways, he forbade others from doing so as well. Again, brilliant!"

"And now we come to the finale," said the pope. As he pulled the cameo from the velvet, he paused, looked at Michelangelo and said, "I do not understand. I am looking at myself, and I am flattered by the depiction of me, but what about the sin of pride?"

Michelangelo reached for the box and said simply, "May I?"

"By all means," said the Pope.

Taking the chain from his neck, Michelangelo said to the Pope, "We are all body and soul, devil and angel, virtue and vice. Should you ever wish to meditate upon humility, you have but to gaze upon your own image. However, should temptation rear its ugly head, simply insert these keys like so, with the word 'virtutus' facing up on both. Turn them to the right, and you can now flip the image to see the personification of pride. Would you like to try it, Your Holiness?"

"You are full of surprises, aren't you, Michelangelo?"

The pope took the chain, inserted the keys, released the locks and turned the cameo over. As he gazed upon the image of Cardinal della Rovere, he remained silent for a full minute. Turning, he embraced Michelangelo, "I think with these cameos, you may have saved my immortal soul, and perhaps helped me curtail my wayward Curia."

"Am I on the reverse of all the cameos?" the pope inquired.

"Indeed," said Michelangelo, "but in different poses and with different settings – each appropriate to that particular virtue."

"I shall examine those at a later date," said the pope humbly.

Deciding the force the issue, Michelangelo said, "Your Holiness, I beg you. If the other cardinals see what I have done, I am a dead man."

"I can protect you, my son."

"If only that were true."

"Are you not surrounded by traitors and those seeking to usurp your authority? If they dare to trifle with you, they will have no qualms about dispatching me, Your Holiness."

The pope nodded, looked at Michelangelo, and said, "But what's to be done?"

"If I may speak frankly, Your Holiness," said Michelangelo.

"Of course, my son."

"There is quite a disparity in our ages."

"True," said the Pope. "I will be 71 in a few months. And you are…"

"Twenty-six, Your Holiness."

"Yes, I suppose you are right," said the pope. "At best, my protection would be rather limited. So, what do you suggest I do?"

"Do as you told me you would. Use the cameos like prayer beads when you need to be reminded that the path to eternal glory is difficult and the descent to hell is easy as Virgil tells us."

"To use my own words against me," laughed the pope, "You would have made a wonderful Spaniard."

"I shall do as you wish, my son, for several reasons. First, because I feel that you have an incredibly bright future. Second, because, as you point out, you did these at my behest. They are better than anything I could have imagined. Yet, you did them knowing full well the danger inherent in the task. Such bravery is to be rewarded, not extinguished because of an old man's folly. Finally, I shall do as you wish because my daughter admires you, and I would do anything to avoid hurting her."

The pope paused then resumed, "Do you have any objections if I leave them to my successors, so that they might benefit from them as I have?"

"Only one, Your Holiness?"

"And what is that, my son?"

"What if Cardinal della Rovere should become pope?"

"You raise an interesting point. I have no doubt that he would nothing more than to be successor, but I believe that I may have devised a way around that. Would you like to hear it?"

"Yes, Your Holiness," said Michelangelo.

Pope Alexander then explained his plan, and when he had finished, he looked at Michelangelo, and asked, "Have I overlooked anything?"

"I don't believe so, your Holiness."

"Splendid; now let me put these in a safe place and then we shall dine and discuss our next steps."

Chapter Thirty-nine – Rome, 1901

The evening went splendidly. The food at the *osteria* was simple but hearty and eminently satisfying. Although we were surrounded by workers from the nearby slaughterhouse and various other tradesmen, they made us feel at home. Holmes returned the favor by deducing their occupations and other pertinent facts about their daily lives. As you might expect, they were amazed at his ability.

As for the opera, suffice to say that I was more impressed with the soprano than Holmes. Overall, however, the production was on a par with anything that we might have enjoyed at Covent Garden.

The next morning we rose early, packed and ate a hearty breakfast in the dining room. As we left, Holmes tried to make an offering for the convent, but Sister Angelica refused to accept it. "You are doing the Lord's work," she told us, "as am I. No compensation is needed as the labor is its own reward."

After walking through the square, we hailed a cab and headed for the train station. Holmes purchased two tickets for Milan where we would transfer to a train for Calais. We had about 20 minutes until our departure, and while I explored the station, Holmes sat placidly, reading a three-day old copy of the London Times.

After boarding the train, we ensconced ourselves in our compartment, but it wasn't until we had pulled out of the station that Holmes spoke: "I shall return shortly, Watson." After about 15 minutes, he entered the compartment, looked at me, and stated: "You saw him, of course."

"Who?" I asked.

"He was quite tall, with a full head of black curly hair and a neatly trimmed moustache. He had on a dark blue suit, white shirt and a neatly knotted dark bowtie. I noticed him loitering near the front of the square, and when we hailed our cab, he did likewise. I saw him again at the station, watching us from a distance behind a copy of *Corriere della Sera* and trying to appear inconspicuous."

"An agent of Giolitti's?"

"I've no doubt," said Holmes. "However, he is not on the train, so I can only hope that he reports our departure to his employer."

* * *

"What news Giuseppe?" asked Giolitti.

"I did as you ordered. I took up my position outside the convent at 5 a.m. They left about 7:30, got into a carriage and went to the train station. I followed them in another cab." "Did they see you?" asked Giolitti.

"I am certain they did not. After waiting in the station for some time, they boarded a train for Milan. I spoke to the ticket agent, and he told me they had inquired about connections from Milan to Calais."

"Did you watch the train depart?"

"Si, Signor. I stood on the platform, no more than 30 feet from their compartment. I can guarantee that when the train left the station, they were aboard."

"You have done well," said Giolitti. "Go home and get some well-deserved rest. I shall contact you tomorrow."

Left alone, Giovanni Giolitti could hardly contain his glee. "With Sherlock Holmes out of the picture, I can see a clear path to the prime minister's palace," he thought.

His reverie was interrupted by a knock at the door. Opening it, he saw a young boy.

"Are you Signor Giovanni Giolitti?" the boy asked.

"I am," he replied.

"I have a very important message for you," said the youngster, handing Giolitti an envelope. Opening it, he saw inside a second envelope that had been sealed with red wax which bore the imprint of the papal ring.

Fishing in his pocket, Giolitti handed the boy a few coins.

"I was told to wait for a response," the messenger said.

"You must give me a few minutes then," Giolitti said. Closing the door, he sat at his desk. With a letter opener, he cut through the wax and fished out a single sheet of paper that had been folded in half. Opening it, he saw a single sentence. It read, "I hope that you are free to meet with me tonight at 7 so that we may put this business behind us."

Rising, Giolitti pulled open the door. He handed the boy a five-lira note, and said, "Tell your master I will be there."

* * *

About a third of the way to Florence, our train made its first stop. As we pulled into the station, Holmes said, "Come on, Watson. We don't have much time."

"I'm right behind you," I said.

We dashed across the platform and with just minutes to spare boarded a local train headed back to Rome. It was around 11:30 a.m. and when we purchased our tickets, Holmes learned from the conductor that the train would make several stops and we should arrive in Rome around 6 p.m.

"We're taking no chances, Watson," said Holmes. "We will get off at the Roma Tiburtina station rather than the Roma Termini. If Giolitti has agents in both stations and can keep them there from morning to night then perhaps he deserves to win this round. However, if all goes according to plan, any agent that might spot us will hopefully find it impossible to tell Giolitti of our return since he will be meeting with the pope."

"Splendid, Holmes, but what if we are seen and the agent waits outside the papal palace until Giolitti comes out?"

"Watson, your friend Capt. Tritini has been asked to detain anyone seen loitering in the vicinity. Apparently, the *carabinieri* have unearthed a plot by a group of anarchists to place a bomb in St. Peter's Basilica."

"Bravo, Holmes!"

"No, Watson. It's simply a matter of planning. One tries to consider what moves your opponent may make and then devise a method to circumvent them. It's a chess game, and if Giolitti is two moves ahead of me, then I must remain three moves ahead of him."

* * *

Giovanni Giolotti arrived at the papal palace at exactly 6:55. He informed the priest who answered the door that he was expected. He was led into a waiting room, and after a few minutes, Cardinal Oreglia arrived. "Signore Giolitti, the pope is waiting for you."

Giolitti rose and followed the cardinal up a flight of stairs and down a long hallway into the pope's study.

The pope, who was seated behind his desk, rose when Giolitti entered the room. He came out from behind the desk and extended his hand. Giolitti knelt and kissed his ring.

"We have much to discuss," said the pontiff.

"Indeed," said Giolitti. "May I ask why Your Holiness has changed his mind on the Roman Question?"

"I have not changed my mind as you suggest, but you have placed me in a rather untenable position. Were I to remain steadfast, the church might suffer an enormous embarrassment. My fervent hope is that even though I have been forced to capitulate, Catholics will continue to recognize that Holy Mother Church cannot be subject to the laws of man."

"Perhaps they will," Giolitti said, "but I hope you can appreciate the fact that the people of Italy cannot have two leaders – especially if they should someday find themselves working at cross-purposes."

"If that were to happen, shouldn't the Italian people have the right to choose whom they wish to follow?" asked Pope Leo.

"Not if such a choice could lead this nation to the brink of civil war," said Giolitti. "After generations of city-states and internal strife, we finally have a united Italy – the dukedoms and principalities are no more. I think the only way that Italy can survive and progress is by having a single leader, who holds sway over *all* Italians."

"Such as yourself, signore?"

"If that is the will of the people," said Giolitti as modestly as he could.

"Then I shall pray for our nation and our leaders," said the pope.

"So then you are prepared to resolve the Roman Question?"

"When you have returned the cameos to me, I will settle the question in your favor," said the pontiff, with more than a hint of resignation.

"Excellent," said Giolitti. "But I do have one question before I retrieve them?"

"Yes?" asked the pope.

"What has become of Mr. Sherlock Holmes?"

Chapter Forty – Florence, 1501

Word of the pope's sudden and unexpected rift with Michelangelo spread quickly through the city. For days, it was the primary topic of discussion – both at the Vatican as well as in the marketplaces and the *tavernas*.

Those who claimed to be in the know stated with certainty that the pontiff had found Michelangelo's works unworthy of a place at the Vatican. They said that Pope Alexander had been so incensed by Michelangelo's creations that he had smashed them to bits with a hammer right in front of him. Though, of course, no one could say with any kind of certainty what it was that the pope had allegedly destroyed.

Some claimed it was an ornate chess set that His Holiness had requested while others believed it to be miniature statues of the pontiff and his children.

For his part, Michelangelo would only say was that he was terribly sorry that he had disappointed the pope, but that he had warned His Holiness prior to accepting the commission that he had never attempted anything like that before.

A few days later, Michelangelo suddenly left Rome. He returned to Florence, where he resumed work on the enormous statue of David that he had started just months before his brief sojourn in Rome.

Rumors abounded about the artist and his work, and some even made their way north to Florence. According to some reports, he had left the papal commission and returned only when the Florentine officials had demanded the return of the rather large advance they had given him for the David.

Others insisted that he had been persuaded to take up the hammer and chisel and finish the work by Leonardo da Vinci. And a small but vocal minority attributed Michelangelo's change of heart to the influence of his old friend Sandro Botticelli.

At any rate, Michelangelo worked on the statue almost nonstop, seldom venturing from his workshop, and entertaining only a few visitors.

Perhaps a month after he had resumed work on David, there was a knock at the door late one morning. Michelangelo thought about ignoring it, but the caller persisted, banging incessantly.

Finally, he heard a familiar voice say, "Michelangelo! I know you are in there! Open the door!"

Realizing that he had no other option, Michelangelo decided to oblige his visitor, and when he did as he had been commanded, there standing before him in a cassock of brilliant red with a large *saturno* on his head was Cardinal Giuliano della Rovere.

Before Michelangelo could say anything, the cardinal began, "And must I journey from Rome to Florence every time I wish to see you?"

Genuflecting, Michelangelo kissed the proffered ring and said, "My deepest apologies, Your Eminence."

"I am confused," said the cardinal. "I thought we had an understanding. I thought we had become friends."

"We are, Your Eminence."

"Then why did you depart without stopping to say farewell?" asked the cardinal.

"I did write you a letter," said Michelangelo, by way of explanation.

"I received it, and I read it many times, trying to comprehend it, but I must confess, its meaning eluded me."

"There was no hidden meaning, Your Eminence."

"Then why did you leave so quickly?" asked the cardinal.

"There were a number of factors that contributed to my sudden return to Florence," said Michelangelo. "I was humiliated and embarrassed by the pope and his criticism of my work. Also, I had accepted a rather sizable advance on this commission and there was talk of revoking it and giving the task to someone else unless I returned."

"You already know what I think of Pope Alexander," said the cardinal. "And if you had followed my lead, you would still be in Rome, working for me."

"You are too kind, your eminence."

"No Michelangelo, I am a realist. Just because one cardinal is incapable of appreciating genius, do not ascribe that shortcoming to all us."

The cardinal continued, "Alexander will be 71 on his next birthday. I will be 58 on mine. I told you in Rome that one day I would be pope. Do you still believe me?"

"I do, Your Eminence."

"Excellent, because when I ascend to the Throne of Saint Peter, I am going to do things that Alexander dared not imagine. I have already spoken with Donato Bramante about designing a new St. Peter's Basilica."

"You can't be serious!" exclaimed Michelangelo. "The basilica is more than 1,000 years old."

"Yes, and for the past decade, it has been polluted by Pope Alexander and his demon offspring. The church will need a new start after the Spaniard is gone, and I cannot imagine a better way to bury the past than by destroying it."

"I also have some very special projects in mind for you," the cardinal added.

"Would Your Eminence care to elaborate?" asked Michelangelo.

"All in due time, my son. Right now, they are little more than hopes and dreams. After our present pope has gone to his judgment, I will be more than happy to elucidate my plans. However, I will tell you this: As much as I admire your works in stone, I know that your first love is painting."

"That is true, Your Eminence. Even when I am sculpting, I try to find time every day to paint if I can."

"And do you paint, as you sculpt, for the greater glory of God?" asked the cardinal.

"I do, your eminence."

"Splendid. I assure you that we are going to have a long and beneficial relationship, my son. But it will require your returning to Rome."

"First, I must finish my work here. After all, as I said, I have taken their money. Also, I think you would agree that sculpting David, God's own warrior, is certainly a worthy undertaking."

"I would think it more worthy were you executing it in Rome," laughed the cardinal, "but I do admire your loyalty."

"Thank you, your eminence."

"How long do you think it will take before you are finished?"

"I was able to finish the Pieta in less than two years," said Michelangelo. "This may take a bit longer because the marble is badly weathered and must be treated much more carefully. I cannot work as fast as I might."

"I understand," said the cardinal, "I suppose there is no need to rush. I am powerless while Alexander overshadows our present. All that I can do is plan for the future and wait for his demise."

"Stay here," the cardinal continued, "Take your time and let David be a monument to your skill and your love of Our Lord. All I ask is that when I become pope, you promise to carry out my commissions – even if it means letting another artist finish something that you may have begun."

"You have my word, Your Eminence," said Michelangelo.

"Splendid," said the cardinal. Looking at Michelangelo, he said, "May I ask you a personal question?"

"Of course, Your Eminence."

"You are not afraid of heights, are you?"

Although mystified by the question, Michelangelo answered, "No, your eminence. They do not frighten me." "Just as I thought," said the cardinal. "Be well, my son," and with that the cardinal climbed into his carriage and drove off.

As he watched della Rovere depart, Michelangelo could only muse, "What an odd question."

Chapter Forty-one – Rome, 1901

Our train pulled into the Rome Tiburtina station at exactly 6:54, just as the sun was setting. Located in the northwest section of the city, the Tiburtina station is less than three miles from the Roma Termini – the main station.

As we stepped off the train, I noticed the platform was empty except for three other passengers who were also disembarking. Looking at Holmes in the twilight, I could discern a slight smile of satisfaction on his face.

"Giolitti should be meeting with the pope right about now," Holmes said. "If His Holiness can keep him there for an hour, we should have plenty of time to get into place." "What place are we getting into?" I asked.

"All in due time, Watson. Now, let us see if we can find a carriage."

Walking outside the station, we saw two cabs for hire. Holmes selected the brougham and told the driver to take us to the Piazza Barberini.

"It's less than five miles to our destination, and it's such a pleasant night that I suppose we could have walked and still arrived in time; however, if the pope is unable to detain Giolitti, we could be cutting things very close."

We drove down the Via Tiburtini, with Holmes pointing out the occasional landmark. I was impressed by how much of the city he had committed to memory in such a short time. As we turned onto the Via Bari, Holmes remarked that we were getting close. After another turn at a roundabout, we moved from the Via Nomenata onto the Via Vente Settembre.

A few minutes later, we turned onto the Via Barberini, and shortly thereafter, we arrived at the Piazza Barberini. After Holmes had paid the driver and asked him to deposit our bags at the convent, we walked the short distance to the Via Veneto.

As we turned the corner, we crossed the street and continued walking until we came to the Via dei Cappuccini, a small side street, not much more than an alley. Holmes turned into the passageway, and I followed him, nearly tripping over two boys, one of whom I recognized as Lucca, hiding behind trash cans. They were both dressed in dark clothing and just about invisible to anyone not looking for them.

"Anything to report?" asked Holmes.

"Not yet, signore," said Lucca.

"Who else is watching?" asked Holmes.

"Fredo and Antonio are at the entrance to the Via di Saint Isidora, but where it begins on the Via Liguria, while Phillipo and Francis are keeping watch from the Via Molise. If anyone sees him, he will dispatch his partner to alert the rest of us. So far, everything is quiet."

"How long have you been here?" asked Holmes.

"We started at 6 – just as you instructed signore. Everyone brought something to eat and a bottle of coffee. We will stay here all night, if necessary."

"Hopefully, that won't be the case," said Holmes. Looking at me, he said, "Let's settle in, Watson, and I'll bring you up to speed on everything."

* * *

Giolitti waited for the pontiff to answer.

After a prolonged pause, the pontiff said, "Mr. Holmes is no longer in the employ of the Vatican."

"A very wise move, Your Holiness. May I ask what precipitated his termination?"

"There were a number of factors," said the pope.

"Indulge me, Your Holiness," Giolitti persisted.

"I decided that as long as Mr. Holmes remained in my employ, things would remain at an impasse."

"That's quite true," said Giolitti. "I must tell you that he gave me quite a start when I opened my office door and found him waiting in my sitting room the other day. He is quite the formidable adversary."

The pontiff merely shrugged his shoulders, and said nothing.

"Would Your Holiness like me to return the cameos tonight, or shall I bring them in the morning?"

"I should much prefer them in my possession as soon as possible. In fact, if you would like, I can have two members of the Swiss Guard accompany you."

"That is certainly not necessary," said Giolitti. "Just give me an hour or two, and I will bring the cameos to you."

"As I said, Signore Giolitti, when *you* return the cameos to me, I will sign whatever you like in order to resolve the Roman Question."

"We can do that tomorrow after you make the formal announcement," said Giolitti. "That will allow me time to notify the press that it has been resolved."

"And you would return the cameos before then?" asked the pope incredulously.

"If I cannot trust the pope to keep his word than whom can I trust?" asked Giolitti.

"Are you sure you wouldn't like the guards to accompany you, signore? I would feel much better if they did."

"Now, it is you who must trust me, Your Holiness."

Although the pope pressed his case for the guards, Giolitti stood firm.

As he left the papal palace 20 minutes later and walked across St. Peter's Square, Giolitti checked several times to make certain that he was not being followed.

Hailing a cab, he ordered the driver to take him to the Palazzo Chigi. Giolitti had long admired the palace turned embassy, and he had promised himself that were he to become prime minister again, the Austro-Hungarian ambassador would have to look for a new residence. Built in the 16th century, the Palazzo Chigi is five stories high and offers an impressive view of the Piazza Colonna and the Via del Corso. "Such a building should be the seat of Italian government, not a home for a wayward diplomat who mangles the language every time he opens his mouth," he thought.

However, Giolitti had chosen the Palazzo because of the large open square in front of it. Were anyone following him, Giolitti would surely detect their presence here.

After paying the driver, Giolitti looked around. He saw a few people strolling aimlessly, but no one that caught his attention. No eyes were furtively averted, no backs turned suddenly; all was as it should be. Best of all, there was not a single youngster to be seen.

Striding to the front door, he rang the bell. When it was answered by a butler, he pulled a letter from his pocket and asked the servant to deliver it to the ambassador. The letter was simply a request for the minister to contact him regarding the particulars of a trade agreement that was in the works, but were anyone following, it might give them pause.

He then started walking along the Via del Tritone. He stopped frequently – to tie his shoe, to light a cigarette, to look in the window of a shop and adjust his tie. Each time, he carefully scanned the faces, and after he had walked the first mile, he decided that he was not being followed.

However, with the prize this close, Giolitti decided that taking even the slightest chance was out of the question.

Had he walked straight along the Via del Tritone, he might have arrived at the church in about 25 minutes, but he turned the two-mile walk into a four-mile excursion. He cut down various side streets. He entered the front of a restaurant on the Via del Pannettria and exited it on the Via dei Maoniti.

Satisfied at last that no one was dogging him, Giolittii decided to carefully reconnoiter the streets around the church before entering. Making his way to the Via di St. Basilio, which runs parallel to the Via Veneto but behind the church, Giolitti considered turning down the Via Molise but decided instead to go the extra block and check out the Via Versilia.

He would examine the Via Molise as he neared the church on the Via Veneto.

The street was empty and as he turned left onto the Via Veneto, he was all eyes. When he had walked the short distance to the Via Molise, he entered the street and walked all the way back to the Via di St. Basilio, but he saw no one and had no cause for alarm. He also examined the Via di St. Isidoro, walking almost to the Via Liguria, and he again came up empty. He was debating whether to investigate the Via de Cappucini. He had been gone far longer than an hour, but he knew the pope would wait and decided two more minutes of caution might make all the difference.

He walked to the street and ventured halfway down. Again, he saw no one and although he felt a bit silly, he knew he was too close to the finish line to take any chances.

Retracing his steps, he pulled open the door of the church of Santa Maria della Concezione dei Cappuccini and entered. After his eyes had adjusted to the glow of the candles, he looked around and was pleased to discover that the church was empty.

After hiding in a confessional for a few minutes to see if anyone entered, he made his way to the stairs, put the "Closed for repairs" sign in place and descended into the ossuary below.

* * *

We had been waiting in the street with the boys far longer than an hour, when all of a sudden we saw two youngsters sprinting down the Via Veneto in our direction. They turned into the alley, and after he had caught his breath, one of the youngsters blurted out, "Signore Giolitti just walked past our street on the Via di St. Basilio. I think he is checking all the streets and alleys."

"I'm sure you are right," said Holmes. "You have done excellent work. Now, I need all of you to go home and be safe. Lucca, I want you to take a very roundabout route to the Via Liguria and give my message to Fredo and Antonio. If, by chance, you should encounter Signore Giolitti, just ignore him. Do you understand?"

Holmes handed the boy a fistful of notes and said, "This is for your trouble. You have proven every bit as resourceful as Sister Angelica promised you would. Now, good night, boys. I will be touch tomorrow."

After they had left, Holmes said, "Giolitti is almost home free. I don't know how desperate he is, but I could never forgive myself if anything happened to any of those brave lads."

We lapsed back into silence, and Holmes seemed to recede deeper into the shadows, occasionally sneaking glances around the corner, while I remained pressed against the wall. After several minutes, he tugged at my sleeve and motioned for me to follow him. I could sense his urgency but could only wonder what might have happened.

We hurried down the Via dei Cappucini to the next side street the Via della Purificazione. After we had turned the corner, Holmes motioned me get up against the wall, and then he threw himself upon the ground. Every few moments, he would peer around the corner. Finally, he rose, turned to me and speaking softly, said, "He gave me a fright, Watson. I saw him heading our way on the Via Veneto and knew that he would examine our street next. After we left, he started down the alley, and I was afraid to move from the ground, lest any motion attract his attention. He came about half way down the alley and then looked at his watch. I guess he was satisfied, for he then turned back to the Via Veneto. I think Signore Giolitti finally believes that he is alone."

He continued, "From now on, it all depends on us. Let us hope that the pontiff's prayers are answered."

With that, Holmes headed up the Via dei Cappucini towards the Via Veneto. As we turned the corner, he looked at me and whispered, "I probably should have better prepared you for what you are about to see but I am not totally certain that words could do it justice."

"Holmes, I am a doctor. I can assure you that I have seen my share of bones."

"As you say, Watson. Just let me stress that silence is paramount. Even before we enter the church, I want you to remove your shoes."

With a million questions running through my mind, I pulled off my boots and watched as Holmes did the same. We laid them next to the steps. Then, very quietly, Holmes inched open the church door and motioned for me to enter and slide to the right. I did so and then Holmes eased the door closed without making a sound.

The church seemed little different from any of the others I had visited, and I wondered why my friend had carried on so in describing it.

Holmes then motioned for me to follow him and we made our way to a staircase that was guarded by a sign that read "Closed for repairs."

Holmes cupped his hands around my ear and whispered, "If we should make even the slightest noise now, all is lost."

He continued, "Despite your training, you may be startled by what you see, but remember, the only dangerous thing down there right now is Giovanni Giolitti."

With that, he turned and began to creep down the stairway. I followed, bracing myself for the unexpected and endeavoring to be as quiet as possible.

However, when we reached the bottom, I must admit that I was ill unprepared for the sight that awaited me.

Chapter Forty-two – Florence, 1503

Michelangelo remembered the day well. It was August 22, and it was very hot and the humidity was oppressive. He had been toiling in his workshop when a messenger, sent from the town square by Botticelli, arrived to tell him that Pope Alexander had died four days earlier. The messenger also informed him that the pope had been sick for several days before he died. Cesare, too, had fallen ill, but he was expected to recover.

While the thought that they might have been poisoned immediately crossed his mind, he was more focused on how long it would take the convocation to elect Cardinal della Rovere to succeed Alexander.

Every day, after working on David, he would go to the Piazza della Signoria in search of news, and while many people speculated about the next pope, the days passed without any announcements. As days turned into weeks, he began to wonder if Cardinal della Rovere had miscalculated his influence among the other members of the Curia.

Finally, on the morning of September 27, a messenger arrived to spread the word that that Cardinal Francesco Todeschini Piccolomini had been elected pope and had taken the name Pius III, in honor of his uncle Pius II.

Michelangelo wasn't sure whether to be relieved or disappointed. He suspected that Pius III might have been a compromise candidate or a "caretaker" pope, but all he really knew about the new pontiff was that he had been born in Sarteano, that his uncle had been pope and that he had been present at Alexander's infamous ball.

With his return to Rome seemingly delayed, Michelangelo pondered his immediate future. Although there was no shortage of commissions offered to him, allowing him the luxury of picking and choosing, none possessed the allure or the prestige of a papal assignment.

So while he worked on David, smoothing the imperfections, tinkering with the mouth ever so slightly and then the hands, and polishing the marble, he wondered what he might do next.

He had just about finished the statue of the boy warrior, and having worked on it for nearly two years from the time he had first begun, he had grown quite tired of it. In fact, the only real question that seemed to remain was where the statue would be placed.

The town – and its artistic community – were divided. One very vocal faction, supported by Leonardo, believed that the statue needed to be placed under a shelter of some sort because the marble had been badly weathered even before Michelangelo started the work. They had decided on the Loggia dei Lanzi on the Piazza della Signoria. Had he been asked, Michelangelo would have said he preferred that location because he was enamored of the wide arches. However, even though it was his work, no one had sought his opinion.

Another faction opined that David should be placed at the entrance to the Palazzo della Signoria, the city's town hall. While it wasn't ideal as far as he was concerned, the truth was that Michelangelo really didn't give a damn where they put it as long as they took it out of his workshop.

No, he was just about done with David. Perhaps another few weeks and then he could move on to something else. He wanted to paint, and he had been offered the opportunity to execute a fresco.

If he wished, he could paint the Battle of Cascina for the Palazzo Vecchio. He knew that Leonardo had already painted the Battle of Angiari, which immortalized the struggle between the armies of Florence and Milan some 70 years earlier.

The more he thought about it, the more the prospect intrigued him. Surely that would quench his desire for something new – and the idea of matching wits with the Old Man once again excited him.

He had made up his mind to do it, when on the morning of October 18, a messenger arrived to ask for prayers for Pope Pius III, who had been called home to God. He also informed the townspeople that a convocation had been assembled to elect a new pontiff.

And so the waiting began again. The days of uncertainty once again grew into weeks, and finally on November 28, the messenger from Rome brought the news that the conclave had elected Cardinal Giuliano della Rovere to the Throne of St. Peter, and that he was now Pope Julius II.

Two days later, another messenger arrived at his workshop with a letter from the newly elected pope.

The note was brief and to the point. It said simply: "Come to Rome as soon as possible." It was, Michelangelo thought, written in the same imperious style that he had come to expect from the man.

Michelangelo wrote back and said,

"I have just about finished with David. As soon as it is completed, I shall be on my way.

Your humble servant,

Michelangelo Buonarotti"

Two weeks later, the statue of David was completed.

As he packed his bags that night for the next day's journey, it suddenly occurred to Michelangelo to wonder about the fate of the cameos. Was he being summoned to Rome so that della Rovere could exact his vengeance in a very public way?

Although he tried mightily, he could not escape the fear that lurked in the back of his mind.

For the next five days, Michelangelo was in a foul mood. Each step of his horse brought him closer to Rome and caused the doubts and fears to grow and multiply. Finally, he arrived at the gates of the city.

He crossed the Tiber and made his way slowly to St. Peter's.

As he climbed down from his horse, he saw Captain Bari approaching. "Signore artista," the captain said, "His Holiness has been asking about you daily. He will be so pleased that you have finally arrived. Please wait here while I inform the pope."

A few minutes later, the captain returned and said simply, "Follow me. His Holiness will see you now."

A few minutes later, Michelangelo found himself standing in a rather large chapel.

The pope, who had been talking with two other cardinals, left them as he entered. As he approached

Michelangelo, he extended his arm, Michelangelo genuflected and kissed the ring.

"I told you that someday I would be pope," he laughed. "And now I am."

"And may your reign be long and prosperous," Michelangelo said.

"Do you know where we are, my son?"

"This is the old Cappella Magna, is it not?" Michelangelo asked.

"Indeed it is," replied the Pope. "It was restored by my uncle Pope Sixtus IV in 1482. It is now the site where popes are elected. This is the building where I was chosen as the successor to St. Peter. Do you notice anything about it?"

Looking about, Michelangelo saw the frescoes that Botticelli, Ghirlandaio, Perugino and Rosselli had executed adorning the walls. "The artwork is inspired," said Michelangelo.

"Yes, you can certainly see God's hand guiding the artists' brushes as they labored over the story of Moses and that of Our Lord, Jesus Christ." The pope crossed himself as he uttered the savior's name.

"But I think it is incomplete. Something is missing, don't you agree?"

"I am not certain that I follow Your Holiness," said Michelangelo.

"I am going to leave you now, Michelangelo. I would like you to join me for dinner this evening, but in the meantime,

I should like you to look at this building. See if God touches you, as I believe he has touched me. Will you do that for me?"

"Of course, Your Holiness."

"Splendid. Then I shall see you in an hour," he said. The pope turned and began to walk away as Michelangelo studied the building and tried to divine what the pontiff had in mind.

Suddenly, the pope turned and began walking toward him. "Just one more thing, my son ..."

"Yes, Your Holiness."

"Do you have any idea what became of those cameos that you executed for Pope Alexander? No one here seems to know a thing about them."

Chapter Forty-three – Rome, 1901

With Holmes in the lead, we crept down the stairs in absolute silence. A task that under normal circumstances might have taken but 10 or 15 seconds took us at least two full minutes. As we walked and waited, the stone beneath my stocking feet felt cold and rough.

There was very little light in the long hallway. There were one or two candles glowing softly and although I didn't know it at the time, I would later learn that the darkness was a blessing in disguise.

We crept past the first room, and despite the dimness, I could make out the painting of what I believed – and later confirmed – was Jesus raising Lazarus from the dead. Surrounding it were piles of bones – legs, arms, pelvises and skulls. "Nothing to be scared of here, old man. Nothing you haven't seen in anatomy class or the examining room," I told myself.

Then we passed a second room. It had an altar but as far as I could tell there were no bones, and I was beginning to think that Holmes had greatly exaggerated the grotesqueness of the place.

However, my opinion quickly changed as we crept past the third alcove – the Crypt of Skulls. I must admit suffering a nasty jolt when I was greeted by a trio of robed figures who seemed to be walking toward us. They had been posed against a backdrop of hundreds, perhaps thousands, of human skulls. On either side were two more figures in the supine position. If you weren't expecting it, and I was not, I think it could prove rather unsettling.

As we were about to pass the next crypt, we heard a scraping sound emanating from the end of the hall. Suddenly, Holmes bolted down what remained of the corridor past two more crypts. As you might imagine, I was in hot pursuit. As I passed one, I saw a dirt floor with crosses protruding from the ground.

As we reached the final room, which Holmes had told me was the Crypt of the Three Skeletons, I saw that a candle had been lit and placed on the altar. Everywhere I looked, I saw bones. The complete skeleton of a child had been affixed to the ceiling and surrounded by other bones – thighs, femurs, even tiny finger joints. As I gazed at the altar, I saw that hundreds of skulls had been placed strategically about it.

However, my attention was drawn to the floor, where I saw Holmes snatch up a velvet bag that was being pushed out from beneath the altar by a walking stick. A few seconds later, a hand appeared from the beneath the altar, and a man slowly began to emerge from some hidden chamber.

"Allow me to give you a hand, Signore Giolitti, lest you get your suit any dirtier than it is."

"Holmes, you bastard!" exclaimed the man.

"Such language in the house of the Lord," Holmes reproved him.

"I've come too far and worked too hard just to give up now," said Giolitti.

"Ah, signore, I am afraid you have no choice. This is checkmate," said Holmes.

"But why are you here?" asked Giolitti. "The pope told me that you were no longer in the employ of the Vatican." "He spoke the truth," said Holmes. "I am doing this *pro bono*. I think you might have been better-served had you asked the pontiff if I were off the case altogether."

"Equivocating bastard," roared Giolitti. "Give me the cameos, Mr. Holmes. This is none of your concern."

"Signore Giolitti, you made it my concern when you tried to blackmail the pope. You also threatened the family of a nun. That you would use the sins of the past to advance your future and torment innocent souls in the process to achieve your ends makes you a blackguard, sir!"

"I repeat, Mr. Holmes. Give me the cameos," said Giolitti very quietly.

"And if I refuse, as I most certainly intend to do?" asked Holmes.

"Then I shall be forced to take them," he answered.

"Signore, you do not frighten me. I have been threatened and tested by far better men than yourself. I suggest you resign, accept defeat and go about your business. Your reputation will remain unsullied, but if you persist..." Holmes left the implied threat hanging.

"And if I tell the world about the cameos? What then, Mr. Holmes?"

"You could certainly attempt that approach and see what happens. However, I can assure you that is also a losing strategy," replied Holmes.

At that point, Giolitti pulled a long blade from his walking stick and placed the tip at Holmes' throat.

"If you do not give me the cameos, I shall be forced to kill both yourself and Dr. Watson. Believe me Mr. Holmes, I shall do so with little regret, and you two will be buried in an unmarked grave, then we shall see if anyone can solve "The Mysterious Case of the Disappearance of Sherlock Holmes.""

Holmes simply smiled at him, ignoring the blade at his neck, and said, "Signore Giolitti, it is over. If you do not lower your blade, I shall have Dr. Watson shoot you." Turning to me, Holmes said, "If it should come to that Watson, try to wound rather than kill him. I would hate to see you brought up on charges here, and I should certainly like to see Signore Giolitti stand trial."

"You're bluffing," snarled Giolitti.

"Actually, he's not," I said as I pulled my service revolver from my pocket.

Giolitti looked at me incredulously. Then he shifted his attention to Holmes and said, "This is far from over, Mr. Holmes. I have a great many friends – a number of whom live in London. I should sleep with one eye open if I were you."

"Signore Giolitti, I too have a great many friends, including some very powerful ones, who reside right here in Rome. Let us just say goodnight and goodbye," said Holmes. "I do not think that we shall meet again."

As Holmes turned to the stairs, Giolitti made one final effort to snatch the cameos from him. He lunged desperately at my friend while attempting to stab him with the blade. Despite clutching the bag, Holmes managed to employ one of his baritsu moves and easily send the man sprawling.

With a torrent of threats and profanities in Italian, Giolitti unleased all his frustration, and finally said, "You are wrong, Mr. Sherlock Holmes of 221B Baker Street. Our paths will cross again."

Leaving Giolitti to rant and rave, we quickly made our way upstairs and retrieved our shoes. We were pulling them on, when a carriage bearing the papal coat of arms on the door rounded the corner from Via Molise.

"Our cab is here, Watson. Don't tarry."

* * *

Thirty minutes later, we were seated in the pope's study with Cardinal Oreglia. As you might expect, the pontiff had been extremely excited to see Holmes. Every few minutes, he would examine one of the cameos, which Holmes had reversed for him so that the 'virtuous' sides were showing, and then utter his appreciation anew.

A priest arrived after a few minutes carrying a tray laden with pastries, a coffee pot and a kettle.

The pope smiled at Holmes and said, "I understand you are not fond of our coffee, so I had the staff prepare a pot of tea."

"You are too kind, Your Holiness," murmured Holmes.

"Now, tell me, Mr. Holmes, how you managed to accomplish this miracle," asked the pontiff.

"After our conversation about Signore Giolitti, I put him under constant surveillance, using the former students of Sister Angelica. On one occasion, a youngster followed him to the Church of Santa Maria della Concezione. As you know the Capuchin Crypt is located beneath the church."

"On a few occasions, I dressed as a priest so that I might thoroughly examine the church. One afternoon, the boys warned me that Giolotti was coming while I was searching. I pretended to be asleep, and he actually had the temerity to wake me up. I had rehearsed just enough Italian so that I was able to make my escape and not arouse his suspicions. When I returned to the church a few minutes later to retrieve my missal, he was nowhere to be seen. Since he had not left, I determined that he must have hidden the cameos somewhere in the crypts below."

"I climbed to the bell tower, and after he did depart, I descended to the crypt, but despite my best efforts, my searches proved fruitless. I knew the cameos were there, but I had no idea where he might have concealed them."

"At that point, I decided the only way to find them was to have Giolitti lead me to them. That is why I had you dispense with my services and why Watson and I had to pretend to leave Rome."

"Mr. Holmes, the Vatican is eternally in your debt," said Pope Leo. "If ever the church or I can render you a service, please do not hesitate to contact me."

"The work is its own reward, Your Holiness," said Holmes.

"Yes, but you incurred certain expenses while you were here," and with that the pope handed Holmes a check.

Holmes looked at it and murmured, "You are entirely too generous," before thrusting it into his pocket.

"No, Mr. Holmes. You have saved me and the church. I do not know how the Roman Question will ultimately be resolved, but I can only hope that when it is, the pope making the decision will be allowed a free choice and not be coerced, as I nearly was."

"I understand," said Holmes. "Before I leave, you will understand if I want to make certain that the cameos are in a safe place."

Smiling broadly, the pope led us to his office and opened the door to a closet where we saw a new safe. "It arrived today," said the pontiff proudly, and the only ones with the combination are the locksmith and myself."

"Excellent," said Holmes. "Well then, Your Holiness, we will be heading home to England in the morning."

"Before you depart, I should very much like to give you and Dr. Watson a small token of my appreciation." With that he opened a draw in his desk and pulled out two small boxes. He handed one to Holmes and the other to me.

"Open them, gentlemen, please," said the pope.

I heard Holmes laugh, and when I flipped back the top, I saw a replica of the chain that Leonardo had constructed as the key to the cameos, complete with two tiny amulets, inscribed with the words "virtutus" and "vitium."

"Despite my anxiety, I never doubted you Mr. Holmes. I think they will double as pocket watch chains," said the pope.

"Well done, Your Holiness. I shall treasure it forever," said Holmes.

"As will I," I added.

"Then, gentlemen, I guess this is goodbye," said the pope, extending his hand to Holmes, this time with the palm perpendicular to the floor. He shook both our hands warmly and wished us well.

Cardinal Oreglia escorted us to the square, where we bade him farewell.

As we walked across the square to the convent, I said to Holmes, "You know, there's one thing that bothers me."

"What's that, Watson?"

"Michelangelo depicted Cardinal della Rovere, who became Pope Julius II, as the personification of pride."

"Go on," said Holmes.

"It was hardly a flattering image, and yet Julius commissioned Michelangelo to paint the ceiling of the Sistine Chapel and do a great deal of work on St. Peter's Basilica, did he not?"

"Someone's been reading his Baedeker," laughed Holmes.

"Well, if you had an artist render you in such a manner, would you hire him for more work? I wonder how Julius overcame his pride and what he thought of the cameos."

"Those are fine points, Watson, but I'm afraid that is one mystery that will never be solved. As I've told you before, it is a capital mistake to theorize before one has data. Insensibly one begins to twist facts to suit theories, instead of theories to suit facts. We have no data, no clues and without them, we cannot develop a theory. No, Watson, the best I could do would be to hazard a guess, and you know how I feel about guessing."

"I know," I repeated with him, "I never guess. It is a shocking habit — destructive to the logical faculty."

Epilogue – Rome, 1513

Cardinal Guglielmo Tosonotti was just preparing to draft a letter on behalf of Pope Leo X to the French cardinals. The election of Giovanni de Medici to the papacy had come as something of a shock to Cardinal Tosonotti. He had been certain that Cardinal Riario would carry the day. Although the selection of a layman as pope was not without precedent, in this case it was rather unusual in that he was already a member of the College of Cardinals.

Elected to the papacy on March 9, Giovanni was ordained a priest a priest just six days later and consecrated as a bishop just two days after that. A traditionalist, Cardinal Tosonotti did not approve, but he held his tongue.

Still, he had to admit that Giovanni was extremely bright. Because of his family and their influence, Giovanni had been named a cardinal-deacon at age 13 and a full cardinal three years later. The world was changing, Tosonotti thought, and he didn't care for the direction in which it was headed.

He was just about to put pen to paper when there was a knock at his door. Grasping any excuse to put off the writing, he asked, "Who is it?"

A young priest came into the cardinal's study. "I am sorry to disturb you, your Holiness."

"What is it Father Bruno?"

"There is a woman at the door who insists upon seeing His Holiness."

"Did she give her name?"

"No, your eminence. She says she has something to give the pope and she will allow no intermediaries."

"Is she a noblewoman?" asked the cardinal.

"I believe she is. She arrived in a fine carriage with footmen, and her clothing is quite splendid."

"Show her in. Perhaps I can handle this without disturbing His Holiness, but tell her that she must give you her name."

A moment later, there was a knock on the door. Father Bruno reappeared with the woman. "Your Eminence, may I present the Duchess of Ferrera."

Cardinal Tosonotti found himself staring at an old acquaintance. "Lucrezia? Is that you?"

She curtseyed and kissed his ring, "Your Eminence, it has been a long time, has it not?"

"What brings you to Rome, my dear?"

"A promise that I made my father on his deathbed."

"And what did you promise him?"

"That I would deliver a package to His Holiness," she answered.

"Let me see if the pontiff is free."

Cardinal Tosonotti returned a few minutes later. "He will see you now, Lucrezia."

As she entered the room where Pope Leo X was waiting, her mind flashed back to that incredible night when she had been a spectator at the "Ballet of Chestnuts."

"Lucrezia," exclaimed the pope, "I haven't seen you since you were a teenager. You look wonderful."

"You are too kind, Thank you, Your Holiness. And thank you for seeing me."

"As if I could refuse the daughter of a pope. Tell me, my child, what brings you to Rome?"

She looked about the room. "I promised my father that I would tell only you."

Waving his hand, the pope dismissed Cardinal Tosonotti, "Leave us, Guglielmo. I do not think Lucrezia poses a threat."

After Tosonotti had departed, the pope looked at her and said, "I understand that you have something you wish to give me."

"Yes, Your Holiness," she said as she handed him the box she had been carrying.

Opening it, he looked inside. "My god," he exclaimed. "Are these the cameos that Michelangelo executed for your father?"

"They are, your Holiness."

"You know, he came to me before he even began working on them. My family owned a very old bowl that is carved on both sides. It's called the *scutella di calcedonio*."

"I have heard of it," she said, "but I have never seen it."

"It is breathtaking," said the pope.

"And you said it was carved on both sides?"

313

"I did,"

"So are these," she said. Taking a chain from around her neck, she took the cameo that depicted her father as humility personified, inserted the keys, and flipped it, so that the pope was now gazing at the image of a naked Pope Julius II."

"That is obscene," exclaimed the pope. After a pause, he took another look and, having regained his composure, remarked, "And yet, it looks just like him."

"I know that you and my father had your differences. I also know that my father came to love Michelangelo, seeing in him an undeniable genius. My father came to regard him as a gift from God. Although he could not bring himself to destroy these, my father was afraid of what Cardinal della Rovere and others might do to Michelangelo if they learned of their existence."

"Shortly before he died, he gave me the cameos and this letter and made me promise that I would give them to a pope after della Rovere had died – as long as the new pope was an man of integrity."

She continued, "You know that I was at that ball and so was Cardinal Piccolini, your predecessor. That eliminated him as far as I was concerned."

She stepped back, looked at him, intently and asked, "Are you honorable, Your Holiness?"

"I try to be my child."

"Then here is a letter from my father, and the key that allows you to choose between virtue and vice. I entrust them to you, Your Holiness because I believe you and because I believe in you."

Choosing his words carefully, the pope said, "Michelangelo and I grew up together. He has been one of my closest friends since childhood. I have watched with pride as he has labored in the service of the Lord these many years."

He continued, "I have no doubt that the ceiling of the Sistine Chapel is God speaking through man. Were the existence of these cameos – and more important their subjects – to become known, it might well mean his life.

"I promise you, Lucrezia. Your secret is safe with me."

Author's note:

Although the Vatican Cameos, as I have described them, do not exist to the best of my knowledge, the sections of the book set in Renaissance Italy are loosely based on actual events.

There really was a "Ballet of Chestnuts," which was presided over by Cesare Borgia and his father, Pope Alexander VI. Sometimes referred to as the Banquet of Chestnuts, an account of the fete is preserved in a Latin diary by Pope Alexander's Master of Ceremonies Johann Burchard, which he titled *Liber Notarum*. However, in all fairness, the accuracy of his account has often been disputed.

Although Michelangelo and Leonardo were contemporaries and did know each other, to the best of my knowledge, they never collaborated on a project. However, they did compete against one another in 1503 when both were commissioned to paint frescoes for the new Palazzo Vecchio.

The character of Cardinal Giuliano della Rovere, who would become Pope Julius II also existed, as did Cardinal Giovanni de Medici, who ascended the Throne of St. Peter as Pope Leo X. The character of Salai is also well-documented as are his roles as Leonardo's servant and erstwhile model.

Visitors to Rome may want to stop by the Capuchin Crypt, which is a fairly small space made up of several tiny chapels and located beneath the church of Santa Maria della Concezione dei Cappuccini on the Via Veneto.

Giovanni Giolitti also existed, and his stints in public office were marred by scandal and charges of corruption.

Finally, the Roman Question was settled in 1929 when the Lateran Treaty was approved by Pope Pius XI, King Victor Emmanuel III and Prime Minister Benito Mussolini. Under its terms, the Holy See acknowledged Italian sovereignty over the former Papal States while Italy agreed to recognize papal sovereignty over Vatican City.

The Holy See also revised its request for indemnity for the loss of the Papal States and of ecclesiastical property that had confiscated by the Italian State, settling for much less than would have been due to it under the Law of Guarantees.

Acknowledgements

Writing is a lonely task made easier by the encouragement and patience of the following who contributed in no small measure to this book.

Sharon Cohen, who was one of the first to read "The Vatican Cameos," and who provided invaluable feedback and a much needed shot in the arm.

Bob McCormick, who volunteered to edit the manuscript and whose suggestions made the book that much better.

Deborah Annakin Peters, who saved me from committing an egregious anachronism and helped me format the manuscript.

My brother Edward, who really does own a house in Scotland near the Old Course, and who provided some much needed local knowledge about the Old Course at St. Andrews and customs in Italy.

Finally, to Lauren Esposito, whose offhand remark one evening started this whole process in motion.

To say that I am in their debt doesn't even begin to scratch the surface of my gratitude.

About the author

Richard T. Ryan is a native New Yorker, having been born and raised on Staten Island. He majored in English at St. Peter's College and pursued his studies, concentrating on medieval literature at the University of Notre Dame.

After teaching high school and college for several years, he joined the staff of the Staten Island Advance. He currently serves as the publications manager for that paper although he still prefers the title, news editor.

He has written three trivia books, including "The Official Sherlock Holmes Trivia Book." He is also the author of "Deadly Relations," a mystery that was well-received during its off-Broadway run.

He is also the very proud father of two children, Dr. Kaitlin Ryan and Michael Ryan.

He has been married for 38 years to his wife, Grace, and continues to marvel at her incredible patience in putting up with him and his computer illiteracy.

He is currently at work on his next novel, also a Holmes tale that he hopes to have finished by year's end.

Also from MX Publishing

MX Publishing is the world's largest specialist Sherlock Holmes publisher, with over two hundred titles and one hundred authors creating the latest in Sherlock Holmes fiction and non-fiction.

From traditional short stories and novels to travel guides and quiz books, MX Publishing caters to all Holmes fans.

The collection includes leading titles such as *Benedict Cumberbatch In Transition* and *The Norwood Author* which won the 2011 Howlett Award (Sherlock Holmes Book of the Year).

MX Publishing also has one of the largest communities of Holmes fans on Facebook (with regular contributions from dozens of authors.

www.facebook.com/BooksSherlockHolmes

www.mxpublishing.com

Also from MX Publishing

The American Literati Series

 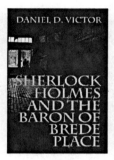 

The Final Page of Baker Street
The Baron of Brede Place
Seventeen Minutes To Baker Street

"The really amazing thing about this book is the author's ability to call up the 'essence' of both the Baker Street 'digs' of Holmes and Watson as well as that of the 'mean streets' of Marlowe's Los Angeles. Although none of the action takes place in either place, Holmes and Watson share a sense of camaraderie and self-confidence in facing threats and problems that also pervades many of the later tales in the Canon. Following their conversations and banter is a return to Edwardian England and its certainties and hope for the future. This is definitely the world before The Great War."

Philip K Jones

www.mxpublishing.com

Also from MX Publishing

The Missing Authors Series

Sherlock Holmes and The Adventure of The Grinning Cat

Sherlock Holmes and The Nautilus Adventure

Sherlock Holmes and The Round Table Adventure

"Joseph Svec, III is brilliant in entwining two endearing and enduring classics of literature, blending the factual with the fantastical; the playful with the pensive; and the mischievous with the mysterious. We shall, all of us young and old, benefit with a cup of tea, a tranquil afternoon, and a copy of Sherlock Holmes, The Adventure of the Grinning Cat."

Amador County Holmes Hounds Sherlockian Society

Also from MX Publishing

The Detective and The Woman Series

The Detective and The Woman
The Detective, The Woman and The Winking Tree
The Detective, The Woman and The Silent Hive

"The book is entertaining, puzzling and a lot of fun. I believe the author has hit on the only type of long-term relationship possible for Sherlock Holmes and Irene Adler. The details of the narrative only add force to the romantic defects we expect in both of them and their growth and development are truly marvelous to watch. This is not a love story. Instead, it is a coming-of-age tale starring two of our favorite characters."

Philip K Jones

www.mxpublishing.com

CPSIA information can be obtained
at www.ICGtesting.com
Printed in the USA
FFOW02n1030310517
36177FF